UNGENTLEMANLY
WARFARE

HOWARD LINSKEY

NO EXIT PRESS

First published in 2019 by No Exit Press,
an imprint of Oldcastle Books Ltd,
Harpenden, UK

noexit.co.uk

A CIP catalogue record for this book is available from the British Library.

This is a work of fiction. Names, characters, places, and incidents either
are the product of the author's imagination or are used fictitiously, and any
resemblance to actual persons, living or dead, businesses, companies, events
or locales is entirely coincidental.

ISBN
978-0-85730-320-2 (print)
978-0-85730-321-9 (epub)

2 4 6 8 10 9 7 5 3 1

Typeset in 11.5pt Minion Pro
by Avocet Typeset, Somerton, Somerset, TA11 6RT
Print   f S.p.A

For   imeuk

For Erin & Alison

PROLOGUE

'Now, people rise up and let the storm break loose!'

Joseph Goebbels, 1943

Galland was in the foulest of moods. He should have been with his men, debriefing the day's sorties, not undertaking this trivial errand for Goering. Galland's FW 190s had fared well against the RAF that morning but two more pilots had been lost and the supply of good men was far from inexhaustible. What could they learn from the engagement? How could he prevent the deaths of yet more pilots? These were the thoughts that preoccupied Galland as his plane taxied to a halt on the runway at Peeneműnde on a bright and cloudless morning.

The Reichsmarschall would be irritated by his lateness but Galland cared more for the well-being of his men. The *General der Jagdflieger* had downed 94 enemy pilots in dog fights over three countries; first Poland, then England, now France and his principal reward for such gallantry? An order never to fly with his men again. The Fatherland preferred its heroes undamaged. They wished to keep him safe for the newsreels. But what did they expect their fighter ace to do when he was not shaking hands with the Fűhrer for the benefit of the cinematograph; pace the runway like a mother hen, waiting for his charges to return each day? It didn't bear thinking about. So Galland repeatedly disobeyed this order, not lightly but knowingly and with no lasting regret.

Galland wore his Knight's Cross with Oak Leaves for the demonstration. The ludicrous Goering would expect it. As he walked from the plane he wondered what unflyable new contraption the head of the Luftwaffe had become fixated upon this time.

The group was assembled in a glass-fronted observation room at the far end of a runway. As soon as Galland entered, he picked out the unmistakeable figure of Goering, surrounded by a band of fawning acolytes. Today the Reichsmarschall's imposing bulk had been squeezed into an expensively tailored bright, white uniform, his large belly straining against its buttons like a badly stuffed cushion. To Galland, he looked like the ringmaster of a cheap, three-ring circus.

'You're late, Galland.' Goering spoke as if this were a deliberate affront to him personally. Then he waved his diamond-encrusted swagger-stick at the assembled group, 'We started without you.'

'My apologies, Reichsmarschall. The RAF detained me longer than anticipated,' before adding, 'they were unaware of our appointment.'

He's like a sulking adolescent, thought Galland, as he caught the eye of a brother officer who shared an unflattering view of Goering. Shegel was still a comparatively young man in such exalted company but he looked a good deal older than the last time the two men clapped eyes on each other. Galland wondered what trials he had undergone since then to cause the lines on his face and the premature greying of his hair. Shegel's reaction to the unedifying spectacle of Goering's sulk was confined to the merest flicker as his eyes met Galland's.

There were Luftwaffe men of senior rank in the room, whom Galland recognised, and some in civilian garb that, ominously, he did not. A number were dressed in white lab coats and stood before machines that clicked and whirred in a seemingly random fashion. Occasionally they made marks in pencil on their clipboards. Men in white coats, thought Galland, perhaps they have finally come to take the lunatic away.

Goering spoke to everyone and no one in particular, 'Dolfo thinks I don't know he still flies combat missions, despite my express orders,' and he arched his eyebrows significantly, 'and those of the Führer. What are we to make of him, eh? How many is it now?'

Galland's heart sank. Although he expected word of his insubordination would eventually reach Goering, he'd hoped the fog of war might protect him a little longer and he bridled at Goering's use of a nickname acquired from fellow officers; comrades he held in high regard. Admit nothing, Galland told himself, stand up to the man, don't quake like a schoolboy in the headmaster's study. He isn't going to have a 'hero of the Reich' taken out and shot. Not today at any rate.

'The Reichsmarschall knows I would never defy an order, least of all from the Führer, unless the circumstances were critical to my squadron, the base or my country and I was unable to directly communicate with him prior to take-off.'

Goering frowned and seemed intent on continuing their verbal joust but, before it could escalate to dangerous proportions, he was distracted – a high-pitched rushing sound from outside of the building made them all turn towards the window.

'Here she is!' cried one of the technicians. Galland stepped forward to witness the demonstration and he was almost too late; such was the speed of the object hurtling towards them. To this master of aerial combat, the little silver vessel was a shocking sight. To begin with, it was far smaller than any aeroplane Galland had ever seen. The tiny craft seemed barely capable of accommodating a man and the space-age object had no propellers. Galland was aware of experimental work on jet propulsion engines; the concept was hardly a new one but the reality always seemed to reside in a far-off, future land. Despite this, the new prototype flew by the watchtower at an impossible speed, making the windows rattle as it screeched by. One of the scientists punched the air exuberantly and there was unrestrained cheering from his colleagues. Galland merely stared in open-mouthed astonishment. Adolf Galland was not prone to incredulity but even he could not contain his wonder.

'What in heaven's name was that?'

Goering had never looked more smug or superior, as if he had personally invented a method for turning base metal into gold.

'That, Galland?' he enunciated the words slowly for maximum effect, '*that* is the future!'

1

'The woods are lovely, dark and deep
But I have promises to keep
And miles to go before I sleep.'

Robert Frost

Even in the subdued glow of the moonlight, Emma could
see the fear in the Frenchman's eyes.

'How much further?' asked Etienne Dufoy. His hand
gripped Emma's shoulder as he peered at her through thick
lens glasses, 'Are we lost?'

'Not far now,' she tried to sound reassuring, 'we are close to
the landing zone. You must be quiet.'

Etienne did not seem entirely happy with the young girl's
answer. Reluctantly he released his grip and turned his head
from her. As the owlish eyes became downcast he tried to
contain his fear.

'Don't worry, Etienne,' she smiled at him then, 'this time
tomorrow you will be in London, drinking Scotch and
complaining about the weather. Just like an Englishman.'

Etienne managed a weak smile in response. They had
stopped again on this mud track for what seemed like the
hundredth time, listening for a sound that should not be
there. The path snaked its way over the fields and through the
dense woodland that covered this little corner of Normandy.

Every noise was amplified by the stillness of the night. The constant stop-start was beginning to unnerve the resistance leader.

Emma looked at Etienne again. He seemed more like a frightened office clerk than one of the most wanted men in France. Maybe even the fearless Etienne Dufoy could feel fear and who could blame him after an interrogation at the Avenue Foch, the Gestapo HQ in Paris. Etienne Dufoy knew the names and code names of resistance fighters in the capital and had personally set up cells all over France. His capture could have been a disaster but, somehow, he had found the courage to elude his captors, jumping from a moving truck on his way to Fresnes prison.

Now the man from Marseilles found himself deep in the Normandy countryside, waiting for an English plane to land in a field in the dead of night and rescue him. And who does he have to deliver him to his salvation this night, thought Emma; a bodyguard provided by the local resistance, who is barely able to shave, and a 22-year-old English girl, the only member of the Special Operations Executive within miles. Emma Stirling had carried out precisely two previous missions in occupied France. In each of these, Emma, code name MADELEINE, had acted merely as a courier of papers. Never before has she been tasked to bring men out, and it probably showed. Is it any wonder Etienne's nerves are shot through, she thought?

As they moved off, she became acutely aware of how incongruous their little party must have looked. Emma wore a raincoat two sizes too big for her, to disguise the Sten gun slung on her shoulder. Her long, dark hair was worn up, obscured by a man's hat and tonight she wore trousers instead of a skirt but Emma could never be described as boyish. A few short months ago, she was on the SOE training program, learning the Morse code, sabotage and silent killing. Now she was leading a boy and a man in his middle forties across a mud track in a foreign land, towards their appointment with a Lysander, which would fly Emma and her most important charge to safety.

Olivier, their bodyguard, was young but not so young he had failed to notice Emma. As she stooped on one knee to check a map reference he clearly tried to peer down her shirt front.

'Stay alert, Olivier,' she told him sharply.

'Of course,' he replied, his young pride affronted.

The local resistance leader had assured Emma that Olivier was a good man but he was so effusive in his praise she had begun to wonder if the boy was a relative. Emma was nervous, for Etienne was a highly wanted man. How the Gestapo would love to catch him tonight, and anybody with him. Emma had to remove the stories of torture from her mind – worse for the women even than the men – or she would be completely unable to function as an agent.

'They like to rape the girls,' a local Maquis leader had informed her, 'so they have power over them. Or mutilate them if they won't talk,' and Emma had not slept that night.

She guided the men along the muddied track for another hundred yards or so then a shadow crossed the horizon and Emma froze. Had she seen movement or was it just the wind stirring the trees? Perhaps it was merely instinct that caused her to halt suddenly in front of the copse directly ahead of them? Her left hand went out to the side, the signal for her companions to halt.

'What is it?' whispered Etienne nervously.

'Ssshhh.' Emma brought the Sten higher but kept it pointing low, just as she'd been trained, to allow for the upward tug of the recoil. She aimed directly into the trees. Emma froze, her stance rigid, the silence around them as complete and unchanging as the darkness. Neither of the men dared break it, even though they could see nothing but trees ahead of them. Emma stared into the shadows. Someone was there, standing in the trees, she knew it.

Emma's hand went to the Sten and, as quietly as she could, she pulled the bolt back to cock the weapon. Emma could hear her own heart now; she almost forgot to breathe. Was her mind playing tricks? Get a grip. The patch shifted shape. No, she was right, there was someone there. Emma brought the Sten up with a jerk, her finger tightening on the trigger.

The silence was finally shattered when Emma heard a familiar voice, deep and resonant. 'Careful, Madeleine, that thing goes off accidentally and you'll have the whole German army down on us.'

'Harry?' asked Emma disbelievingly, 'Harry Walsh? Is that you?'

The unseen figure took this as his signal to emerge from the trees, forming into view like an apparition. A tall, well-built man with clear sharp eyes and a shock of straight, dark hair, he was dressed in a dark civilian raincoat, black leather gloves and a plain scarf to shield him from the cold. His face was prematurely aged with the knowing, slightly jaded look of the combat veteran and he had a dangerous air about him. Something about the way he carried himself hinted strongly at the capacity for violence.

'Don't use that name here, Madeleine,' it was spoken quietly but there was steel in his voice. Walsh walked up to the little group as if his anomalous presence was both expected and entirely normal. He turned to the older man.

'You must be Etienne Dufoy?' and he held out his hand in greeting.

'Yes,' answered Etienne who seemed bemused by this stranger, but the Englishman appeared to know his pretty guide and Etienne reached out to shake his hand.

'What are you doing here?' Emma asked, the question

tinged with anger. Damn it, couldn't Baker Street trust her to complete the mission on her own without sending Harry Walsh to nursemaid her. 'No one told me about a change of plan.'

Ignoring Emma, Walsh tightened his grip on Etienne's hand and yanked the smaller man towards him. Etienne gasped as Walsh wrapped a burly arm around the Frenchman's neck and forced him down, on to his knees, facing away from Walsh. There was a further strangled gurgle of alarm from Etienne before Walsh put his full weight behind the next move, as his knee went into the older man's back and he jerked Etienne's head sharply backwards, snapping his neck in an instant. He let the body slump to the ground under its own weight.

'My God, Harry, no!'

'That is not Etienne Dufoy,' explained Walsh, as calmly as if Emma had chosen to board the wrong bus, 'we need to get going. This wood will be full of Germans in minutes.'

Olivier stood rooted to the spot, staring wide-eyed at the lifeless body of his charge on the woodland floor.

'Come on, lad,' the Englishman's voice jerked Olivier out of his stupor, and he scrambled frantically in his coat pocket for the ancient Lebel revolver his uncle had given him. The youth brought the gun up and pointed it into Walsh's face.

'Do not move,' he stammered, but the Englishman calmly advanced towards him.

'Don't be bloody stupid, boy,' Walsh commanded in accent-less French, 'it's a trap, a Gestapo trap. That is not Dufoy and if you want to get out of here alive you will do exactly as I tell you.'

'Don't shoot,' begged Emma.

'Stop, stay back,' hissed the startled young man as he cocked the revolver.

'Do as he says, Olivier,' Emma was worried the inexperienced boy would simply gun down Walsh in his panic, 'he is with us.'

But Olivier did not lower his gun. Instead his confused eyes darted between them; from Harry to Emma, then the prone and lifeless body of the man he was escorting, now back to Emma once more, as if seeking guidance from her that he was still too scared to accept. Walsh waited till the boy's eyes were on Emma's then he took a half pace forward and in a blur of movement snaked out his left hand, rotating the palm so that it reached the boy's revolver on the inside of the barrel. In one fluid movement, he pushed it outward and away, levering it from the young man's grasp. Walsh brought his right hand up smartly, in time to receive the handle of the gun as it spun from Olivier's hand. Emma marvelled at the speed of movement and the boy found himself staring down the barrel of his own gun. He let out a startled whimper, assuming the next breath would be his last.

'I'm not going to shoot you, boy, but I will leave you here if you don't follow me now.'

Olivier felt like a foolish child. He started to edge back down the path.

'Olivier, no, come with us,' said Emma, 'it's the only way,' but Olivier would not listen. He turned and ran.

'Don't go back that way. They'll find you,' but Walsh was talking to himself for Olivier had fled.

Walsh took Emma by the arm. 'This way,' he said.

But Emma did not move. She stood rooted to the spot, staring at the lifeless body of the impostor lying in the mud.

'Let's not make it easy for them,' and he steered her towards a gap in the trees.

2

*'The agents should die, certainly, but not before torture,
indignity and interrogation has drained from them the last
shred of evidence that should lead us to others. Then and only
then, should the blessed release of death be granted to them.'*

SS Reichsfűhrer Heinrich Himmler on the
treatment of captured SOE agents.

Galland relished the rare tranquillity of a night sky
free from enemies. He had forgotten how calming it
could be to fly a plane back to base without having to
constantly alter its course or keep a ready eye out for Allied
fighters.

There had been no hostile presence over Peeneműnde that
day but the end result had been the same. Another burned
pilot dragged from the wreckage screaming. No one could
doubt the man's courage; agreeing to fly that thing was like
offering to be strapped to a Roman Candle. Possibly the pilot
imagined a career elevated to dizzying heights, following
a successful display in front of the Reichsmarschall, and
perhaps it could have been but not now; and what a terrible
price to pay when the test flight ends in failure. Of course, the
scientists will go back to their drawing boards but the pilot
will never fly again.

Maybe he'd simply been one of that special breed of men

who willed themselves beyond natural boundaries, defying God, fate and gravity, to fly higher and faster than any one before them. In a way that would be even worse; for how could such a man ever adapt to wheelchairs and hospital beds, to limbs permanently frozen by burned tendons, fingers melted together by flames?

Galland knew it served no purpose to dwell on such things but, try as he might, he was unable to remove the image of the horribly injured pilot from his mind. By the time the medics reached him the hair had been burned away, along with the eyebrows and lashes, and much of the skin on his face, making him unrecognisable from the fresh-faced, recklessly hopeful youth he'd been moments earlier.

There were operations these days, or so Galland understood, that could make you resemble a man again, after a time. He himself had seen old comrades transformed into walking waxworks, which is why the sight of the ill-fated pilot made him shudder involuntarily. Goering had caught his frown of distaste and misunderstood.

'He was a volunteer!' as if that made the smoke-choked screams, as they led the man away, any less pitiful. Before Galland could even consider an answer, Goering rounded on the scientists he blamed for yet another delay to his miracle weapon.

'What in providence happened? You said it was working!'

'It was… it did, Reichsmarschall,' stammered a youthful technician, clutching a clipboard defensively to his chest as if it was a shield, 'it flew perfectly…'

'Flew perfectly?' Goering was apoplectic now, 'it fell out of the sky like a kite when the wind drops and you say it flew perfectly!!' Goering brought his swagger stick down on to the nearest desk with such force he almost broke it in two, 'I demand to know what went wrong!'

'It's possible…' the young scientist looked terrified, 'it is likely... the plane is still too heavy. At low speed, without altitude, it is unable to cope with the extra weight of the liquid-fuel, rocket-powered engine.'

'Gaerte said this would happen, he warned me but I chose to ignore him. Instead I listened to you... children! Very well, if you are incapable of providing me with an operational jet fighter we shall relieve you of your duties and you can make your contribution somewhere less comfortable than here.' For soldiers this was usually code for the Eastern Front and Galland wondered what Goering had in mind for the unfortunate scientists.

'Get me Gaerte!' Goering was screaming like a spoilt child, 'get him here now!!'

While the Reichsmarschall raged, Galland quietly proffered his excuses and made to leave. Nobody seemed to notice his departure. If the injured pilot received half as much attention as Goering's tantrum he might even pull through, thought Galland. The memory of the disfigured young man would stay with him, as it did whenever one of his brotherhood was killed or maimed.

Goering had been predictably unstable that day and remained a liability to them all but he had been right about one thing. When the new Messerschmitt Me 163 Komet tried to land it tumbled out of the sky. It did not make Galland think of a child's toy but instead of Icarus, flying too close to the sun and fatally burning his wings. The pilot corrected the worst of the dive and managed a crash landing of sorts but the impact still churned the stomach. The squealing noise, as metal plates and rivets twisted then broke free from one another, made it sound as if the plane itself was screaming in protest as it was thrown down the runway. When it finally came to a halt there was a second's calm, until the Komet abruptly ignited and the pilot's fate was sealed.

What could not be denied, however, was the Komet's

prowess in the air before its sudden, untimely demise. In free flight, the plane screeched unstoppably across the sky at twice the speed of a normal fighter. In that regard, it really was 'the future'.

Galland had come to the not unreasonable conclusion that, if this Professor Gaerte was half as good as his reputation, he might just be able to work out a way to land the Komet safely. If he could accomplish that, it followed logically, then perhaps Germany could still win this war after all. Aerial domination was the key to the conflict. With a few squadrons of Komets, surely even Goering could not mess that up.

Galland did not know it but someone else shared his view; a German officer who did not enjoy the consoling notion of a Luftwaffe miracle weapon. Shegel wasted no time that day. Just like Galland he slipped away unnoticed, for he had an important message to convey. The Komet, cured of its teething problems, could keep Germany in a war it was patently losing. Air superiority could leave her armies safely embedded in France for years. Shegel knew there were other wonder weapons in development and they, in turn, would buy more precious time for their deranged Führer. The longer he remained in control the more likely it was that Shegel's beloved nation would be dragged down into the abyss.

The imminent arrival of the eminent Professor Gaerte, to replace the naive young fools Goering once favoured, was a startling development. If Gaerte succeeded in turning the Komet into a viable fighting machine then Hitler's promise of a thousand-year Reich might come true after all and the nation would be lost forever. Shegel had seen the Komet with his own eyes, could easily imagine its effect against conventional enemy fighters. It would be like pitching a squadron of Spitfires into the Battle of Waterloo. So Gaerte must not be allowed to succeed. Shegel was determined to stop him, even if it meant treason, even if it meant death.

As both a Christian and a Prussian aristocrat it outraged Shegel's sensibilities to see the historic, God-fearing German nation being systematically destroyed by an unhinged, atheistic little corporal. Slowly, over time, Shegel had become convinced there was only one way to save his country; rid Germany of Hitler and all of his gangster friends once and for all. A conditional peace could then be negotiated with the allies from a position of strength, before the whole country was reduced to rubble.

There had always been dissenting voices amongst the officer class but they were few in number and lacked influence while the military campaigns went well. But the tide of war had slowly turned and, following the disaster of Stalingrad, it had been easier to find those with a similar view – that for Germany the war was unwinnable. Some very senior men indeed now agreed; the mad little corporal had to be stopped. A secret line of communication had already been opened with London, through neutral Switzerland. The allies had yet to promise them anything but nor had they rebuffed the plotters. They would welcome the coup when it came, Shegel was sure of it, but a gesture was needed in the meantime, something that would underline the importance of their group, making them a force to be respected and reckoned with.

Shegel would give them the Komet.

Emma flinched as the first shots were fired but Walsh showed no reaction. He was used to being shot at and instinctively knew the gunfire was some way from them, aimed at a less fortunate fugitive.

'Looks like they have found your young friend.'

'Better they chase him than us,' Emma was determined to show no sentiment in front of Harry Walsh.

Walsh snorted. 'He'll identify us both. I should have killed him. If they do catch him, he'll wish I had,' and he pressed ahead.

They were striding across the damp fields, keeping to the low ground so their silhouettes wouldn't break the horizon and mark them out to pursuers. Emma was breathless but managing to keep up with Walsh, belatedly grateful for the hours of PT she had endured in training. The land around them seemed empty but they remained on high alert. When they spoke to each other the words came out quickly in a breathless half-whisper.

'Harry, what about the plane?'

'I know the pilot, travelled with him before, got him to bring the flight forward a day. Alan didn't want to fall into a trap.'

'So, where is it?'

'He used an old landing zone, a couple of miles from here and I hitched a ride. We flew in last night, covered the Lysander and laid low. All I had to do was trek back to the original landing zone, stake out the approach road and hope you'd come by before the Germans. I assumed you'd be early.'

'But how could you know?' Emma was irritated he could predict her actions so effortlessly.

Walsh seemed amused at her consternation. 'I didn't but you're a cautious one. It was a fair assumption you'd check out the area before the plane came – and you did.'

'And if I'd forgotten how to be cautious I'd be as good as dead right now?'

Walsh frowned. 'You could say that about any of us, Emma.'

'If you hadn't dropped in to save the day I'd be sitting in a cell waiting for the Gestapo. Is that it?'

'Probably. You've good instinct but the odds were always stacked against you on this one.'

'But Etienne was vouched for,' she protested.

'I know, and when we trace that one back somebody will

have to account for it. There's a traitor, Emma, at least one. Until we find out who it is nobody in the networks is safe.'

'And the real Etienne Dufoy?'

'Most certainly dead.'

'Jesus.'

Walsh grunted, 'Had absolutely nothing to do with it.'

'Keep your atheism to yourself, Harry Walsh. At least until we are safely back in England.'

It was as if Emma had inadvertently cursed them with her thoughts of home. As soon as she uttered the words the calm of the night was shattered once more. This time it was the sound of tracker dogs barking in the middle distance.

'Damn it, come on, Emma. Run.'

3

*'All murderers are punished unless they kill
in large numbers and to the sound of trumpets.'*

Voltaire

The Lysander was as ideal for this kind of work as it was unsuited to conventional warfare. Nicknamed the Flying Carrot, the little plane was achingly slow. With a top speed a fraction above 200mph it was no match for enemy fighters. However, this two-seater, high-winged monoplane was an indispensable tool for the SOE, because it could take off and land on a five-pound note. The Lysander needed just two hundred yards, sometimes less, to get into the air, turning the smallest field into an impromptu landing strip.

Flight Lieutenant Alan Collins waited nervously by the plane as a silhouette formed on the horizon. It had to be Walsh and the girl, and they were running. Collins cursed, for he had not yet dared to remove the camouflage from the Lysander and it would surely delay their escape. He began to pull the netting free, struggling as it caught on its tail and propellers. He looked back at Walsh, still some way off but waving at him frantically now. Walsh wanted him to start the engine, which meant the Germans must be close. A wave of panic swept over him. It would surely be impossible to get the camouflage netting clear, the engine running and take-off completed in time. The net refused to budge. Collins thrust a hand deep into his pocket, grasping frantically for the knife. He began to slash at the netting in a desperate attempt to free it.

Walsh was running hard now and Emma Stirling started to fall behind. Inwardly, she cursed her lack of speed as Walsh pulled ahead of her.

The dogs had their scent. German voices could clearly be heard as their pursuers closed in. It's going to be close, thought Walsh, very close. He turned back and reached behind him, grabbing Emma's arm and pulling her along by her sleeve in a stumbling run. What the hell was Collins playing at? Why didn't he start the damned plane? Had he not seen the frantic wave? Tell me he's not asleep, thought Walsh, his anguish increasing with every stride.

Shouting to the pilot was a risk but so was waiting till they reached the plane before revving the engine into life. Walsh could pick out individual German voices as they called to each other in the trees, like huntsmen closing in on a fox. It sounded like half a battalion was out there looking for them. There was no choice, he had to risk it. And so, Walsh called.

'Alan! Start her up, man! Now! They're right behind us!'

There was an immediate cacophony from the hunters but no response from the pilot. The Germans heard Walsh's cry and knew they were close.

Unbeknown to Walsh, Collins was wrestling with the last remaining scrap of netting, which snagged in a tight thread around one of the propellers. The Flight Lieutenant normally subscribed to the adage that more haste led to less speed but now, in his panic, he began to hack the net free with the lock knife. Sweat formed on his brow, for he too had heard the dogs.

'What's wrong? Where is he?' asked Emma, desperate now.

'Keep going,' was all Walsh said in reply. It was all he could offer, for he had no idea himself what had gone wrong. There wasn't even the prospect of an alternative plan. How far could they realistically get in this countryside, with dogs snapping at their heels, if Collins was not there for them? He made his decision then. Letting go of Emma's sleeve, he ran, leaving her trailing in his wake. Emma felt a surge of panic. He was actually going to leave her behind. They said he was a ruthless bastard.

Then came the crack of the first German rifle. Walsh could still not make out the Lysander in the darkness but he had to be in the right spot. Surely it couldn't be far now but what was closest, the plane or the Germans?

Finally, gloriously, there was a roar as the Lysander's 870-horsepower engine suddenly burst into life ahead of them. Walsh and Emma were sprinting flat out. A lone dog was set off its leash at the sound and it burst free, racing ahead to tackle them. Walsh could hear the Doberman's bark as it drew nearer. The din of the Lysander increased as Collins brought the plane towards them, its door opened invitingly.

Walsh sprinted towards it, reached the plane first, put a hand on the door to steady it, as the Lysander taxied slowly forward, and shouted back at Emma.

'Come on!'

Emma Stirling ran the last remaining yards flat out. Walsh bent low and put out a hand. Without breaking stride, she planted her boot right into it. Walsh ignored the dark shape careering towards him across the field. Instead, he hoisted Emma into the air and she pitched into the plane head first, landing heavily. Walsh immediately followed her straight through the door just as the dog finally reached him, leaping to snap at his leg. The dog jumped and missed, close enough for him to feel its presence. Walsh was half in and half out of the plane as the dog jumped again. Instinctively he kicked out, his boot connected with something fleshy and the attack dog was knocked senseless. It let out a high-pitched yelp, as Walsh's blow sent it arcing away from the plane.

'Go man!' but Collins needed no further urging. He was already pushing the throttle even as Walsh clambered inside, slamming the door shut behind them. The Lysander set off along the ground as the advance party of soldiers appeared at the edge of the field. A command was hastily barked and the soldiers levelled rifles, aiming at the onrushing plane as it gathered speed.

Collins had brought the plane to them; the right call or the Doberman would have mauled Walsh in the dirt, but there was surely a good deal less than two hundred yards before the trees now. As the shots rang out, Collins pushed the throttle hard, pulling the plane upwards. Its whole frame seemed to shudder as it rose.

A German bullet clipped a wing, another took out a corner of glass from the cockpit but the volley of hastily aimed fire did not prevent the Lysander from slowly rising.

Walsh knew the plane had to gain height quickly or there would be nothing left of them for the Gestapo to arrest. At least the end would be quick. Emma and Walsh both held their breaths as trees filled the view ahead of them. It was going to be close.

4

Bullets zipped past the wing tips and the engine coughed alarmingly, making the tiny plane fall momentarily then rise again at the last moment as Collins struggled with the controls. All Emma could see ahead of her, through the misted glass of the cockpit, was the dark clump of trees. They were far too close. There was no way they could make it now and she closed her eyes, bracing herself for the inevitable crash.

But Collins had not given up on the Flying Carrot. He gave the plane one last push and its Bristol Mercury engines drove it miraculously clear of the treetops, while the tips of the uppermost branches scraped against the wheels, like hands trying to drag it down. More shots flew harmlessly by as the Lysander left a field full of frustrated cursing Germans behind it.

Emma let her breath out in relief then put her face down into her palms. 'I really didn't think we were going to make it,' her voice was muffled by her hands.

'If you want the truth,' said Walsh, 'neither did I,' and he exhaled heavily before calling forward. 'Well done, Alan.' Collins simply nodded dumbly. He was in his own little world now, peering nervously at the sky around him for enemy night fighters.

Emma shivered involuntarily. 'Do you still carry that flask of rum around with you? I don't know why after all that running but somehow I'm bloody freezing.'

Realising Emma Stirling was probably in the throes of shock, Walsh reached into his inside pocket, produced an ancient and battered silver hip flask, unscrewed the top and handed it to Emma. 'Calvados,' he said.

'What?'

'Rum in England, Calvados in France. In case I should have the misfortune to be stopped by the authorities. Calvados is more authentic and just as effective at keeping out the cold.'

Emma took a large swig to steady her nerves. 'Is there anything you don't bloody think of, Harry?' and she handed back the flask. He took a sip of the apple brandy. 'Cheers,' she said, 'and it's good to see you again, Captain Harry Walsh, whatever the circumstances.'

The Channel crossing was happily incident-free. It had been a long night and they were all relieved by the lack of enemy contact. Perhaps God really was an Englishman, mused Emma, who'd had more than enough excitement.

'How did you know that wasn't Etienne Dufoy, Harry?'

'Because I met him once,' he said, 'I heard you were bringing him out. They told me he'd been arrested by the Gestapo but escaped. I thought it unlikely. Don't misunderstand me, he was an impressive and brave man in his own way, but I doubted he was capable of making a break from the Secret State Police.'

'Then why not get a message to me?'

'There was no time and I wasn't certain. You might have killed an innocent man. I had to see for myself.'

'Who was he then?'

'No idea. Some creature who'd gain from helping the Gestapo; a man who'd bait a trap for his own countrymen and their allies. No great loss in other words. The Germans would have followed you all to the landing zone then waited for the plane to arrive. That way they get the plane and pilot, the boy from the resistance and you. A few hours' persuasion and you'd have betrayed the whole network. Don't look at me like that, Emma, everybody cooperates eventually. It's just a question of time, until you run out of cover stories. You know that.'

'Yes, you told me at Arisaig, remember?'

'I remember.'

Walsh decided now was the time to bring her into his confidence.

'There is just one thing, Emma.'

'What's that?'

'I wasn't here tonight. London can't know.'

'What? Why? I thought Baker Street knew all about this.'

'No,' Walsh paused, as if measuring how much of the truth he could afford to tell her, 'I asked for approval to come but it was denied.'

'By whom?'

He shrugged, as if to say, *who else*? 'Price.'

'Bastard,' she said with some feeling.

'Yes, I'm beginning to think that he is.'

'But you came anyway?'

'Evidently.'

'You disobeyed a direct order.'

'SOE is not like the regular army,' said Walsh, 'I should know. We're meant to think for ourselves. Besides, Price did not actually say "I order you not to go".'

'What did he say?'

Walsh adopted a high, pompous nasal tone as he mimicked his immediate superior, the Deputy Head of 'F' Section. 'Don't be a bloody fool, Walsh. The *gel* will be fine. It would be a damn fool errand and only a complete and utter fool would attempt it.'

Emma laughed. 'What does that make you then?'

Walsh's face broke into a smile for the first time. 'At least three types of fool by all accounts.'

'Did he say anything else?'

'Only that flying out to meet you would be "the thin end of the wedge".'

'My God, he sounds just like my father.' Her tone made it clear to Walsh this was not a good thing. She turned away from him then and looked out of the window, 'Thank you, Harry, you saved my life tonight.'

'You'd have done the same.'

'Yes, I would,' she said it firmly, still not looking at him.

Emma fell silent for a long time. Walsh took another swig from the flask then closed his eyes. The only sound now was the dull purr of the Lysander's nine-cylinder, air-cooled engine. That, combined with the tots of Calvados, threatened to lull him into a sleep.

'But, Harry?' Emma turned back to him.

'What?' His eyes still closed.

'How am I going to tell London I returned without Etienne Dufoy, that we... that *I*, sorry... killed an impostor and left his body in the woods for the Gestapo to find? Oh yes, and that we have a traitor in the networks.'

Though Walsh kept his eyes firmly closed, Emma could clearly discern the outline of a smile.

'You'll think of something.'

'Thanks, Harry. Thanks a bunch.'

The English coast finally came into view, its chalky cliffs a dull silver hue in the moonlight but Emma could not enjoy the spectacle. She was too preoccupied with her plight. However was she going to explain this one?

Emma knew Walsh was never going to respect the 20mph speed limit imposed by the blackout and they made short work of the journey from RAF Tangmere. At least he had taken the trouble to fit an adapted lamp, which dimmed the motorcycle's beam, projecting it downwards, as they sped through the darkness of the capital's empty roads. The Norton growled one last time as Walsh steered towards the kerb then it fell silent. Emma let her arms slide from his waist and she climbed from the motorcycle.

'How do you get the petrol to keep this old thing running? No, actually, don't answer that, I probably don't want to know.'

'*This old thing* happens to be a 1933 Norton. A Model 30, 499cc, racing-adapted "International". In other words, it's a classic and a bloody quick one.'

'I shall have to take your word for that,' she said dismissively, 'but thanks for the lift.'

'All part of the service, miss.' Walsh stayed astride the bike. He seemed reluctant to ride away.

Emma sighed. 'At least come in for a drink, Harry. It's so late, one drink won't make any difference,' she said before adding, 'I'm grateful for the ride but bloody freezing again now. Come on, I've some real rum in the house.'

Walsh climbed from the bike and followed Emma up the steps of number 34 Devonshire Place, a dwelling she'd chosen primarily for its proximity to SOE headquarters in Baker Street. The building had changed since Walsh last visited Emma Stirling there. Its iron railings had been taken away and melted down for scrap to help the war effort.

'That friend of yours not in?' asked Walsh trying to sound unconcerned.

'Knowing Lucy, she'll be gadding about somewhere. If she is in bed we'll just have to be quiet, won't we? I'd hate to damage your reputation, though why I'm more concerned about yours than mine I'll never know.'

They dragged two armchairs up to the dying embers of a coal fire and Walsh prodded it back into life with an iron poker. They drank Emma's rum from enamel cups. It tasted sweet and warmed the backs of their throats.

Suddenly Emma shuddered.

'You all right?'

'Yes,' she replied, 'I mean I will be.'

'You had a bit of a shock tonight,' he conceded, as if the notion had only just entered his head.

'I feel better than I thought I would to be honest. Nothing like the realisation you are close to death to make you appreciate life, eh?'

'True.'

'How many times have you been over there now, Harry?'

Walsh looked down at his boots as if checking them for mud. 'I don't keep count.'

'Why? Superstitious? When did you first go over – back end of 1940? How have you coped with this life for three years?'

Walsh wished Emma wouldn't remind him of his diminishing chances of survival. 'I try not to think about it. I just do the job and come home.'

Walsh gave the coals an absent-minded prod with the poker. They both watched as sparks danced from them. There was a silence while each waited for the other to speak.

'Do you keep an eye on all of your little protégés these days?'

'Meaning?'

'Nothing, I just wondered how often you fly over to help them complete missions.'

He knew where she was going and doubted he could prevent her. 'Like I said, I knew Dufoy and this one just didn't ring true.'

'So tonight had nothing to do with "us"?'

'Us?'

'There was an "us", once. I can carry on pretending there wasn't if you'd prefer.'

'Emma, I am married, you know that. You knew that…'

'And how is Mrs Walsh?'

'You say that as if you know her?'

'No, but I know you, and I know what we had, even if it was just a few weeks on a miserable, rain-lashed Scottish estate. It was still something *worth* remembering. A girl is allowed her memories, isn't she? Even in the SOE.'

Walsh remained silent.

'I didn't imagine it, did I? You had feelings for me then.'

'Yes, I had feelings for you but what use are feelings when one of us is married.'

'For just over a year as I remember.'

'I made a mistake.'

'Seeing me or marrying her?'

'Seeing you.'

'You said that very quickly, Harry.'

Walsh sighed, 'Would you rather I'd not come out to get you, Emma; is that what you're telling me?'

'God no, I hate to think where I'd be right now if you hadn't. It was a big risk you took tonight; I just want to know if you would have done it for every agent you trained?'

'I would, yes,' and he said it emphatically, looking directly into her eyes.

'Well then, I suppose I'm lucky to know you, Harry Walsh.' She took a sip of rum before adding, 'And so is the rest of my intake.'

They drained more of the rum as the room warmed up around them until Emma felt able to go barefoot. She pulled the coarse, woollen men's socks she was wearing from her feet, slumped low in the old armchair, stretching her legs out in front of her and flexed her toes at the flames. Her hair was unruly now; a combination of the relaxing properties of alcohol and the reclined position she'd adopted. The effect was a positive one. It made her look more attainable somehow, like a woman and less a young girl. 'Just-fucked hair' thought Walsh, that's what Tom Danby would have called it and he instantly told himself to banish such thoughts before they became too appealing.

He drained the last of his rum, 'I should go.'

Walsh rose and quickly put on his coat. Emma followed.

'You can stay if you want. Of course you know that,' she was trying hard to sound casual, 'and I'm not drunk, well maybe just a little, but that's not the reason.'

They were at the door now and before he could open it she reached out and took his hand, 'Harry, you saved my life tonight and I want to wake up next to you in the morning and... I'm not doing a very good job of this am I? Out of practice you see.'

'No, you're doing far too good a job, which is why I have to go. If it was just bed it might be different but it's not and I can't give you anything more than that.'

She leaned in closer and Harry picked up the familiar sweet smell of her hair, something sharp like lemon juice and fresh like the rain. 'And what if I settled for just bed?'

5

At that exact moment in the local headquarters of the Geheime Staatspolizie in Rouen, Olivier was screaming in agony.

'That was just one,' assured his interrogator, 'imagine how it will feel if I order him to remove them all.' And Captain Kornatzki nodded at the Gestapo corporal who had just torn Olivier's fingernail out of its roots as calmly as if he were removing the top from a beer bottle.

'Please no,' and the young man's voice cracked into sobs. 'I'm trying to help, I'm trying to remember but I don't know anything.' His voice carried a slight echo in the damp stonewalled cell.

'Tell me again about the English girl,' asked Kornatzki, 'her name, Olivier, what was her real name?' The interrogator was annoyed he had not been granted the opportunity of a personal appointment with Emma; the women were always more satisfying to work on than the men. He was beginning to view the whole of that night's operation as something of a failure.

It had seemed promising enough at the planning stage. A single impostor would trap an entire network. By now Kornatzki should have been on the telephone to the Colonel, happily informing him that a British pilot and his plane had been captured, a female agent was under interrogation and soon he would be in possession of the names and whereabouts of Normandy's key resistance fighters. But it had all gone very badly wrong. An interfering Englishman had murdered the impostor, a petty career criminal persuaded to replace the late Etienne Dufoy, who had been so scandalously allowed to die in custody before revealing all of his secrets. The promise of an amnesty and a little money had led that insignificant crook to an early unmarked grave and the Wehrmacht's finest soldiers had failed to follow their targets closely enough. Now all the Gestapo had to show for their efforts was this snivelling boy.

'I don't know,' the boy was sobbing hard now and staring at the bloodied stump that used to be his finger. Kornatzki had experimented with countless forms of torture but you could rarely surpass the visual impact of a torn-out fingernail. 'We knew her only as Madeleine. Please, I'd tell you if I knew.'

'I'm starting to believe you, Olivier, I am. You've been most cooperative so far but I need names,' and Kornatzki clasped his hand against the back of the boy's neck then pulled his face forward so it was less than an inch from his own. He spoke in a low whisper, coaxing the boy to talk, 'If I get the names you keep your finger nails, it's very simple. So tell me now about the Englishman.'

'He came out of the trees.'

'He came out of the trees,' sighed Kornatzki, 'yes, you said that. Like Tarzan perhaps, swinging on a vine?' and he let go of the boy and retreated. The Gestapo corporal rolled up his shirt sleeves and advanced once more to take his place.

'No,' Olivier protested weakly.

'But I must have his name, Olivier, otherwise I cannot keep you alive, you understand that don't you, it will be out of my hands. You have to help me if you want me to help you.'

'I don't…' and Olivier began to shake his head in wordless protest at the injustice of it all. All he wanted to do was leave this place, go back to his mother and father in the village, walk across the fields with his girlfriend and never think about war or the resistance again. This was all so unreal somehow; all of it apart from the searing, burning pain in his finger, which was very real indeed.

'Take another finger nail, Corporal.'

'Please! His name, yes, I think I can remember. It was Harry!'

'Harry?' Kornatzki snorted, 'is that all you give me? What use is that to me? There must be a hundred thousand Harrys in England. Do it, Corporal.'

'No! It was Walsh. The girl called him Walsh! Harry Walsh!'

'Did you say Harry Walsh?' asked the astonished Major.

'Yes. The girl… she said it, she called him Harry Walsh.'

Kornatzki waved his henchman away and left the boy to his sobbing. He walked briskly out into the corridor and went straight to the nearest telephone. The Colonel must hear of this immediately. Had a drunken Colonel Tauber not once told him bitterly how he would now be a general were it not for an Englishman named Harry Walsh? Poor Olivier, thought Kornatzki, the Colonel was about to take a very personal interest in his questioning.

Mary was sleeping soundly when Walsh looked in on her. There was no need to wake his wife, for she was used to the long and irregular hours of his 'hush-hush' work. Her endless worrying for him finally receded once he assured her his latest posting meant he was desk-bound and would never have to leave the country again.

The light from the landing bathed Mary's face but she did not stir. Instead she slept silently on, her breathing soft and regular. She was classically beautiful, Walsh had to admit. On the dressing table nearby lay the silver brush and comb set he had bought her on their honeymoon. Every night without fail she would count out fifty brush strokes on either side until she was satisfied with the condition of the long, dark hair. Next to the brush lay her Bible and a silver-framed picture of her older brother, Harry's friend Tom, the man who had brought them together and now, in a bitter irony, seemed destined to keep them apart.

Walsh closed the door and trod gently down the stairs. Not even close to tired he thought; too full of adrenalin, fear and rum to sleep tonight. So much so he had almost stayed with Emma, a particularly tempting notion now he was in the cold and lonely living room, with its long-dead fire, but he told himself he had done the right thing.

In any case Emma Stirling was not his biggest problem. A new day was almost upon him and there would be a reckoning to pay; an account must be given for the night's actions. He knew Emma would play her part well but really, the more Walsh thought on it, the more convinced he became that there could be only one outcome. They'd been waiting for an excuse and this time he would likely be kicked out of SOE for good.

Walsh poured himself a generous measure of whisky, sat down in the easy chair and waited for morning to come.

6

'The Baker Street Irregulars.'

Name given by Sir Arthur Conan Doyle to the band of
youngsters who helped Sherlock Holmes solve his mysteries
– adopted as a nickname by SOE for its own operation.

Walsh turned the collar of his coat up against the
downpour as he joined the line of pedestrians
shuffling along Baker Street. The pavement shone
beneath them, coated by an incessant rainfall, turned slippery
under the footfall of soldiers home on leave or housewives
looking for a queue to join.

There were as many horse-drawn carriages on the road as
petrol vehicles these days. Horses needed food but not fuel,
and petrol was in shorter supply, so many tradesmen now
preferred the older methods to ferry their bulkier wares
around London. Baker Street was a peculiarly Dickensian
scene, one which Sherlock Holmes himself would have had
little difficulty in recognising.

Walsh passed a teashop with a window boarded-up in
anticipation of an air raid. Some enterprising amateur
artist, the owner perhaps, had painted the accoutrements
of a traditional English afternoon tea on the boards as an
invitation to passers-by, as if to imply such delights actually
awaited them inside. Walsh knew there was little chance of

that. The only scones or cakes likely to be found here were of the painted variety.

As Walsh traversed Baker Street, he was assailed by posters urging him to 'Buy War Bonds', 'Dig For Victory', or simply 'Eat More Potatoes', then ardently reminded that 'This firm is entirely British' by a barber who had once been proud of his Italian heritage before the outbreak of hostilities.

He finally reached the plain sandbagged door of 64 Baker Street and instinctively checked to see if anyone was taking an unusual interest in the building. Passers-by did not pause, nor were there suspicious-looking souls loitering on street corners, surveying the property. Nobody walking by this large, innocuous-looking building could have guessed it housed the highly secret organisation known as the Special Operations Executive.

Walsh went straight to the third floor – the home of 'F' Section and the spartan office to which he had been summoned. SOE divided itself into departments, each representing the country in which its operations were based. France had four sections; one run by Gaullists and another by Poles, a third was an escape line for captured airmen and finally there was 'F' Section, the British-run outfit to which Walsh belonged. The SOE had been hurriedly formed in July 1940 when Winston Churchill instructed Hugh Dalton, the Minister for Economic Warfare, to 'Set Europe Ablaze' and Harry Walsh had been, if not exactly a founding father, at least one of the earliest waifs and strays through its doors.

Walsh rapped on an office door and the familiar public-school voice of Major Robert Price answered him.

'Come in,' murmured the deputy head of 'F' Section and Walsh obeyed. 'Sit down, Walsh,' he said, without looking up from the papers he was reading, affording Walsh a perfect view of his superior's balding head, interrupted only by a thin ginger wisp of combed-over hair. He said nothing further, so

Walsh took the vacant chair that faced Price's well-ordered desk. Like all of the furniture in the building, it was basic and functional.

Price kept him waiting in what Walsh took as a display of authority. The younger man looked placidly beyond Price's shoulder, watching as an improbably bulbous spider patiently span a web in the window outside. He wondered how it had managed to climb this far up the building.

Price was wordlessly writing notes across a pile of memos. Finally, but still without raising his eyes to meet Walsh's, he spoke, 'Madeleine came back with the most extraordinary story.'

Walsh wasn't sure what was expected of him in response but when the Major failed to elaborate further he said, 'Really, sir?'

Price did look up then, 'Yes "really, sir",' he answered in a chiding tone. Price was a squat rotund man, just the wrong side of forty but looked considerably older. When he became annoyed – as he had a tendency to do when Walsh was in the building – his face burned a deep red, instantly becoming the most colourful thing in his drab little office. Today he appeared calmer but Walsh knew it was unlikely to last. 'I must say I just don't know what to make of it. It turns out Etienne Dufoy is very likely dead and the man she was sent to collect almost certainly an impostor; or should I say, he *was* an impostor, as I ought to add that the bloody inconvenient woman killed him.'

'Well, I'm sure she had good cause, sir.'

'She did apparently, or so she says. Madeleine tailed our man to a café where she overheard him speaking into the telephone in German to an unspecified contact. She understood just enough of this conversation to realise he was about to betray the exact time and location of the landing zone then she killed him. Strangled him with the phone cord evidently and not a soul noticed until she was clean away.'

'Really?'

'You keep saying that, Walsh, yes really.'

'Remarkable lady that one.'

'Oh she is, definitely. Of course, her story is complete and utter twaddle.'

'I'm sorry, sir, I'm afraid you've lost me.'

'Let's just say I shall dig deeper. If I find you had any involvement whatsoever in this then you are in a truly enormous amount of trouble. You'll beg me to return you to the wilds of Scotland to take up permanent residence as an instructor.'

'I doubt that very much.'

'Well don't, because I can dream up a hundred less attractive postings than that one, believe me.'

'I'm sure you can, sir, but I don't know…'

'Have the decency to be quiet while I'm rollocking you, lad. Now you may have managed to cover your tracks on this one, for now; the pilot swears there was only a young woman on board the Lysander that night, nobody saw you at the air field and of course Madeline is hardly going to be disloyal to the "legendary" Captain Harry Walsh now is she?'

'I barely know the girl.'

Price carried on as if he had not heard Walsh, 'But I'm not partial to legends, particularly ones who disobey my orders as regularly as you do. Ever since that little incident involving the diamonds I've had my eye on you, Walsh, and frankly I've had a belly-full of your dumb insolence.'

'Permission to speak, sir?'

'Permission granted,' answered Price suspiciously.

'I was sent to repatriate a large consignment of industrial diamonds from occupied France, under the noses of the Germans, and I did just that. I completed my mission and we benefited to the tune of some £60,000.'

'That's just the point, isn't it? The consignment was valued at £70,000 and you know it.'

Walsh felt his blood beginning to boil, 'By a crook, a convicted fraudster and counterfeiter, *he* valued them at £70,000.'

'We utilise the talents of many such men in SOE, Walsh. You are not averse to using them yourself from time to time.'

'I'll use that kind to get the job done but I don't believe every word they tell me. Your man Maurant spent more time in prison than out of it. He is not only a crook but a singularly unsuccessful one. I would take every word he said with a hefty pinch of salt if I were you.'

'But you're not me, Walsh, which leaves us with the mystery of the missing £10,000 in diamonds. Where can they be, I wonder?'

'No idea,' offered Walsh defiantly, 'have you looked under Maurant's mattress?'

'Don't be obtuse; you know the Gestapo caught up with him. I would imagine if he had taken the diamonds they would have found a way to persuade him to hand them over before he died, don't you?'

'Undoubtedly.'

'So, we're back to you again, Walsh.'

Walsh felt his indignation rising. Price might be his commanding officer but he had no good cause to distrust his subordinate, nor any new reason to question him on the disappearance of the mythical diamonds. 'And I am not going through it all again. Your superiors cleared me of any wrongdoing and the whole thing happened more than two years ago, so I won't answer any more questions unless you make them formal. Are you making this formal, sir?'

Price looked as if he was about to explode at the tone of Walsh's carefully worded defiance but, realising he was on shaky ground with his unproven accusations, he gathered as much dignity as he could muster and replied through gritted teeth.

'Not for the time being.'

'Will that be all for now then, sir?'

'No, it will not,' and Price sighed as if trying hard to contain his exasperation, 'there is another matter I wish to discuss.'

'And what would that be, sir?' Walsh was relieved Price had managed to uncover so little of his clandestine adventure with Emma. Good girl, he thought to himself, got your story nice and straight. Later he would enjoy a smile to himself at the thought of Emma Stirling strangling someone with a phone cord, not because she was incapable of such a violent act, far from it, but because she had clearly anticipated Price's need for a full and vivid account. She had certainly supplied it, complete with a traitor's lifeless body left in the darkened corridor of a French café to be discovered by the startled owner. Thanks to her, it appeared Walsh had survived.

'The use, your use, your unauthorised use to be precise, of some of our very precious equipment. I have a few questions to put to you, Walsh, and I want some straight answers.'

'Sir, I would never dream of giving you any other kind.'

Professor Gaerte wore a grey suit that morning but no lab coat. The civilian clothes would underline his authority, making him stand out from the white-coated subordinates now back under his heel. As Gaerte entered the room, Schiller intercepted him. He had been expecting something from Schiller; the bright, young, doe-eyed, obsequious, treacherous youth.

'May I say what a pleasure it is to have you back on the project, Herr Professor...' Gaerte stopped him with a raised finger, warm smile and friendly sing-song voice completely at odds with his words,

'Don't be absurd, Schiller. You conspired to have me

removed me from the project, you must realise I know that.'
He raised his voice to address the score of young scientists
in the room. 'You are all worried men and so you should be.
You've had things all your own way for a dozen wasted weeks
and what have you achieved apart from a handful of roasted
pilots? Nothing. The Komet is still too heavy. I said it all along.
Now you will work for me, tirelessly and without complaint.
At the end of our time here the Komet will be ready for combat
testing. I have promised the Reichsmarschall this. Those who
reach my standards in the intervening weeks will accompany
me to France, those who do not will be reassigned,' and
Gaerte's eyes flicked over the cohort of worried faces.

There was complete silence. Good, just the right
combination of fear and hope. They were all scared witless
yet had been given a glimpse of salvation and how they would
work to achieve it. All except Schiller that is, he would work,
by God, harder than them all, Gaerte would see to that, but
his fate was already sealed. Schiller's reassignment had been
approved. They were always looking for men of science to
conduct experiments on the *Untermensch*. Schiller would
spend the rest of the war at one of those God-forsaken camps
in the east, inserting needles into filthy Jewish arms, with the
stench of the place always in his nostrils. He would rot there.
Gaerte would see to it.

'Good,' he said when no answer was forthcoming, 'then let
us begin!'

Selwyn Jepson reached into the briefcase and retrieved the
buff manila folder, placed it carefully on the desk in front
of him, opened it and began to read. 'Now then, yes, Harry
Walsh, here we are. Do you want to know everything, sir, or
just the interesting bits?'

Major General Colin Gubbins sat impatiently opposite
him in an office not two floors from where Walsh was, at that

very moment, being harangued by his deputy section head. 'Give me what you think I need to know,' said the Executive Head of the SOE and he frowned at Jepson bringing two dark bushy eyebrows almost together as he did so. Gubbins was a small man but no less imposing because of it. A Scot, with no discernible trace of an accent thanks to a lifetime of received pronunciation of the King's English, first at public school then in the army. He looked every inch the British officer, right down to the precisely clipped, caterpillar-shaped moustache he favoured.

'Right you are, sir. Back then, like every potential recruit, he was interviewed by Major Lewis Gielgud.'

'Oh yes, his brother's the actor, Shakespeare and so forth.'

'Indeed he is. Walsh was regular army, like most of our early intake; distinguished himself fighting a rearguard action at Dunkirk and was made captain with a battlefield promotion.' Jepson frowned. 'There was something a little odd about that I seem to remember but I could never quite put my finger on it during our follow-up interviews. I conducted a number with our surviving veterans you see, sir, to try and build a picture in my own mind of what constitutes a good field man.'

'Odd? How so? A fair number of men were promoted on that battlefield, chiefly to replace the ones that died there.'

'Yes, but far from being flattered or proud, Walsh seems rather to… I'm not sure how to explain it.'

'Please try, Jepson.'

'Well, sir, to resent it, if I'm honest. I probed him on this obviously but he simply clammed up. I did think it was odd that a man decorated and promoted to the rank of captain should be shuffled out of his regiment with such unseemly haste.'

'You had your doubts, so why did Gielgud take him do you suppose? Why not just show him the door?'

'Other attributes. His father worked in France before the

war and his mother was French, so he speaks the language fluently. His decision-making at Dunkirk bordered on the inspired but he's far from rash. Thoughtful, I'd say.'

'Ruthless? I mean if need be?'

'Without a shadow, sir. He caused a rare amount of carnage out there for the first wave of Germans. Maybe that's why the regiment didn't want him. He doesn't fight by the usual rules.'

Gubbins sighed. 'You know there are still intelligent, seemingly rational men in this country who would rather we lost to the Germans than win if it means fighting dirty. Meanwhile the whole bloody world descends into darkness around them. Where can I find this Walsh?'

'Well, he's here today as a matter of fact. I saw him earlier and assumed you'd sent for him.'

'Good. Look, I asked you for an opinion on Walsh. I know him by reputation alone. Do you think he fits the bill?'

'He seems exactly what you're looking for.'

Not necessarily what *I'm* looking for thought Jepson and once again he remembered the forceful, enigmatic message.

Only Harry will do.

7

*'Oh what a tangled web we weave
When first we practise to deceive.'*

Walter Scott

Jepson made enquiries as to Walsh's whereabouts and less than five minutes later Gubbins walked into Price's office.

'Price! Sorry to barge in but I need to borrow Walsh.'

'Good morning, sir! I had no idea you were even in the building,' and Price was out of his chair so quickly he banged his knee on the side of the desk. 'How are you, sir?'

'Well, thank you, Price, but if I could just have Walsh.'

It belatedly dawned on Price that Gubbins' visit had absolutely nothing to do with him and everything to do with the presence in his office of the oafish Harry Walsh. Trying hard, but largely failing to disguise his displeasure, he answered his chief.

'Of course, sir. Jump to it, Walsh, you heard the CD.' Price used the familiar abbreviation of the SOE head's title. 'Off you go. We can finish that other business later.'

'Come on, lad,' urged Gubbins, 'a spot of lunch while we have our chat?' It was a rhetorical question.

Lunch with the CD thought Price bitterly as they left him. He would have killed for the prospect of such a thing. But no, instead it is Harry Walsh who is afforded this inexplicable honour. Pearls before swine.

Price waited till they had both removed themselves from his office and there could be no prospect of his being overheard. 'Probably can't even hold a knife and fork,' he said bitterly.

Kornatzki reached for the glass by the water jug in his office. He wiped it with his handkerchief then went to the desk, opened the window behind it then sat down heavily in the leather chair. He needed some air.

The Captain pulled open the bottom drawer of his desk and reached blindly inside. Though it had been deliberately hidden from view under a mound of innocuous papers, he found the bottle immediately by touch. Kornatzki would normally not have opened the schnapps this early but he had just discovered the profound difference between wanting a drink and needing one. That day he needed a drink.

Kornatzki poured a generous measure of the clear liquid then gulped half of it down. It burned the back of his throat but that was the least of his concerns. He had just come from the fetid cell that housed young Olivier.

Kornatzki had seen many men tortured in his time with the Geheime Staatspolizei. His Gestapo superiors felt he possessed the stomach for this unpleasant yet highly necessary work and he gained satisfaction in extracting information from the enemies of the Reich. Some were easy, turning into snivelling wretches who pleaded for their lives before the inquisition had even begun. All one had to do was strap them securely into a chair and the feeling of helplessness would completely overwhelm them. That alone could take the fight and spirit away. Kornatzki would then ensure the instruments of their torture were placed before them. The movements of the inquisitor might seem slow and routine as he rolled out his linen bag, with a separate pocket for each of his sharp tools, until it lay flat on the table but they were deliberate and premeditated. As the victim's gaze went to the scalpels, pliers, hooks and saws, resistance would drain from them along with the colour in their face. The actual torture could become almost unnecessary but the prisoner would be subjected to it just the same; to soften him up and ensure the whole truth was extracted. Kornatzki would watch as all hope, loyalty to friends, or faith in God vanished from them. It could be that easy.

Others took longer in the breaking but Kornatzki had never dealt with anyone who would not tell him at least a partial truth following a few hours in his care. Even the toughest ones were realists, trying desperately to buy time with fabricated names and false accounts, so their comrades could make good an escape and continue their cowardly terrorist activities. This would present quite a challenge for Kornatzki; one in which both sides would become wholly preoccupied with the clock. There was an art to breaking a man in enough time to sweep up his comrades and if Kornatzki had not yet perfected that art, he felt he was damn near close.

Witnessing the questioning of Olivier, an interrogation that was wholly controlled by the Colonel, had been a different matter, however. Never before had Kornatzki seen such malevolence, such delight in a man's pain as this. The Captain always felt he could retain a small semblance of honour in his grisly work for, if the truth be known, he seldom actually enjoyed it. On the whole, Kornatzki was content enough when the prisoners broke down and confessed their crimes, implicated fellow conspirators, betrayed the whereabouts of friends and eventually received the merciful blessing of execution.

The Colonel it seemed was made of different material; for he appeared to gain a deep, almost spiritual satisfaction from the process. No, not spiritual; more disturbing than that thought

Kornatzki. Tauber was a sadist. Frankly the Colonel in full flight was a profoundly disturbing spectacle.

When Kornatzki had called the Colonel and given him the name 'Harry Walsh', the SS man came to the cells immediately to personally interrogate Olivier. There were protracted beatings, which continued long after the boy would have sold his entire family to end the pain, applied at such regular intervals they could serve no purpose except for their own sake. The hours thereafter seemed to constitute little more than a form of personal revenge on the part of the Colonel for the humiliation once bestowed upon him by an English officer.

Olivier was left with a bloody, discoloured and permanently damaged face that had barely an unbroken bone in it. The swollen flesh matched the broken, crushed hands he now held limply on the arm rests of his chair. The woman who bore him into this world would have been incapable of recognising Olivier by now. There was no further need to hurt the boy thought Kornatzki. Just give him a mirror and let him see his face, it would surely be enough to break him.

Tauber gave specific orders Olivier was not to clean himself, so the stench in the small cell grew.

'Tell me about the Englishman,' Colonel Tauber demanded and Olivier shrank back into his chair in terror. The physical torture was handled by a couple of the Colonel's own men; Kornatzki's were deemed insufficiently ruthless for the task, but Olivier had quickly worked out who was in control of his pain.

'I've… told you… I keep telling you,' he spluttered the words through newly broken teeth. He could barely bring himself to match the Colonel's gaze.

Colonel Tauber was responsible for all matters of security for Rouen and the surrounding area. He was a tall, gaunt man who wore the sinister black uniform of the Schutzstaffel. As he bent over the boy, he looked like a malevolent crow. The Colonel never once removed his black jacket though it was suffocatingly warm. Kornatzki watched as he leaned in closer to his victim. 'Tell me again,' he hissed and Olivier was forced to relate the same story over and over. The colonel made him recount it endlessly and, after each telling, set his dogs loose upon the boy once more. They worked with enthusiasm, oblivious to Olivier's screams.

'When is he coming back, Olivier? When will I meet this Harry Walsh again? I'm so looking forward to it,'

'I don't know, I don't know,' protested the boy.

'Will he come for me next time, this English assassin?'

Olivier was beyond hearing the question. 'Please let me go... take me back... I want to go home,' he pleaded, 'I've told you everything I know.'

Finally the Colonel sighed and said, 'Yes, I think you probably have,' and he thought for a moment. 'Take him out back and shoot him. Don't give the body back to the parents.'

Olivier realised all of his agonies had been for nothing. 'No... no... you said you'd let me go if I told you... I helped you... I helped you.'

Colonel Tauber was already at the door but he turned back wearily, to indulge the boy. 'I said I would help if you cooperated, Olivier. You have been most cooperative and now I am helping you. Soon your pain will be at an end,' and with that he walked from the room.

Kornatzki quickly followed him, followed by the boy's anguished screams as he was dragged to his feet for immediate execution.

'Well, that was a waste of my valuable time,' said the Colonel.

Then why did you prolong it, thought Kornatzki, though he was certainly not foolish enough to say that.

'This Walsh will come again,' continued the Colonel, 'he's been here before and keeps returning. He cannot stay away, can't live without the danger. I know his sort. I almost caught him before and we would have had him this time if your scheme with the impostor had been handled correctly. Instead it was a dismal failure.'

'Yes, Standartenführer,' replied Kornatzki, who correctly surmised blind agreement was his safest course.

Tauber stopped walking and turned to Kornatzki. 'Do I have your full attention, Captain?'

'Of course,' and Kornatzki rather unnecessarily illustrated the point by coming sharply to attention in the corridor.

'I want this Harry Walsh. I want him more than a promotion or the Knight's Cross with Oak Leaves and Swords, more than dinner with the Führer himself. Is that understood? Because that Englishman embarrassed me. He made me appear ridiculous. Have you got that, Kornatzki, because if he escapes again your next posting will make Stalingrad seem like a quiet rural backwater in the south of France.'

Kornatzki recalled those words now as he took another large sip from the glass. The memory of the undoubted pleasure Olivier's torture afforded the colonel still disturbed Kornatzki but not nearly as much as the prospect of a posting less enviable than Stalingrad. That would tax the colonel's imagination right enough but it was far from beyond him. Kornatzki knew he would have to get very drunk indeed that night in order to sleep. Far more so even than usual. He refilled his empty glass and took a large bitter swallow.

They dined at Gubbins' club, where the waiter handed each of them an ostentatious, yet clearly ageing leather-bound menu, assembled in a more optimistic era before the outbreak of war. The main courses were handwritten in a fussy, calligraphic lettering.

'Recommend the Beef Wellington,' said Gubbins absent-mindedly as he perused.

They ate well enough considering the shortages. Walsh knew poor Mary would stand in line an hour or more for a couple of sausages and think herself blessed if they were still there when she reached the front of the queue. Little evidence of rationing here, though.

'I hear they gave you a gong for that bayonet charge at Dunkirk,' said Gubbins.

'The DSO,' Walsh confirmed.

'Dick Shot Off, eh?' It was a well-worn joke.

'Mercifully not, sir.'

'Indeed, wouldn't want to be a chap without a chap,' and Gubbins chuckled to himself, before deciding to come to the business in hand. 'You are wondering why I wanted to see you.' Gubbins leaned forward conspiratorially, 'I may have a job for you, laddie,' his eyes narrowed, 'if I think you are up to it that is.'

8

*'No occupying power can break the spirit and blunt
the retaliatory power of a patriotic and proud people.'*

Colonel Maurice Buckmaster, Head of F Section, SOE

Gubbins continued his probing throughout the meal.
The questions were matter of fact but Walsh knew he
was being tested.

'Worked with the Yanks before, have you?'

'On occasion,'

'Successfully?'

'When our interests coincided, yes.'

'And when they didn't?'

'I barely got out of Yugoslavia alive.'

'Mmm,' Gubbins reacted, as if Walsh had just commented
on the changeability of the weather, 'harbour any resentment?
One might.'

Walsh shrugged, 'They weren't too keen on sponsoring Tito
and his communist pals. I wasn't convinced about their man
Mihailovic. You could say I got caught in the middle.'

'But you made it out. Any qualms about working with them
again?'

'I'd work with the Abwehr if I thought it would bring the
Germans down any quicker.'

'A realist, good. I want you to go to a meeting with Colonel

Buckmaster and the OSS.' Maurice Buckmaster was head of 'F' Section. Gubbins was clearly leaving nothing to chance, delegating only as far down as a section head. That'll please Price, thought Walsh.

'The Yanks have all the resources but were a little late coming to the party,' Gubbins continued, 'so we have experience they can benefit from.'

'You want me to tell the Americans how they should be fighting a covert war? That'll please them.'

'It's not that simple.'

'No?'

'Cooperate with our American cousins, give them the benefit of your wisdom but do it tactfully. You can be tactful can't you, Walsh? Without their seemingly endless supply of equipment we'd have nothing to fight this war with, even if it rather pains us to admit it.' Gubbins paused then and he looked Walsh straight in the eye, 'I need somebody to go into France in a couple of weeks. Been there lately?'

'Not recently, sir, but I'll go if it's needed.'

'It is. This is important, Walsh. The second front will come eventually, as we all well know and, when it does, the invasion has to work or there'll be no second chance. I believe our humble organisation can play a big part. Our boys and girls can train and mobilise the Maquis and the new German labour laws are a very effective recruitment drive for our cause.' French males between twenty and twenty-three were now required by law to go and work in Germany. Unsurprisingly, thousands opted to head up into the mountains instead. Gubbins was right, there was a ready-made army in France, right under the noses of the enemy. It just needed equipment and training.

'I think they can cause the Germans all sorts of trouble. Our friends in Six disagree.'

'MI6 are involved in this operation?' asked Walsh.

'No, in fact they would really rather it didn't happen at all.

SIS consider us a band of bungling amateurs.'

Walsh bridled, 'It wasn't us that lost a cipher machine.'

'Good point. I shall have to remember that next time Menzies collars me over a pink gin.' Gubbins pronounced the SIS chief's name correctly as 'Mingiz'. 'But suffice to say our very existence is an inconvenience for "C" and all who sail with him. Every time we blow something up, dispose of a collaborator or bump off a high-ranking Nazi there are reprisals and house-to-house searches. Inevitably the Germans sweep some of their men up, often by accident. I can understand their irritation, I really can, but our work is too important for it to cease. At the moment Churchill and the Americans agree, which is why they want to drop teams in behind the lines when the invasion comes. Each must consist of an Englishman, a Frenchman and an American.' Gubbins frowned, 'I know, it sounds like some awful joke one might hear down the pub.'

Walsh wondered if the patrician Gubbins was familiar with the inside of an English pub but he concurred with the sentiment. 'It sounds like a passport to disaster.'

'Quite, but I'm afraid it's the only way. The Americans insist on being involved and they are paying the piper, so it really is their tune. The French? Well you know de Gaulle; 'France for the French' and all that, so they must be in on this too. Despite the unnecessary complication of the nationalities we still think it can work. Besides, it really is this or nothing.'

'So where do I come in exactly?'

'You are the difference between us saying it can work and proving that it will. The idea is to drop one of these "Jedburgh" teams in early for a specific and very important mission. I need someone who can hurt the Germans straight away, not spend weeks bedding in like a lot of agents do. It must be an individual unafraid to act and prepared to be ruthless. Somebody who can handle the Maquis, cope with the Yanks and the Free French and live with the distinct possibility that MI6 would sell you to the enemy, just to get you out of their hair. Oh yes, and there is the small matter of the Germans, mustn't forget them! In short I need someone who's... how can I put it?'

'A bit of a bastard, sir?'

'Precisely, Walsh, glad you catch on.'

'I see.'

'What's the matter? Don't fancy it, lad?'

'It's not that; there are security issues.'

'Security issues? How so?'

'Our building for a start, a lot of people coming and going all of the time; how many are already secretly working for Six? A few, I'd bet.'

'I don't doubt it for an instant,' conceded Gubbins.

'Then I'd need a free hand to create my own cover stories, false identities and papers. It'll be expensive but it's the only way.'

'I take your point, Walsh, and I'll see what I can do; anything else?'

'Yes, equipment; I just spent twenty minutes with Price being told exactly how much I can and cannot have for ops in occupied France and it's nowhere near enough for a mission like this. If I'm going to link up with the Maquis I'll need a lot of kit; a little to start with and regular air drops to follow, depending on how many men we are talking of supplying.'

'With the Americans on board I don't think equipment is going to be a problem.'

'Not with the conventional stuff but I need access to everything the Thatched Barn has created, including the latest devices they are working on. Elder Wills is something of a genius in my book and I don't want to be told I can only take half a kit bag full of goodies out there because Major Price views me as wasteful.'

'Do I detect a faint atmosphere of friction between you and your Deputy Section Head, Walsh?'

Walsh had long ago realised the folly of giving an honest answer to any one above the rank of captain. 'I am certain Major Price acts with the best of intentions but this mission sounds like it might require some specialist equipment.'

'If you take on this assignment for me I'll keep Price off your back, for now at least.'

'Thank you, sir.'

'But you have got to get me results, you hear?'

'I will.'

'Good,' Gubbins had been won over by Walsh. The Captain might just be suitable after all. He would have to be in fact. *None but Harry, only Harry will do.*

'I want you to go out there and create something for me, Walsh.'

'And what would that be, sir?'

Gubbins smiled. 'Havoc.'

9

'The mass of men lead lives of quiet desperation.'

Henry David Thoreau

Price was seething. He marched angrily down the street, grinding his teeth as he went, stabbing his umbrella at the damp pavement with each step, as if the cause of his indignation was the very ground he walked on. But no, the reason for his foul mood was far more prosaic; none other than Harry Bloody Walsh.

Initially Price had been delighted to see Gubbins once more, as the CD entered his office for the second time that day. Back from his lunch with Walsh and wants to bring me into his confidence with a briefing, thought Price. Well, I'll tell him what I think with nothing spared. But the conversation went very differently from the way Price had hoped. When Gubbins informed him that Harry Walsh had been selected for an important mission in France the Major decided it was right to speak up.

'Are you sure that's wise, sir, I mean after all...'

'Yes, quite sure, Price,' interrupted Gubbins tetchily, 'I have had the man checked out.'

You didn't check him out with me, thought Price but he did not voice this sentiment aloud. Instead he chose the diplomatic route, the course of least resistance, the one he had always followed. 'Of course, sir, I am sure he will be up to the job, it's just…'

'Spit it out, man. If you have reservations let's hear them.'

Price was rattled by his superior's harsh tone. He felt his train of thought diverted by such plain speaking. 'Well, you see it's… I mean…' Price found himself beginning to waver under the stern gaze, 'well there is that little matter of the diamonds. I really do think…'

'Nonsense, Price, we looked into that business ages ago and there wasn't a shred of evidence against the man. Walsh has proved he can be trusted time and again. This foolish innuendo has been hanging over his head for too long. Now, is there anything else?'

'Well… er…' Price felt that a mission of such obvious magnitude surely warranted a man with a more solid background at the helm. Someone who had not lost the stabilising influence of a father so early in life and been raised largely by an aunt, somebody who received better than a barely decent education at a very minor school – and that only due to the advantageous passing of a scholarship. Not, in other words, a man like Harry Walsh, an officer who was always going to be some way short of a gentleman, fortuitously promoted thanks to the fluctuating fortunes of war, a man with secrets. Price wanted to say a man who is not like us, sir, but immediately thought better of it. He knew Gubbins had no qualms about who he used to win this war; even women, damn them. In his mind, Walsh was probably faintly respectable compared to some of the ne'er-do-wells and reprobates SOE employed to carry out its dirty tricks. Gubbins cared nothing that one of his own officers had a father who, when it came down to it, was little better than a travelling salesman.

'… No sir,' Price conceded eventually, 'I think you have covered everything and I am sure Walsh will do admirably.'

The words stuck in his throat as he pronounced them. But that was far from the end of it. Price belatedly realised he was in for a lecture.

'I'm going to give Walsh a free hand on this one,' – a free hand thought Price, but I'm his commanding officer – 'I don't want him subjected to the usual supervision. The normal rules cannot apply on this assignment for reasons of security.' Price was being sidelined and he knew it. Just when he thought his humiliation could grow no deeper, Gubbins stuck the knife between his ribs, 'I am sorry I cannot permit you to know the details but you of all people must understand why.'

But Price did not understand. Far from being a favoured acolyte of the great Gubbins, a status he had craved till now with every fibre of his being, it appeared he was little more than a very small cog in a large and unforgiving wheel, a cog that represented a security risk to boot.

What had Walsh been saying to the CD during their cosy little chat over lunch? It must have been truly damning for Gubbins to feel the need to march into Price's office, his own office, damn it, and warn him to keep his nose out of Walsh's business. Oh, that was what Gubbins meant sure enough. He reckons I can't be trusted, concluded Price as his paranoia and resentment grew. Gubbins thinks I'm windy, not good enough for his little cabal. Don't think I haven't seen them sipping whiskeys down at Whites or the Berkeley while I get barely a nod as I pass by, let alone an invitation to join the gang. It was just the same at school, thought Price bitterly and the familiar feeling of exclusion settled over him like a dark cloud. Well, it's not good enough, he decided, not near good enough.

The remainder of this insultingly short meeting was largely concerned with the need to let Harry Walsh do just as he damn well pleased, probably right up to the point where he personally strangles Adolf Hitler, or carries out some other

Herculean task Gubbins has so cavalierly set him. So, Price is not allowed to know eh? Then he will damn well make it his business to find out. Gubbins would see. He'd learn. There was something not quite right about Harry Walsh. Price had detected it early, could almost smell it in fact. It would all come crashing down around them eventually and Price would be there to pick up the pieces when it did. Then Gubbins would know who was of real value to his organisation. Walsh would live to rue the day he tried to stall Robert Price's career. He hadn't become a major by allowing men like that to get in his way. And he'd show Gubbins as well. He'd show the CD just what a big mistake he made the day he put all of his trust in Harry Bloody Walsh.

10

'Is the last word said? Has all hope gone?
Is the defeat definitive? No.
Whatever happens, the flame of French
resistance must not die and will not die.'

Charles de Gaulle, 18 June 1940, on BBC Radio

It was a pleasure to take the Norton through the countryside instead of sitting on the morning train with a carriage full of those too old or infirm to fight. The day was bright, autumnal, and the roads were dry. Walsh opened up the bike and it responded eagerly, the engine purring as he sped along the country roads. The bushes flashed by, blurring into green borders either side of him

The rare sense of freedom couldn't last but at least he wouldn't have to contend with Price today. It wasn't just the Major's open dislike of Walsh the younger man found irksome, for he had never been popular with his superiors. Nor was it Price's unfounded belief in Harry's ability to comfortably moonlight as a diamond smuggler, based on evidence no more damning than his instinct and the word of a former conman. No, Walsh disliked his regular appointments with the Deputy Section Head because he realised it would never matter what he said or did. The Major was never going to accept him or his continued presence in 'F' Section. Walsh was simply not 'the right sort' and knew Price would never rest until he had been thrown out of SOE for good.

The area Walsh sped through was still ostensibly rural, its banks of fields broken by market towns that dispensed produce from the farms nearby. This rustic appearance belied the location's importance to the war effort. Walsh was at the geographical centre of Britain's struggle against Germany. Housed within thirty square miles of Bedfordshire countryside was a plethora of locations variously described as 'secret', 'top secret' and even sometimes 'ultra-secret'. The British SOE and SIS and the American OSS used these bases between them and Bedford now thronged with off-duty American soldiers. Walsh was in a position of privilege working with SOE. He knew more than most what was likely to be going on behind the lace curtains in these isolated country houses or within the barbed wire perimeters of the tiny airfields, but some locations remained a mystery even to him.

Woburn Abbey housed the British government's propaganda unit, the Political Warfare Executive, and at nearby Chicksands Priory the RAF had built a listening post to intercept enemy radio traffic. Enquiries about their work would be fobbed off with a terse reply from the men or women stationed there, some in uniform, some in civilian clothes. They were with the Foreign Office they'd say with no further elaboration.

There was an even bigger secret in a little town not twenty miles from Bedford, judging by the number of civilian workers that had been bussed into the surrounding area. The locals referred to them as 'guinea pigs' because landladies got a guinea a week towards the cost of housing them. They were an unlikely lot. Instead of spies or battle-hardened commandos the tenants were linguists, scholars and mathematicians but even Harry Walsh was not privy to the immense secret that lay behind Station X. Whatever was going on at Bletchley Park was classified too high even for him.

Walsh was more familiar with the area's secret airfields, thanks to his regular missions into occupied France. Cheddington and Chelveston were within easy reach and both used to drop agents, supplies or propaganda leaflets but today his destination was RAF Tempsford though he would not be flying anywhere.

Walsh pulled up by the front gate and handed over his identification papers for scrutiny. Just as he began to wonder if there was a problem with his documents, the sentry saluted Walsh and the barrier was raised.

Walsh rode the Norton along the approach road. All around him there was activity; voices raised in urgency, diverting lorries here and there to unload a precious cargo. Tempsford was the base for the Royal Air Force Special Duty Service, the airfield a supply base for the French resistance, dropping men, women and equipment into occupied territory. Canisters containing arms, ammunition and provisions were driven in from the nearby depot at Holme, to be dropped later by parachute. Lorries came and went and equipment was offloaded at an impressive rate. He found a quiet corner in which to safely leave the Norton and walked briskly into the main building.

Colonel Maurice Buckmaster was already on the base having seen off an agent the night before. Now he was deep in conversation with two other men. Buckmaster was a tall figure with a long nose, a small thatch of remaining hair and a perpetual frown. He resembled an accountant more than a senior army officer. Some questioned if he was too gentle to be head of 'F' Section but Walsh was not among the dissenters. Price jealously guarded access to the Colonel and Buckmaster could appear a distant, unapproachable figure sometimes but Walsh knew the man's work rate. Every day Buckmaster would put in an ample day at the office before cycling across London to his Chelsea home. There he would have an evening meal before returning once more to Baker Street and carrying on, usually well into the early hours. The whereabouts and welfare of some one hundred and twenty agents were always the Colonel's prime concern and that fact alone was enough to earn him the respect of Harry Walsh.

One of Buckmaster's companions wore the uniform of a US army officer.

'Captain Walsh,' said Buckmaster when he saw Harry, 'allow me to introduce Captain Sam Cooper from the Office of Strategic Services.'

The OSS man leaned forward to shake Walsh's hand. Cooper had a powerful soldier's frame and his light brown hair was parted neatly down one side. He looked a shade older than his twenty-five years, thought Walsh, but doesn't everybody these days?

'We've met,' said Walsh dryly.

'Harry, good to see you,' Cooper smiled broadly, 'so glad you made it out of Yugoslavia.'

'No thanks to you, Sam.'

'I never doubted you would.' Cooper was from well-heeled, Boston-Irish stock and family money had bought him into the Ivy League. He was smiling now, as if they were the very best of friends.

'Really? I did, on more than one occasion.'

Buckmaster coughed. 'I see you are already acquainted.' The Colonel was beginning to wonder if he was about to have an incident on his hands but he continued doggedly. 'And this is Monsieur Christophe Valvert of the Free French.' Until then Walsh had barely noticed the nondescript little man in civilian clothes who completed the group.

'I am a delight to make your acquaintance,' Valvert spoke

in heavily accented, broken English. The fellow must have stood no taller than five feet four inches in his stocking feet observed Walsh.

Buckmaster gave them all a short speech on the importance of their undertaking. And Walsh waited impatiently for the exact nature of the mission to be revealed.

'To begin with you will team up with a specially selected band of the Maquis,' Buckmaster continued. 'They have been asking us for equipment and are prepared to accept you into their group,' I'll bet they are thought Walsh, if they've not got a Sten gun between them, 'and they are committed to assisting you with operations in their area.'

'And what is their area?' asked Valvert.

'Normandy,' answered Buckmaster and Walsh inwardly shuddered at the prospect of an early return to the territory in which he recently risked his life.

'You will train the Maquis to assist you in a mission that is vital to the outcome of the war.' Buckmaster pulled a cover from a draftsman's easel behind him, to reveal a charcoal sketch of what appeared to be some form of alien flying machine.

'What on earth is that?' asked Walsh who had certainly never seen the like before.

'Something out of Buck Rogers,' observed Cooper.

'It looks like a toy,' said Valvert staring at its sleek lines and glass-fronted canopy, 'where are the propellers?'

'It doesn't need any,' answered Buckmaster, 'that is the Messerschmitt Me 163, a rocket-powered, fighter plane with a flying speed in excess of 600mph.'

Cooper whistled then leaned closer to the picture, frowning as he peered at it suspiciously.

Valvert reacted to the American's awe, 'That's fast? Really quick?' he asked uncertainly.

'It's fast,' confirmed Walsh, 'a Spitfire can do what?

360mph, maximum?' He glanced at Buckmaster who nodded his agreement. 'This thing is almost twice as quick but the real question is how near it is to full development? Is this a prototype we are looking at or a production model?'

'It's a prototype but production models are not far behind. We have a very well-placed source. He tells us the intention is to conduct battlefield tests on the fighter. There have been problems with it, thankfully. For starters it's too heavy, almost a tonne over its anticipated flying weight. Then there's the engine; a liquid-fuelled rocket-powered unit that is currently proving unstable.'

'Meaning what exactly?' asked Cooper.

'Meaning I would not want to be the first to fly it,' answered Walsh.

'The plane's excess weight makes it prone to crash landings and the liquid fuel has a nasty habit of igniting both the plane and its pilot. However, the engine is being rebuilt by this man,' and Buckmaster pointed to a faded, black and white photograph pinned to the board, of a middle-aged man with the unmistakeable look of academia about him. An emotionless face peered out at them from the photograph through dark rimmed glasses. 'This is Professor Gaerte, the scientist tasked with bringing on the development of Germany's latest miracle weapon, the Me 163 fighter interceptor, also known as the Komet. He must find a way to reduce the weight of the plane and make the unstable engine work before the first batch of some eighty odd production models is completed. If he succeeds the Germans will manufacture hundreds of Me 163s in the new year.'

'Meaning no prospect of a second front,' observed Walsh.

Buckmaster nodded, 'Exactly, any invasion of Europe must be based on complete air superiority or our ground forces will be annihilated before they have even left the beaches.'

'And if they have hundreds of jet fighters flying at that speed they can knock our planes out of the skies before they know what's hit them,' said Cooper.

'Indeed,' answered the Colonel.

Valvert peered at the odd-looking aircraft, 'But it looks so little and puny.'

'Imagine that same small and insignificant plane fitted with twin 30mm cannon,' continued Buckmaster, 'coming at one of our fighters at twice his speed. He would have no chance of outrunning it, let alone shooting it down.'

'So, what are we to do? Destroy this toy?' asked the French man.

Buckmaster did not answer at first. Instead he straightened and walked slowly away from the drawings.

'Why do I get the impression that wouldn't do the job?' asked Cooper. 'If you know where it is, the RAF could drop everything they had on it.'

Buckmaster's tone became appeasing, almost apologetic. 'First, we do not know exactly where it is, only where it is going to be. Eight weeks from now the battlefield trial will commence from an airfield in Normandy. The Me 163 prototype will leave Germany for the first time, to join up with a squadron of Luftwaffe fighter planes. It will go on patrols and have its effectiveness evaluated by scientists attempting to eradicate its remaining faults. Second, destroying the plane would be a setback for the Germans but one that could be measured in weeks not months.'

'So what are we expected to do if not destroy it?' questioned Valvert.

'I think I can guess,' answered Walsh, 'if I am right the Colonel has already shown us our target.'

11

'I think that the dropping of men dressed in civilian clothes for the purpose of attempting to kill members of the opposing forces is not an operation with which the Royal Air Force should be associated.'

Air Chief Marshal Charles Portal on the SOE

The three men who would make up the first Jedburgh team all turned their gaze back on to the unknowing face in the picture.

'Exactly, Walsh,' Buckmaster was nodding, 'remove Gaerte and the delay becomes months.'

'Remove?' asked Valvert.

'He is Germany's foremost expert in liquid-fuelled jet propulsion and will accompany the plane to France,' explained Buckmaster, 'kill the professor and his expertise dies with him.'

'So, it's an assassination, as simple as that,' said Cooper.

'I wouldn't exactly describe it as simple,' admitted the Colonel, 'there are a number of obstacles but we will go through the fine detail in due course.'

A number of obstacles thought Walsh, between them and a scientist who holds the future of the Third Reich in his hands; try half the German army for starters. For now though, he thought it best to keep his own counsel.

Valvert was not so reticent, 'Colonel, how do you get all this information about Germany's top-secret plane?'

Walsh snorted, 'He's hardly going to tell you.'

'Quite,' answered Buckmaster and Valvert felt like a schoolboy whose question has been ridiculed by the rest of his class. 'Let's just say our source has proved reliable in the past.' Though Buckmaster would not admit it, he did not know the identity of the source either. Shegel's information had first been processed by MI6 and reported to Churchill personally by Menzies in one of their weekly briefings. Neither man would accept anything less than the unconditional surrender of Germany but it could do no harm to encourage destabilising forces within the Third Reich, especially when they provided priceless nuggets of intelligence to court favour with the allies. A dialogue with the plotters was worth it, even if they ultimately proved to be little more than a stone in Hitler's boot.

Churchill gave the job of killing Gaerte to Gubbins without telling MI6. In one of life's ironies, Six, as they always did, would now try to undermine an SOE operation they knew nothing about that was based on intelligence they themselves had provided.

'Who will command this operation, sir?' asked Walsh.

'This morning I agreed with Captain Cooper that you will be in nominal operational command, Walsh, based purely on field experience.' Walsh gave Cooper a small nod to acknowledge his concession of command. 'However, we expect each of you to use your respective skills and work together as a team.'

'Of course,' replied Walsh.

'We are still new to this game,' admitted Cooper, 'and we have something to learn about clandestine operations in France.'

Buckmaster turned to Walsh, 'Captain, can you devise a

training program for Monsieur Valvert and Captain Cooper before you leave?'

'Oh yes, sir,' answered Walsh and Cooper was perturbed to see a slight smile cross the Englishman's face.

'Good, now let's go over this in detail,' commanded Buckmaster, 'naturally you'll have questions.'

Indeed, thought Walsh, as he stared into the dull bespectacled eyes on the photograph, chief among them *how am I going to get close enough to kill you*?

They were leaving the building a little over two hours later when Cooper caught up with Walsh. 'This business in Yugoslavia, answer me truthfully, Harry, what would you have done in my position?'

'Probably the same thing,' Walsh admitted, 'doesn't mean I have to like it.'

Cooper nodded as if conceding he had a point. 'And are we going to have a problem working together – that's all I need to know? If you prefer to work with somebody else on this one then you should tell me now.'

Walsh sighed, 'No, Sam, we are not going to have a problem, as long as you consider me not trusting you as far as I could throw you to not be a problem.'

Cooper smiled, 'Thank you for your candour, Harry.'

'I've got to be going,' said Walsh, 'remember to meet me on the early train tomorrow.'

'I haven't forgotten. Where are you taking us or is that something else we're not permitted to know?'

Walsh had almost reached the motorbike but he turned to answer the American, 'I'm taking you to the Thatched Barn.'

'What's that,' Cooper called after him suspiciously, 'one of your pubs?' But Walsh was already astride the Norton. He kicked it into life and roared away.

There was no consistency in the trees. They were a patchwork of bronze, gold and green, as if they couldn't decide between them when summer should end and autumn begin.

Opposite Walsh sat Valvert, staring unblinkingly out of the window as he had done from the moment the train left the station, his face a mask, showing no emotion. He might be on a day trip or visiting his grandmother. Walsh had noted Valvert's ability to disappear quietly within himself with satisfaction, his flat almost featureless face granting him an anonymity that would serve them well amid the hostile occupied streets of his homeland. In another life, it might be considered a handicap to possess what could honestly be described as dull, unmemorable looks but here his inherently conventional appearance was a distinct advantage.

Walsh offered Valvert a cigarette, which the Frenchman gratefully accepted, acknowledging it with a little dip of his head. Cooper meanwhile used the time on the train to doze.

Colonel Elder Wills was waiting for them inside Station XV, an anomalous building known to all as the 'Thatched Barn'. The large white-brick, thatched-roof dwelling had three chimneys, numerous out-of-proportion windows and a flag pole by its entrance way, which bore an ever present Union Jack. For a reason no one could readily explain a number of ornate bird tables were lined up like sentries in front of its walls. The whole muddled construction would have seemed more at home in the middle of an alpine ski resort than a quiet corner off the Barnet bypass. This former film studio near Elstree provided SOE with its 'props' as Colonel Wills liked to refer to them.

Despite his rank, Elder greeted Walsh like an old friend, for he was still a civilian at heart. 'Harry! Come in you scoundrel.'

The Colonel conceded to his early forties, weighed at least

18 stones, walked with a limp thanks to a wound received at Dunkirk and was deaf in one ear. To compensate for this condition, he had a tendency to issue instructions at little short of a bellow, which merely added to his larger than life demeanour.

'And who are these fine fellows with you?'

Walsh made the introductions and was amused when Cooper seemed taken aback by the ebullient Colonel Wills. The former film director was certainly no shrinking violet but Walsh was long used to him. Walsh produced the letter of authorisation from Gubbins. Elder read it intently then looked up, alarmed.

'Good God, Harry, what are you planning?' he declaimed with an almost Shakespearian grandeur. 'Starting the second front all on your own?' and he turned to Cooper, 'I wouldn't put it past him.'

'Never you mind, Colonel.'

'Need to know, eh? Yes, all right,' it was enunciated sadly, as if Walsh had spoilt his fun, 'well, at least you have a letter.' Men had tried to take items from the Thatched Barn before without completing the necessary paperwork but none had succeeded. Instead they were reprimanded sternly and at length while Elder stood over them like an aggrieved headmaster.

Elder reached into his pocket and withdrew a small leather-bound notepad and a worn pencil. 'So what exactly do you need, Harry?'

'Tyre bursters,' Harry began while Elder scribbled on the pad, sticking out his bottom lip as he wrote, 'and Gammon bombs. Also clam charges, with time pencils. The ones with the half pound of plastic explosive.'

'That sounds like some major firework display, Harry,' said Cooper, 'though I haven't heard of any of this stuff before.'

'It's all been specially developed for our kind of work,' explained Walsh, 'there's no point sending pieces of artillery, bazookas or rifles over to France when they are wholly unsuited to the task and easy to find during searches. Colonel, would you be good enough to show Captain Cooper around?'

'Delighted, dear boy, as long as he's authorised of course. You are authorised, aren't you, Captain Cooper?'

'Of course,' replied the American.

'I can vouch for that,' confirmed Walsh.

Elder took them to a large wooden trestle table set aside from the main part of the room and picked up a pen. 'This is quite useful. It's a basic, working fountain pen but inside there's a .38 calibre ampoule of tear gas. All our 'Joes' take them into the field now. If you're stopped or arrested you trigger it like so,' and he pressed his finger lightly against the catch to show them without actually activating the weapon, 'there's enough gas in here to seriously inconvenience any annoying German.'

Elder took them further down the table and Cooper recoiled at what appeared to be a large pile of decaying rodents.

'My God,' exclaimed the American.

'Don't be alarmed, Captain, they are perfectly safe and entirely disease free.'

'But they are… rats. Aren't they?'

'Yes, well sort of. Dried and cured rat skins to be exact, stuffed with plastic explosives until they have regained their original shape then sewn back up, neat as you like. Insert a standard primer and it's an explosive device that looks to any casual observer like, well, a dead rat,' and Elder smiled at the seeming absurdity of it all. 'The device can be triggered with a simple time delay fuse or by the flames from any boiler; though you'd better not hang around once you've chucked it in. Unusual I'll grant you but highly effective,' and he beamed proudly. 'We do exploding coal as well you know,' he mused, 'and turds; camel turds so far, for the North African campaign. Not much use in France though, camel turds,' he ruminated.

'No, not much,' agreed Cooper.

'What have we got these days in the way of silent killing?' asked Walsh.

'Silent killing?' mused Elder.

He was already striding over to another part of the workshop. The American followed dumbly and Walsh found himself enjoying his perplexity. Cooper had seen a lot in a short, quite spectacular career with the OSS but he had never come across anything like the Thatched Barn before.

'It's like something created by a demented Walt Disney,' he spoke softly to Walsh as they walked, shaking his head at the Thatched Barn, 'and here are all the elves.' They passed two dozen workbenches, each one manned by an industrious craftsman intent on welding, sawing or hammering some unconventional weapon into shape. The din was akin to that of a much larger factory floor producing a rush order for armaments. Walsh wondered which of these creations would ever see operational use and how many would be rejected because they were deemed more dangerous to the user than his target.

Elder turned abruptly back to face Walsh, 'Do you think he could handle the Welrod?' He was referring to Cooper as if the American were not in the room.

'Absolutely,' replied Walsh.

'Good. Then follow me, Captain Cooper, and we will see what you are made of.'

12

*'Three may keep a secret,
if two of them are dead.'*

Benjamin Franklin

Elder led the way down a dark and curving metal staircase into the bowels of the building. As they reached the bottom the air turned stale. They walked through large windowless rooms with low curved ceilings made of brickwork that resembled the underside of railway arches. Temporary lights had been rigged up and every surface dusted and scrubbed – in a manner beloved of the British army – until years of grime had been removed, though the distinctive smell of age and musty dampness still remained. Once used to house unwanted furniture and a generous stock of wine, the huge cellar had been cleared for a new purpose.

They finally reached their destination, a low room, which housed a shooting gallery. A long trellis table supported half a dozen weapons, along with ammunition of various calibres. Man-sized paper targets were pinned to large planks secured against sandbags against the far wall. Spent cartridges littered the floor. The room was filled with the smoky aroma of spent gunpowder. Elder issued instructions and two men removed the debris from a morning of weapons testing. A new box of 9mm ammunition and fresh paper targets were provided.

Finally, something resembling a violin case was set down on the table.

Cooper watched as Elder opened the box and removed a weapon with a distinctly unorthodox appearance. It seemed nothing more than a long, bulbous length of steel tubing with a rudimentary trigger guard attached to its underside. Elder took a short, squat magazine, loaded six of the 9mm rounds then slotted the magazine up into the barrel behind the trigger guard. He handed the weapon to Cooper, who took it gingerly.

'The Welrod, Captain Cooper. What do you think?'

'Looks like a piece of drain pipe with a trigger,' said Cooper flatly.

'Yes, well, appearances can be deceptive,' answered Elder. 'This is a fine example of British engineering. Possibly the most effective example of suppressed weaponry in the world.'

'Suppressed,' asked Cooper, 'you mean silenced?'

'Indeed I do. Almost inaudible in fact.'

Cooper regarded the weapon in a new light. Elder leaned forward to point out the gun's features. 'It's a remarkably simple device. You have a fourteen-inch steel cylinder for the barrel. The weapon is bolt action, with the bolt in the rear and the expansion chamber for the suppressor housed in here,' he tapped the middle of the barrel. 'The baffles and wipes are at the front which causes the suppression of sound. The magazine doubles as the pistol grip.'

Cooper raised the weapon and aimed it towards the sandbags, 'Range?'

'Theoretically, thirty to forty feet but I wouldn't actually recommend using it unless you are quite close to the target.'

Cooper lined up the two basic sights on the barrel of the gun, balanced its two and a half pounds in loaded weight carefully in his hand, allowed for the drag of its protruding barrel, took a breath, held it then fired. A slight popping of air signalled the discharge of the weapon. Cooper lowered the Welrod and placed it on the table. A technician retrieved the paper target and the group gathered round.

'Right in the throat,' noted Valvert.

'Good shooting, Captain Cooper,' said Elder as they surveyed the bullet-sized tear in the paper.

'Nice weapon, Major Wills,' acknowledged the American.

'And quieter than a nun's confession,' said Walsh.

They each took a turn with the Welrod; Walsh reacquainting himself with a weapon he had used to good effect on enemy sentries, though never before to murder a civilian in cold blood. Like Elder Wills, Gaerte spent his time in laboratories and factories with clipboard and pencil. Unlike Elder, he had probably never fired a gun in anger in his life but if his work was allowed to continue, many thousands of Allied soldiers would perish. That was justification enough to see him removed him from the world.

It was time for Valvert to take his turn. They soon realised that, whatever military background he had, he was unlikely ever to have been lauded for his marksmanship.

'High, wide and handsome,' said Elder dryly when they surveyed his blank target, 'you're a danger to low flying aircraft, Monsieur Valvert. Whatever it is you are good at, I suggest you stick to it. Leave the shooting to these two, eh?'

'It's too damn long,' said Valvert, as he frowned at the barrel and swore in French.

'Come on, I'll escort you from the premises,' Elder's abrupt announcement signalled the end of their tour, 'to make sure you don't steal the family silver.'

'Are you certain you have everything we need?' asked Walsh.

'It's all here, Harry,' said Elder and he tapped the notebook confidently.

On his way out he turned to Cooper, 'Being an American I expect you are partial to films, or should that be "movies"?'

Cooper seemed keen to avoid offending his host, 'On occasion, yes.'

Walsh found it hard to picture the straight-laced Cooper enjoying a Hollywood melodrama. He wouldn't be able to sit still for long enough.

'Then perhaps you have seen some of my work. I was a director before the war you know. Familiar with *Song of Freedom* at all? That was one of mine?'

'Er... I'm afraid I don't think I know it.'

'Really? Quite a big hit that one, back in '35, starred Paul Robeson as a matter of fact.'

'I may have been posted abroad around then.' Walsh knew Cooper would still have been studying at his Ivy League university in 1935 but decided against pointing this out.

'Oh, well what about *Tiger Bay*? I wrote and directed that one.'

Cooper looked as if he did not know what to say.

'Mmm, don't remember it either,' Elder said a little sulkily. 'It seems I may not achieve immortality through the big screen.' He appeared genuinely sad about that for a moment. 'Still, my little inventions might end up in a glass case somewhere one day.'

'They are one of a kind, Colonel, just like you.'

'Thank you, Harry, although I must say I wouldn't have the stomach to use a single one of them up close. I don't envy you that task. My war seemed more gentlemanly somehow. I was in the Royal Flying Corps during the last show, Captain Cooper. We shot at each other from our planes and it was terrifying and bloody but at least there were rules, a code you could understand. Damned Nazis certainly put an end to that, which is why we have to fight fire with fire. I know that, of course, but I don't think I'd be able to do it myself. No,' he nodded emphatically, 'I'll leave all that dirty fighting to you chaps.'

Having made his point Elder strode magisterially ahead of them, having spotted something else to divert his short span of attention.

'Your Colonel Wills is quite a character,' announced Cooper with classic understatement.

'He is,' agreed Walsh, 'but his props can save your life when you are in a tight spot. There's many a Joe returned from a mission thanks to one of Elder's little gadgets working just the way he said it would.'

'I wonder how many did not return,' mused Valvert, 'because one of them did not work the way he said it would.'

'That, Valvert, we will never know,' conceded Walsh.

Elder was walking back to them now, in animated conversation with a stranger. He was a tall blond athletic-looking man in his mid-thirties with a distinctly rakish look, dressed in the uniform of a naval commander. There's a man who looks as if he knows how to enjoy life, thought Walsh.

'Harry, Captain Cooper, Monsieur Valvert, there's someone here I would like you all to meet,' announced Elder with genuine enthusiasm, 'he's another of you cloak and dagger boys down for the day to examine my wares; from Naval Intelligence; right-hand man to Admiral Godfrey no less. I rather think you two would get along, Harry. He comes down here all the time to look at my little gadgets.'

The stranger stretched out a hand to Walsh. They shook hands firmly and the naval commander said, 'The name's Fleming. Ian Fleming.'

Save for themselves, the railway carriage was empty on the return journey. The English countryside rolled passively by outside.

'Of course we will need clothes, equipment, documents…' observed Valvert.

'You can leave all that to me,' assured Walsh, 'I know some people,'

'Aren't we coming along?' asked Cooper.

'Not this time, Sam. My contacts are a little shy. They deal only with me.'

'Meaning we have to trust you on this one, right?' Cooper sounded distinctly uncomfortable at the prospect.

'That's right,' said Walsh, enjoying the American's unease.

'And what will we be doing while you are meeting these nervous individuals?' asked Valvert.

'Completing your education. I've arranged some time at Beaulieu.'

'And what is Beaulieu?' asked Valvert suspiciously.

'A beautiful, old English country house.'

'Sounds nice,' said Cooper, 'so why are you smiling?'

'Because it's an experience you are unlikely ever to forget, Sam.'

13

'This is war not sport. Your aim is to kill your opponent as quickly as possible. So forget the Queensberry Rules.'

Major William Fairbairn, SOE expert on silent killing.

Sam Cooper faced his assailant resolutely and attempted to rein in his anger. He had come off worse so far and his body throbbed from the punishment it had taken but Cooper was a determined man and he would never give in lightly. He climbed slowly to his feet then suddenly launched himself straight at Fairbairn, feinting with a right hand to the torso then checking it and bringing a crashing left fist into the other man's solar plexus. Fairbairn simply stepped lightly away from the blow, caught his assailant off-balance on the follow-through, and then grabbed Cooper's arm, twisted it and somehow pulled Cooper further off his feet, before succeeding in his principal aim of lifting the American right off the ground and propelling him through the air.

As he was flung forward, Cooper was dimly aware of his audience being exhorted to use their opponent's anger and forward momentum against them to knock an attacker off-balance. Then he crashed heavily to the floor, letting out a considerable groan as the wind was knocked from his body. Cooper rolled over on the mat but Fairbairn was on him in an instant, drawing back a boot to deliver the coup de grace, as he enthusiastically instructed the room full of candidates, 'Then kick him hard in the testicles!' And he did just that, halting his heavy boot only at the very last moment before impact. Cooper was entirely uninjured by the kick but for a brief alarming second had fully believed it would connect.

'Thank you, Captain Cooper, you've been most helpful,' concluded Fairbairn politely, 'you can take a seat again now.' He held out a hand to haul the American to his feet.

Cooper had just gone several throws with William Fairbairn, the SOE's unarmed-combat instructor, an expert in silent killing, and the former Shanghai policeman had dumped him repeatedly onto the rubber mat. Fairbairn was teaching two dozen khaki-clad candidates of both sexes how to master the ancient eastern art of jujitsu. If it was so ancient and eastern, wondered Cooper ruefully, why did almost all of Fairbairn's moves end with the very British phrase 'then kick him hard in the testicles'?

At the end of the session the candidates all filed from the gymnasium. Valvert caught up with Cooper on the way out to enquire after his well-being. Cooper's torso ached but he shrugged, 'I've had worse.' Certainly that was true but not recently and never in the name of training. Cooper told himself it was in no way a humiliation to be called out in front of an audience, including a fair number of women, to be almost casually disarmed of the razor-sharp commando knife he had been given, then thrown all over the matting like a small child trying to fight a fully grown adult. 'I hope you learned something watching me get slung about in there.'

'Oh, I did,' replied the Frenchman, 'I learned violence is definitely not for me. I will leave all of that to you and Captain Walsh. William Fairbairn is remarkably skilled but I would be surprised if a man such as I could learn too much of that in a week. I fear I may have forgotten most of his instructions already.'

'I haven't,' Cooper assured him. It was the silver lining he would take from the comprehensive beating. 'I remember every last damned thing and God help the first person who gives me an excuse to use it.'

Lunch was typical British wartime fare, a plate consisting largely of potatoes and watery cabbage, accompanied by a small chunk of protein of indeterminate source. Cooper thought it best not to enquire after its origins but he wondered how something so flavourless could give off such a pungent aroma. Even the effort required to stick a fork into it made his aching muscles throb.

Apart from the quality of the food and bruises from the jujitsu, Cooper had to agree Walsh was right. Beaulieu had been a good idea.

'Beaulieu is a sort of SOE finishing school, Sam,' Walsh had explained, 'it will be tough down there but they'll teach you a few things you'll be glad you learned.'

That was true. The American had used the time well, attending talks on everything from escape and evasion to rudimentary safecracking. He concluded that almost all of the lectures were worth staying awake for. Admittedly some of Beaulieu's experts could not, by any stretch of the imagination, be described as charismatic. Some were eccentrics, others had the ability to declaim the most interesting of topics as if teaching advanced algebra to bored boys at a prep school but all had something useful to impart from their experience of clandestine warfare in occupied lands.

One or two of the instructors were even quite compelling. He had heard promising things about the first lecture of the afternoon. 'This fellow's very good you know, considering he's quite new,' confirmed a fellow diner.

Sure enough the speaker was a confident young man with a clipped patrician accent, who seemed entirely sure of both himself and his abilities. He started the lecture punctually and without ceremony, 'I will be devoting the next hour to a talk on the art of propaganda and its practical uses against the enemy.' He spoke authoritatively in a voice that somehow defied you not to listen to him. By the lecture's end, Cooper had to admit he had learned a great deal from a relatively short time in the company of Kim Philby.

Goering's office was large enough to house a small aircraft. Professor Gaerte was seated opposite him in an opulent, handcrafted chair made from soft leather and varnished beechwood, yet he was far from comfortable.

'I promised the Führer the Komet would soon undergo combat testing because you assured me it was nearly ready.' A subaltern tried to bring them coffee on a silver tray but Goering waved him away. 'I brought you back to the Komet expecting great things, Gaerte, yet all you give me is more dead pilots. I hear they have started to call the planes "Buzz-bombs". They tell me the last man was literally dissolved by chemicals. Nothing left to bury. Is this progress?'

Gaerte had time to reflect that Goering had a source close enough to the project to leak embarrassing details to him but that was hardly a surprise. 'That was the new fuel mixture, Reichsmarschall.' The professor was nervous but knew he had to stand firm. 'It is highly corrosive and increases the risk for our brave volunteers.' Gaerte calculated that the welfare of pilots was not high on Goering's list of priorities. He was unlikely to blanch at an increase in casualties if it brought results. 'However, as you know, the previous mixture did not allow enough time in the sky for target selection.'

'As soon as the damned plane is in the sky, the pilot brings it home again. I know that much.'

'Which is precisely why I ordered a change from the T-Stoff mixture to the new Z-Stoff formula.' Goering leant back in his chair and folded his arms. Gaerte knew he could easily lose the

Reichsmarschall's interest; he cared little for detail. 'The correct mixture is essential; previously, at eighty-five per cent hydrogen superoxide, with carbon dioxide, hydrogen and catalysts, we had less than one minute to reach altitude, assuming that is, a forty-five degree climb at 10,000 feet per minute...'

'Enough!' cried Goering, 'I did not order you here to lecture me. I just want to know if the plane is ready to go to France and engage the enemy without running out of fuel or exploding on landing. Can you answer that simple question, Gaerte?'

'Which was the part I was just coming to; yes, Reichsmarschall, trialling the new fuel mixture, combined with the additional work on weight elimination...' Goering sighed and Gaerte went faster, desperate to finish his explanation, '... I predict the Komet will gain an additional sixty seconds of airborne target selection time yet still land safely.' Gaerte raced to the end of the sentence.

Goering nodded, 'Well, I hope you are right. The Führer has a lot of faith in this project, Gaerte. Of all the weapons he is counting on to deliver the Reich from its enemies, this is the closest to completion. If you succeed, there will be a summons to the Berghof and you will be a hero of the Fatherland.' Gaerte risked a small smile. He could not resist the briefest glance towards the framed picture of Hitler on the wall behind Goering. 'If you fail... well, just don't bother to come back.'

On his way out of the building, Gaerte contemplated the words Goering had used. Did he really mean them in a literal sense? By inference, would it be better for Gaerte to take his own life? The conclusion seemed inescapable. The Reichsmarschall really did mean that.

The sign above the door read 'Dickens, Templeman & Marlowe – Antiquarian books and lithographs', and beneath it, in smaller *olde worlde* style lettering, the words 'Specialists in rare first editions' were added, almost as an afterthought.

Of course, there was no Dickens nor was there a Marlowe. Clavelle, the latest proprietor of this specialist bookstore on the Charing Cross Road, had chosen the names purely for their English literary connections. Templeman did in fact exist but he had nothing whatsoever to do with the book trade. He was in fact the first Englishman Clavelle had met upon his arrival; a young army officer who gave the Frenchman a sympathetic debrief in the post-Dunkirk chaos. Poor Templeman had no idea of the true character of the man to whom he had just granted sanctuary.

As the bell above the door rang shrilly, Clavelle looked up from the counter. He showed no sign of recognition as Walsh entered his crumbling shop. Instead he continued with the task in hand, gently coaxing an elderly male customer into parting with twenty English pounds for a rare and ancient edition of *Don Quixote*.

'I can assure you this purchase will never be a cause for regret,' the English words were mangled by a soup-thick French accent but Clavelle practised them often enough to be understood. 'Cervantes is such a solid investment in these uncertain times.' As no doubt was every other author on these shelves, thought Walsh, in case the customer's eyes should carelessly wander to another tome.

Walsh played the part of the browsing customer, lifting books from the old wooden shelves and perusing them, while he waited for the fool and his money to be expertly parted. The room was dark and musty, filled with the aroma of the ancient leather that bound many of the books. It's the smell of decay thought Walsh.

When the man finally left, Walsh turned to Clavelle and asked, 'That a real copy you just sold him or a fake?'

Clavelle smiled, 'What does it matter if it's real to him? Let him tilt at his windmills.'

Clavelle had the wiry frame of the perennial prisoner. Years of successfully avoiding a return to jail had done little to alter his undernourished body and gaunt face. His cheeks were sunken, the lips thin and bloodless; his hair was lank and unwashed and he constantly swept it from his eyes. 'So what is it?' Clavelle's voice was stilted, as if he struggled to conquer the alien language he dealt in. 'Not a first edition. What do you want from me?'

'Everything,' answered Walsh.

Clavelle nodded slowly, then he walked out from behind the counter and locked the front door. He gestured to a curtain, which hung over a door-sized gap at the rear of the shop.

'Then you had better go through, 'Arry.'

14

'Go search for people who are hurt by fate or nature.'

Advice on the recruitment of agents from
a Soviet spymaster

Walsh followed Clavelle into the rear private section of the shop. Here was a storeroom containing, among other things, an overflow of books yet to be sorted for the shelves. There was a small wooden table with two simple chairs and Clavelle removed a pile of books from one of them then gestured for Walsh to sit. There was a tiny stove in the corner of the room with a kettle on it but Clavelle was not the sort to offer his acquaintances refreshment and the people he did business with rarely stayed long. Aside from books, the room was quite bare. Walsh suspected it contained nothing the Frenchman could not leave behind in an instant if he needed to. He wondered if Clavelle spent his solitary evenings in this tiny, cheerless room.

'Whoever said crime doesn't pay.'

'Very funny, 'Arry. I have overheads, you know.'

Clavelle may not exactly be enjoying the good life in London town, pondered Walsh, but at least he possessed the good sense to realise he was unlikely to flourish under the Third Reich. He had fled France under a false name with an equally fictitious letter of introduction, purported to be from the British embassy in Paris, bringing with him enough funds to continue his nefarious activities. These included the faking of rare and ancient books, for which there was still a surprisingly buoyant market even in wartime.

Clavelle had used his skills to forge the necessary papers to spirit himself out of occupied France. His successful escape put him in mind to start a lucrative sideline; forging travel documents for those with a similar incompatibility to the Nazi regime. Passports, travel passes, permits for work and exemptions from it could all be purchased from Clavelle. The majority of these documents were designed to transport people out of occupied France into neighbouring neutral countries. Others would prove just as effective for getting people inside. With a pocketful of Clavelle's documents an entirely new covert identity could be confidently assumed and that is how Harry Walsh came to know the fraudster.

'I need three of the ration books in the new style and driving licences – the *permis de conduire les automobiles* on the pink paper.'

'D'accord, what else?'

'Travel passes for the buses and the trains. The *Société Nationale des Chemins de Fer Français* and the *abonnement réseau urbain*. I'll need ID cards, the *carte d'identité* with the fingerprints and *République française* stamps on them...'

Clavelle nodded gravely, 'They're always tricky.' And he began to stroke his chin as if in deep thought. Walsh took this reticence as feigned; a preparation for the convoluted haggling over price that would surely follow. Clavelle was never the easiest man to deal with but he was the only credible alternative to the regular channels used by SOE. The Special Operations Executive employed a number of talented individuals to forge documents, some naturally of a criminal persuasion, but Walsh had begun to distrust internal security. The finished documents appeared wholly authentic but were of minimal use if their cover names had been betrayed in advance by some rogue section of SIS.

Above all else, Clavelle was discreet, a quality that was based entirely on self-interest, but he was also a lover of money and Walsh always paid on time, so Clavelle was never too disappointed to see him enter the little shop.

'And finally, census certificates, exempting the bearer from compulsory work service.'

The Frenchman whistled at the burden required of him.

'And how long do I have to prepare these crown jewels for you?'

'Two weeks.'

Clavelle spread his palms, 'It cannot be done.'

'Yes it can, as long as I agree to your ridiculously inflated price and I go to the front of your queue. That way I am unlikely to inform my friends at Special Branch that not everything in your shop is a genuine first edition.' As if his contacts in Special Branch would give a damn, thought Walsh, but Clavelle was not to know that.

Clavelle frowned, ''Arry, please, I thought we were friends. Very well, I shall think about my price, which will be fair as it always is, bearing in mind the risks I must take to get hold of the genuine documents for copying plus the latest stamps.'

'It's not your risk, Clavelle. You never leave Charing Cross Road. Your associates in France take all the risks.'

'And since I must pay them, it amounts to the same thing.'

As Walsh left the Charing Cross Road he found himself almost instinctively heading north. When he reached the British Museum he suddenly stopped, checked and turned back towards Russell Street then along the Theobalds Road into Holborn.

The morning's business with Clavelle had gone smoothly enough, so perhaps now was as good a time as any to get it over with. Though the prospect was distasteful to him, Walsh knew he could no longer put it off. He would do it then and do it now and have done with. He would go and visit Jago.

Halfway along Theobalds Road, Walsh stopped abruptly. He moved sharply to cross the street, glancing back the way he had come as if checking for traffic. Walsh could often detect a pursuer with a sudden about turn, even if they were very good. A flicker of hesitation was all he needed. Did anyone move too quickly into a shop doorway, look away abruptly or merely lower their head instinctively to shield the face under the brim of a hat? It could be enough to give them away.

Not this morning. No one seemed to be following him now and there had been no tail on his way to meet Clavelle. He was almost sure of it. Unless the person – or more likely persons – doing the surveillance was really very good indeed, and there were still some out there even at this stage in the war. Six had followed him before but not in a while. Walsh had to concede he probably wasn't worth their time these days. After all they had no inkling of his role in Gubbins' scheme.

Of course there was another possibility. All that time in the field had dulled his edge. Perhaps he was no longer able to tell the difference between a watcher from MI6 and a midshipman home on leave or a housewife clutching her ration book. Walsh put the doubts from his mind. In any case Jago was worth the risk.

These days, Jago lived in a run-down, one-bedroom apartment above a shabby pub on the Gray's Inn Road. 'I do like to be near the street,' he'd explained in that peculiarly resonant voice of his, turned deeper over the years from the excessive intake of whisky and tobacco. 'The street' was nearby Fleet Street but Walsh knew it was the low-level rent that really attracted Jago to the spot. 'I'm back where I belong in the autumn of my years, on the streets of "Sod'em" and Gomorrah, amid the human detritus of dear old London town – and you know what, Harry? I wouldn't have it any other way!' He spoke the words defiantly but with little apparent conviction.

Jago was sitting in the saloon bar of the pub beneath his tiny apartment, as Walsh knew he would be. As the younger man crossed the floor the warped wooden boards creaked in protest, as if they were never designed for treading on. Jago did not seem to notice. He was too busy making notes with an ancient Mont Blanc fountain pen, its nib leaking ink on to the writing paper. Jago wore his crumpled, worsted Savile Row suit and the chain of a gold pocket watch strained against the ample girth of his waistcoat. Walsh doubted it was actually attached to anything. More likely he had already pawned the watch for rent money, an impression that was immediately heightened when Jago squinted at an ancient Cartier wristwatch to check the hour. Like Jago, it had seen better days. Next to his papers was a glass, containing a generous measure of scotch, and Jago reached for it absent-mindedly with yellowing, nicotine-stained fingers that shook visibly. It was a little after eleven thirty.

'Writing your will, Jago?'

The older man looked up in surprise, peering at Walsh from beneath unkempt, bushy eyebrows, 'Harry, dear boy, well I never.' Jago had an aristocratic demeanour and a clipped, cut-glass accent so akin to what an average man might expect of an upper-class gent that it just had to be fake. 'If you say so; shall I leave you all my debts?' He chuckled softly before noticing his glass, as if for the first time, 'Just having a livener, a bit of a pick-me-up. Join me?'

Walsh shook his head – the answering silence somehow more disconcerting to Jago than words could ever be. Walsh towered over the older man, a menacing silhouette that blotted out the little light that was still able to reach them through the grimy windows. Jago seemed to shrink visibly into his chair. He swallowed audibly, his mouth suddenly dry.

'So, Harry,' forced cheerfulness, 'what can I do for you this fine autumnal morning?'

Walsh looked about him. Everything in the bar was decrepit, including most of the clientele. Jago's watch and pen were perhaps the only authentic items in the place.

'You know what I want, Jago,' he said, 'let's get out of here.'

15

'Men are born to succeed, not to fail.'

Henry David Thoreau

'Lamb and Flag's just round the corner, Harry,' suggested Jago struggling to keep up with the younger man's pace, 'or should we have a spot of lunch instead?' he asked hopefully. 'What do you say? How about Wiltons? Haven't had a slap-up one at Wiltons in donkey's years.'

'Really? I thought Emma Stirling took you there three weeks ago.' Walsh knew she had for he had been the one to suggest it.

'Three weeks, was it really?' Jago smiled nervously. 'Well, if you say so, old boy. I mean, time flies. Emma Stirling, ah yes, feisty little thing, a real popsie that one. Thank you for sending her, Harry, brightened my day considerably I must say. What a shame she's so...'

Walsh locked eyes with Jago.

'It's all right, Harry, I was going to say "unattainable". Oh well, honey wasn't meant for the mouth of a donkey.' Then he chuckled. 'Ever tempted to have a crack at her yourself?' Walsh gave Jago a murderous look. 'Course not, you're married and very happily damn you. Lucky man! How is the lovely Mary? Thriving I expect.'

The walk to Wiltons left Jago with beads of sweat on his forehead. When they were finally seated, he dabbed at them with a crumpled handkerchief.

'You'll be wanting to see my latest bona fides,' puffed Jago and he handed over a battered press card as fabricated as he was. It optimistically proclaimed him to be a correspondent for the *Daily Herald*. Walsh barely glanced at it before flicking the card back at him. Jago picked it reverently from the table and placed it carefully back into his wallet. When the wine arrived Jago watched as the waiter poured them both a generous glass and immediately took a large gulp. Seemingly rejuvenated, he completed a survey of the room, his eyes reaching into every corner. When he was satisfied he asked, 'So what is it this time, Harry?'

'I want information, Jago.'

'T'was ever thus.'

'I need you to engage that prodigious memory of yours.'

'What will it be then? Names and addresses of cafés and safe houses on the Rue St Georges, a breakdown of the local Gestapo hierarchy in some obscure little part of the Dordogne perhaps or a quick peep into the life of the latest thug sent by Six to tweak your tail? Knowing you, Harry, it's probably the latter, am I right?'

'It isn't anybody from Six.'

'Relieved to hear it,' and he palpably was, 'they're not too keen on old Jago right now. You'll get me shot one day, you will.'

'That's funny,' said Walsh without a trace of humour, 'always thought you'd end up hanged.'

Jago forced a weak little laugh.

'This time it's closer to home. My boss in fact.'

'Gubbins?' the question came too quickly.

'There are several layers between the CD and me and you know it.'

'Who then?'

'Price.'

'Price?' Jago rolled the name slowly over his tongue as if it were a foreign word he was attempting to translate.

'Major Robert Price,' confirmed Walsh, 'formerly of the Scott's Guards, now Deputy Head of Section "F", Special Operations Executive.'

'I think I vaguely know who you mean.'

'Don't be coy, Jago, it doesn't suit you. You know exactly who I mean. He's hardly low profile.'

'No he's not,' conceded Jago, 'not in this game at any rate. Let's assume I do know him then, but shall we also imagine I get a little nervous when you come to me about your own commanding officer. What's that all about? I mean if you have a question why don't you just ask the fellow?'

'That's my business.'

Jago looked down at his wine then, swirling the contents of his half-empty glass, not wanting to look Walsh directly in the eye, 'And what if I choose not to remember, just this once?'

Walsh surveyed Jago for a long moment. When he finally spoke there was a withering contempt in the quietly spoken words.

'I walk out now and leave you to explain the bill for everything you just ordered. You are known here and I'm not and you haven't a pot to piss in. Then of course I'll stop sending my contacts to seek advice from the oracle. There'll be no more nice lunches or cigarettes, no cash donations towards your retirement fund. We both know you are a pariah in the intelligence world, Jago, and Six are an unforgiving bunch. When they kicked you out they made bloody sure nobody would touch you. I don't actually think the *Herald* would trust you to write the obituary page these days. Without me, you probably wouldn't be able to pay the rent. To be honest I doubt you'd manage.' Walsh drank his wine while Jago digested the words.

'Harsh, Harry, harsh but fair, I'll grant you.'

'Clear?' asked Walsh.

'Abundantly, dear boy,' Jago gave a forced smile and raised his glass in mock salutation, as if he was about to proclaim a toast in Walsh's honour. He took another deep swig of wine before setting down the glass. 'You're absolutely right of course, barely had a word published since the "incident". Years of elegant prose, diligence beyond the call of duty. It all counts for nothing when you are on the rum list. I sometimes wonder what they told the editors. What are my little peccadilloes do you suspect? Am I a Pinko, a collaborator or a nancy boy? Was I caught fiddling with some boy scouts do you think?'

For a moment Jago looked so desolate even Walsh almost felt sorry for him, until he remembered who he was dealing with. 'All of that I should think.'

Jago snorted bitterly, 'Yes, I shouldn't wonder. Whatever it is Six well and truly cooked my goose, I'll say that much. Here's to them.' Another mock toast and he drained his wine. Walsh did not wait for the maître d'. He refilled Jago's glass to keep him pliant. 'Make sure it doesn't happen to you, Harry, that's all I'm saying,' and his mood became sullen. 'Do you know: I was the last English correspondent out of Paris when it fell? Did I ever tell you that, Harry?'

'On numerous occasions.' Walsh needed to halt the self-pity. 'Price,' he said firmly.

'What? Oh yes...'

And slowly Jago closed his eyes then fell silent. He appeared to be concentrating hard. Walsh wondered if this was a necessary trigger for his memory or merely an affectation; a cheap conjuring trick used to impress the likes of Emma Stirling, though she had seen through him right from the start.

'I went to see your chap down the Gray's Inn Road,' and she had shuddered at the recollection, 'he's like that fellow "Mr Memory" from *The Thirty Nine Steps*, only a thousand times more vulgar than anything John Buchan could have created. He had on the wrong school tie for a man who supposedly went to Harrow and half of yesterday's dinner still down it.'

'Did he try to pinch your behind?'

'He tried. I told him if he did it again I'd break his fingers.'

Jago finally spoke then, snapping Walsh back from his memory of Emma. 'Major Robert Price? Let's see, ah yes, born Edinburgh, 1903, educated Winchester and Caius College. He won't like you, Harry, oh no, you're a bit common,' he held up his hands in supplication, 'they would be his words not mine.'

'Tell me something I don't already know, Jago. What makes him the man he is? Where's Price from and where does he think he's going?'

'What makes him tick? There's always a story and if I remember his, which I'm quite sure I do then he'll be jealous of that pretty wife of yours. As a young man, Price had the misfortune to fall in love with a debutante and the way I hear it the damn fool woman felt entirely the same way. "I'm head over heels with you too young, Robert, let's elope together and have a couple of perfect children, one of each flavour. What do you say?"'

Jago was afflicted with the storyteller's need for elaboration and the desire to act it all out. '"Well I'd like that very much indeed, my dear," says he, "trouble is I've no money, not a red cent, and your daddy will never permit the union but have no fear for I have a plan. I'm off to India to make my fortune. It'll only take a couple of years and after all we're still so young. When I return we'll marry in fine style!" "Agreed!" says she, "I will wait for you, my darling, forever and a day!" So off he trots to the subcontinent to make his way in the world.

'You can guess what happens next. Just like time, "Debs" wait for no man. Gone less than a year when she writes him. She has met another and it seems her love for young Robert is not nearly as enduring as he'd hoped. "By the time you return we'll be married" she writes, or some such tosh. Poor jilted Price is devastated, and you would be! Put her on a pedestal you see; should never do it, Harry, at that height no woman can ever resist the temptation to kick you firmly in the teeth.

'Of course Price returns tout suite but all's in vain. She's married and away on the honeymoon. All he's left with is a broken heart and tortured images of his one true love rolling around in another man's bed. Cue much wailing and gnashing of teeth.

'Year later he marries a plain Jane, some stout old maid with broad thighs and an even broader bank balance. Not the prettiest girl in Christendom but her daddy is grateful she's landed a Cambridge man and that's enough for Price, for now. The lady dutifully provides an heir and a spare but it's not a match made in heaven. Now she stays in the country and he lives up town. It's one of *those* marriages, not that I'm an expert you understand, never had the misfortune, no offence intended.

'Price seeks solace in an army career. He was expecting great things but turned out to be not all that good, as I suspect you may have noticed. Struggled to reach his current rank, despite the social connections of his marriage, then Six wouldn't have him, which is how I first got to hear all about the fellow. He was eventually packed off to SOE by his underwhelmed superiors.' Jago got a little gleam in his eye then, 'Happened to a lot of regular army men, so I hear.' Walsh did not react to Jago's jibe. 'In short he's a passed-over major with a chip on his shoulder and they're the worst kind if you ask me, Harry.'

To Jago's surprise Walsh seemed unusually satisfied by his performance, 'Thank you, Jago, that was illuminating.'

Jago was a natural spy who remembered every piece of gossip he heard. Heaven help the nation, thought Walsh, if the Nazis ever worked out how cheap it would be to buy the man and his memory.

When they finally left Wiltons, Jago, buoyed by the meal and his more-than-half share of the wine, said 'Tell me, Harry, I've always wanted to know. Did you really take those diamonds that were meant to be... argh!'

Walsh span Jago round, slammed his cheek hard against the wall and pulled his arm behind him, twisting it upwards. 'Of course not... nnnh... only joking, Harry... I didn't mean anything by it honestly... gnnnhhh you're hurting... just repeating what I heard... please...'

'You've gone sloppy, Jago, you've forgotten yourself,' hissed Walsh venomously, 'or did you just forget what I can do to you? Want me to remind you, "dear boy"? Eh? Should I break your arm? Will that help you to remember?'

'No, Harry, please no, Jago's sorry,' he almost sobbed it and reluctantly Walsh let him go. Jago was breathless and in pain, the skin of his cheek scraped raw from its intimate contact with the brickwork. 'No need to get tough with me, Harry, not with old Jago. Just no need, you hear; not cut out for the rough stuff,' and he sloped sulkily away rubbing his injured arm. Damn the man, thought Walsh. Trust Jago to ruin my mood.

Walsh walked sullenly across Piccadilly Circus where gaudy posters cajoled him to 'Lend a hand with War Savings – they are vital to Victory!' then reminded him 'More Salvage is wanted!'

'Eros' could no longer be seen here now thanks to the bombing, the god of love having been unceremoniously boarded up for the duration.

16

*'Snobbery is the pride of those who are not sure
of their position.'*

Berton Braley

There was a faintly discernible spring in Bill Martin's step that afternoon. What a stroke of luck to bump into old 'Dobber' Price the day before. How thankful he was now that he'd not been quite as beastly to the boorish little man as their fellow undergraduates at Caius.

Martin had been forced to hide his disappointment as Price bounded up to greet him outside Fortnum & Mason. It had been some time since he last had the dubious pleasure of a tête-à-tête with Price it but didn't seem so long.

'Oh, it's you,' was what he wanted to say when Price accosted him on the pavement. Instead Martin replied, 'Robert, my dear fellow, how the devil are you?'

'Well, I've been better as a matter of fact but it's nothing a large snifter won't rectify, which is why I am so glad I bumped into you. Come on, the FO can spare you at this hour surely. I'm buying!' and he said the last part as if it would make a blind bit of difference to a man of Martin's not insubstantial means.

Price's choice of venue left a good deal to be desired. A private 'Gentleman's Club' on the unfashionable fringes of

Soho. The sort of dimly lit den of iniquity, with its red velvet drapes and gilt candelabras, that reeked of new money. Martin could easily imagine its back rooms used by good-time girls to blackmail married minor aristocrats into parting with a slice of their family fortunes. Women who were just one step up from the 'Piccadilly Commandos' who whored their way round the Circus during the night. In short, the place had neither class nor discretion, so it was entirely in keeping with Price. Martin prayed nobody from the Foreign Office had seen him enter the place and took solace from the certain knowledge that none would ever voluntarily darken its doors.

It wasn't long before Price's rose-tinted college reminiscences were replaced by the far-too-frank admission that all was not well in either his private life or career. Martin managed to offer sympathetic musings on the limitations of marriage and he listened patiently as Price waffled on about the lack of common ground with his wife. Martin was waiting.

Price, who seemed genuinely delighted to have bumped into his old college 'friend', had another Gimlet, then another. That was all it took for him to surrender all discretion. Entirely unsolicited by Martin, Price began to share the latest snub delivered by his superior, the blunt and vulgar Gubbins of the Special Operations Executive. Martin fanned the flames with more than one 'poor you' and a well-timed 'really? My dear fellow, that's beyond the pale'. He then hinted that he might be in a position to have a word with a chap he knew, who knew another chap who actually worked with the Secret Intelligence Service. They were always on the lookout for a good sort with the right background. Martin allowed the intimation, that Price could be just the 'good sort' MI6 were looking for, to hang tantalisingly in the air and that was enough to ensnare him. Price spilled it all.

At one point the idiot even said, 'So nice to have someone to talk to that I can trust entirely. I mean it's not as if *you* could be working for the Germans, Bill,' and Price had giggled drunkenly at the very thought. Not working for the Germans no, thought Martin, but on the books of MI6 for nearly twenty years and still you think I just 'work for the Foreign Office'. What a bloody fool, no wonder they were so pitilessly cruel to you at Cambridge.

Martin's superiors would be very interested in SOE's plans to send someone called Harry Walsh into France. Of course, they did that sort of thing all the time, dispatching maverick agents to stir up a hornet's nest, usually where it was least needed. These sledgehammer-subtle operations could undermine months, sometimes even years of patient intelligence gathering. But this mission was different. Walsh's own controller had been pushed out of the loop. Even the Deputy Section Head, was not allowed to know its aims.

Martin was hardly surprised Price had been cut out of the inner circle, merely disappointed, for the whole op could have been blown before it started for the price of a few watered-down Gimlets. But Price had given him a name, which was a start. Six would want to take a close look at Captain Walsh.

From now on Harry Walsh wouldn't be able to make a move without them knowing about it and it was all thanks to good old 'Dobber' Price. What a complete dullard. The very notion of Robert Price occupying a position of responsibility in MI6 left Martin chuckling to himself on his way to the train.

Walsh left the railway station behind him and followed the gently sloping hill down to the high street. He was presented with a tranquil English scene as far removed from war as one could imagine. A week of rain had softened the common land until its grass was now the dark green of a billiard table but above him the sun was peering cautiously out from behind a large downy cloud, as if unsure whether it wished to make an appearance this late in the day.

The scene was a reassuringly familiar one. Harpenden had become his home; their first home, his and Mary's, following years of a nomadic existence, first with his father then the army. Harry Walsh was trying to put down some roots; and he would continue to try.

A passer-by nodded at Walsh. He knew the middle-aged woman by sight but not acquaintance and she offered him a cautious smile. If she perhaps wondered why this able-bodied man still walked her Hertfordshire town, while so many others were away fighting, then she at least had the decorum to hide it.

Some of Walsh's neighbours knew he'd fought at Dunkirk but not all; far fewer that he now held some unspecified, inherently mysterious post that required regular, often lengthy absences from home. Certainly no one had the poor taste to ask questions, for by now everybody instinctively knew that careless talk costs lives.

It wasn't always like that. He well remembered the day a pasty-faced spinster marched up to him in Dean Street and handed him the white feather. It had happened to much older men than Walsh and he was hardly in a position to publicise his contribution to the war effort but he was aggrieved by the gesture nonetheless. He at least managed to infuriate the woman with a smile, as he accepted her ridiculous feather in a seeming good grace, even as the shame burned into him, for he was only human after all. He could have berated her, told her about Dunkirk, rearguard actions and Tom Danby but what good would that have done?

They had posters now, which showed a red-faced father unable to look his son in the eye when the boy asked, 'What did you do in the war, daddy?' Walsh had cheated death by inches with Emma Stirling, yet most of his neighbours thought the closest he came to peril these days was riding the morning train into London.

Walsh was home earlier than usual, in good time for dinner. Mary would pronounce herself pleased. There would be time to sit in the living room and talk beforehand, though he was unable to tell her anything about his day, and she would not enquire. The meetings with Clavelle and Jago would go unmentioned, the afternoon spent with an SOE tailor similarly so. Walsh had ordered the clothing they would take with them. All items would be shorn of manufacturer labels and altered to make it appear they were purchased in occupied France. Then the garments would be aged, so they did not stand out, as new clothes could be conspicuous in occupied territory. None of this could be discussed with Mary.

Walsh decided to call in at the Cross Keys to postpone the stilted conversation; the mundane digesting of Mary's day into its constituent parts, each with its own inconsequential drama; the queues in the grocery store, the woman trying to cheat her way to extra portions of this and that, the barely whispered pregnancy of that weekend's supposedly virgin bride; and he needed time alone to think about his mission. Walsh told himself that was the real reason for diverting into the pub.

He ordered a pint of bitter, counting out coins on the pock-marked wooden bar as the landlord pulled the ale. The price had gone up again – you could no longer buy a pint with a round shilling, it now required an additional penny. 'Cost nine pence when the war started,' observed Albert Anderson sadly from his usual stool at the bar. The doctor had called into the Keys at the end of every working day since anybody could remember. 'Bloody Germans have a lot to answer for,' grumbled the old man.

Walsh nodded his agreement, 'We'll add it to their list of crimes,' but he picked up his freshly poured pint from the bar and walked deliberately away to sit in a corner. Another time he might have indulged the curmudgeonly general practitioner with a conversation but not today. Walsh spread his copy of *The Times* on the table before him and pretended to read it while mulling over the events of the past few days. Something was not quite right.

For some time Walsh had been out of favour, despite his record. Lately he'd been limited to missions of a routine, unimportant nature; courier jobs that could easily be entrusted to a recent graduate of Arisaig not a three-year veteran like himself. This sidelining was down to Price and both of them knew it. The man wanted nothing less than to have Walsh thrown out of 'F' Section and did little to disguise the fact. Price was hardly head boy at Baker Street but he still retained the influence that came automatically with his rank and social position. Walsh could appeal to more senior men, they might even make a show of listening to his complaints but it would be a fruitless exercise. Going over his commanding officer's head was not the done thing. It would merely serve to confirm that Walsh was far from the right sort.

A week ago, he'd have considered himself fortunate if he continued to pick up scraps of work here and there, usually when Price wanted him out from under his feet. Eventually the Major would tire of the younger man's presence at Baker Street all together and consign Walsh to a training school graveyard. He would probably spend the rest of the war teaching novices how to duff up a German sentry.

Then, out of the blue, he is suddenly sent for by the CD himself, taken out to lunch by the top boy, a man he had never previously exchanged two sentences with. Walsh had been entrusted with a mission he would normally have been fifteenth in line for. Something was clearly amiss and it left him with a bad feeling. Walsh could feel the familiar cold draft of betrayal? He had always trusted his instincts but this one made no sense to him. Gubbins hardly knew Walsh but he appeared genuinely committed to making the Jedburgh teams work and the very real threat of the Messerschmitt jet plane meant his mission had to succeed, so perhaps Gubbins was sincere and Walsh really was, however implausibly, back in favour.

Walsh knew he still had a great deal to contend with. They would enter France in darkness, yet another night-time parachute drop on to a landing zone that might already be compromised to the Germans. The moments just after impact on touching hostile soil were always the worst. Walsh would feel his heart stop as he froze and waited for the sounds of ambush; the blowing of a whistle, the barking of an attack dog, the cocking of rifles and shouted German commands. He had not forgotten the traitor responsible for Emma Stirling's aborted mission and would be sure to keep the cyanide capsule close at hand; anything to avoid the horror of capture.

If they survived the jump they would rendezvous with a disparate band of the Maquis and must earn the respect of what would doubtless be a rough and ready lot, who would view him with distrust. If they disagreed with his tactics and methods, they might be tempted to kill him to remove the hindrance from their midst. It would be all too easy to blame the Germans for his demise. The memory of the partisans in Yugoslavia and the cheapness they afforded life was ingrained on Walsh.

He took another swig of beer to offset these sobering thoughts. His mind went to Cooper and Valvert. The latter was a completely unknown quantity; a quiet little man, who could be entirely suited to covert life or might just as likely crack at the merest hint of danger. As always, Walsh would have to trust his life to strangers and ultimately the men who had selected those individuals to work with him. He hoped this time they had chosen well.

Sam Cooper was no stranger. Walsh might even have held a grudging respect for him, if he had not come so close to death because of the American's deeply ingrained desire to put his country's interests first. Would he have really done the same thing as Cooper if he had been in his shoes in Yugoslavia, leaving the man alone and hunted in a foreign land with only his wits and a side arm? Perhaps; who knew for sure? This time at least, their interests were the same and Cooper would have to depend on Walsh's experience of occupied France to get them all safely through.

This mission was no routine sabotage job but an attack on a man who was probably guarded by a battalion of SS. Only now in the sanctity of the quiet, little pub could Walsh allow himself to consider something he'd placed firmly at the back of his mind since the first briefing with Buckmaster; he hadn't the faintest clue how to carry out this mission. How in hell were they going to get anywhere near the scientist let alone kill him; and if they failed? It was not just the safety of three men at stake here. Many more would die if the Komet was perfected.

The doubts returned to plague Walsh now like a child's bad dream. Was he still up to the job? It had been a while since Walsh had been on an extended operation behind enemy lines. True, the hand that steadily gripped his pint hadn't shaken uncontrollably in a while. During his rescue of Emma Stirling he was able to keep the, now familiar, paralysing terror for the most part at bay but he suspected this was temporary. It merely fought a losing battle over his concern for this woman he knew he could never have. His life had seemed inconsequential compared to hers. But Walsh was fatalistic and he knew his extraordinary run of luck had to come to an end eventually, so the fear would stay with him.

It was not too late to pull out but if he turned his back on this one he might as well pack his bags and pay his own train fare to Arisaig. He would spend the rest of the war cooped up in a draughty barracks, teaching trainees how to set time fuses and prime Gammon bombs.

Walsh took another sip, the beer already nearly gone. He did not normally drink so quickly. One more pint then and he counted out the coins on the table in front of him before rising to catch the landlord's eye. It would give him more time to think things through. The peace the pub provided in early evening was just what he wanted.

Walsh was sure his sudden need for solitude had nothing to do with Emma Stirling, even if he seemed incapable of banishing the girl from his thoughts. He had always known there could never be a future with her. Not while Mary Danby wore his wedding band and he'd been right to end it, should never have started with her in the first place. Even so, since the night of their escape from France, in the few idle moments he had permitted himself, he couldn't help wondering what life would be like if he was free to be with her.

'I just can't get ten across,' said Dr Anderson glumly as he looked up from his crossword, 'you any good at solving puzzles, Harry?'

'Sorry,' answered Walsh flatly as he claimed his pint, 'not these days.'

17

'They were in no way conspicuous; the last thing we wanted in them was eccentricity. We denied them glamour, in their own interests; we made them as homely and unremarkable as we could.'

Colonel Maurice Buckmaster, Head of 'F' Section, on the agents of SOE

The house was a simple two-up two-down, red-brick dwelling on a gable end. A white painted fence bordered a tiny front garden in a criss-cross. Rose stems and rhododendron bushes pushed impatiently through it like spectators vying for the best view of a parade. A hand-painted wooden sign on the gate bore the enigmatic name 'Fallow Field'. A previous owner had named their home and Walsh had never bothered to remove it. A slow pall of smoke rose from a single chimney as Walsh pushed the gate open hard and cleared his throat to signal his premature return.

Mary was reading at the kitchen table. A pot simmered on the stove behind her. The door of the walk-in pantry was open and a vegetable pie cooled on a ledge. She put down her book, a much-read copy of *Far From the Madding Crowd*, and rose to greet him. Walsh had read Hardy's novel. He vaguely recalled the story; a woman falls for a dashing soldier with predictably tragic consequences. Walsh realised when he thought of his wife the image he invariably conjured was of her holding a book.

'You're home in good time,' she kissed him automatically. Could she taste the beer on his lips? If so, she said nothing. Drinking was just something men did.

They ate in near silence, struggling to find something from their respective worlds that might interest the other. It was as good a time as any to explain he would be leaving soon.

'They are sending me back to Scotland, Mary. Of course, I'm not allowed to tell you exactly where. They want old hands like me around to show the new ones how it's supposed to be done.' The training school was as good a lie as any and would spare Mary fretful nights.

She took a moment to digest the news, 'They obviously appreciate you, to send you up there again.' Then she added, 'I'll miss you though, of course,' and he wondered if she would truly miss him, surrounded by her books, or if he was somehow an impediment to the neat, well-ordered running of their home.

'When will you leave?'

'Quite soon I think.'

'Oh,' she rose to clear the plates from the table before pronouncing, 'well, we will just have to make the best of it then. I've been saving my coupons. Before you go I'll make you your favourite.'

They had been through this scene before. The night before he left she would make a cottage pie. Afterwards they would make love. It was her wifely duty after all and Danbys knew about duty. Hadn't they all made sacrifices of one kind or another?

Walsh had been on a bus once when two gossiping, middle-aged women behind him were discussing the condition of a seriously wounded neighbour, newly returned from the war.

The unfortunate fellow's wife had confirmed the difficulties in looking after an invalid. This was relayed to the other busy-body in a whisper that was far less discreet than normal conversation. Walsh stared out of the bus window as the woman concluded this tale of woe with its solitary silver lining.

'Still, at least he has stopped "bothering" her,' she said.

At the time Walsh could not help but wonder if Mary saw his need for her as a 'bother', judging by its infrequency. There were some obvious contrasts, the French girl at Dunkirk before his marriage for one. Her need for him had been at least equal to his own desire. Then there was Emma Stirling, who did not seem in any way bothered by Harry's attentions, positively welcomed them in fact. What could they, and the others he had to admit to, see in him that his wife could not, and what, if anything, could be done about it?

'How was dinner?' she asked.

'Perfect.'

She smiled then, 'You're easily pleased.'

Over the next two weeks, Walsh continued his preparations for the mission. Valvert and Cooper were still at Beaulieu, so his time was his own. A priority request for a plane had been formally submitted to the Royal Air Force. One could become available at any time and there was still much to be done. A return visit to Clavelle was his first priority. Walsh had learned never to take anything for granted. The regular army was all about delegation to trusted subordinates. SOE was the opposite. Walsh had learned to trust no one. Whenever possible he would carry out tasks himself, avoiding a reliance on untried strangers. If he had the wherewithal to forge documents himself, then he would not have had to put all of his faith in a small-time con man living in a draughty room above a library of fake books. What would keep Clavelle from discreetly sabotaging his papers one day? The wrong stamp or watermark and the next document check would be Walsh's last. In one simple act the spectre of Harry Walsh could be removed from Clavelle's life forever. What then would it take to insure against this? Fear, thought Harry, with sudden certainty. Fear and greed. Clavelle would be terrified of retribution if Walsh escaped the trap and he was not in the habit of enlisting the German state police to murder his paying customers.

As always, Walsh avoided the underground station closest to his destination. A short walk from Baker Street and soon he was in the West End. The weather was fine enough for it to be more of a pleasure than a chore.

Walsh reached Charing Cross Road and the antiquarian bookstores that lent the street its fame. He fully intended to walk straight into 'Dickens, Templeman & Marlowe', but something made him pause. There was no real reason beyond instinct, a nagging feeling that something was not quite as it should be, that made Walsh walk on past the shop door.

He continued south for a time then cut down a narrow side street that led to St Martin's Lane. Walsh did not turn to look behind him. Instead he finally halted by Trafalgar Square, at the church of St Martin-in-the-Fields. Walsh took out a cigarette and lit it. Standing on the church steps, he faced the square, as if newly impressed by the towering monument to Nelson's victory. He took a couple of drags on the cigarette then glanced about him. Walsh stole a look back the way he had come and spotted him.

There, standing back from the road, staring too intently into the window of a violin-maker's, was a lone, male figure. The man was assiduously ignoring Walsh, though the window's reflection or perhaps his peripheral vision would probably afford him an outline view of his target. It was not that Walsh had met the man before, merely that he recognised the outline: the brown raincoat and grey cap he wore. For the same man had been standing in the doorway of the Sherlock Holmes hotel in Baker Street that very morning as Walsh passed by. The fool had followed him all the way to Trafalgar Square on his own. Walsh would not have expected such an error from a wet-behind-the-ears apprentice, so perhaps even MI6's resources were strained to the limit these days. Maybe Six weren't used to spying on their own side on home ground. That was something their counter-espionage colleagues in MI5 were more adept at but Five wouldn't care about Walsh and his operations in France. No, this was Six alright. They were always desperate to know what SOE were involved in and hell bent on stopping it if they could. Probably someone recalled from occupied Europe just before the Germans marched in and now they were finding him a job to do; keep watch on Harry Walsh to see what he's up to.

Walsh experienced contrasting emotions. The momentary feeling of triumph at spotting his tail soon evaporated, along with the sudden realisation that Six must know at least something of his mission. Without knowledge of the operation, Walsh was not worth the watcher's shifts. What they knew about him and how they knew it would remain a mystery for now. Walsh would just have to hope the entire mission had not been blown before it had begun. Even if he could trap and question his shadow, the man would probably know nothing; his brief merely to report back on Walsh's movements.

At least he had not gone into 'Dickens, Templeman & Marlowe'. If Walsh had called on Clavelle that morning, he would never again be able to use the Frenchman, for this or any other operation. Somehow, he would have to get back to the bookshop without his shadow being aware of it.

Walsh slowly finished his cigarette, as the world and the people in it rolled busily by him; normal people going about their war work and domestic concerns, blissfully unaware of the secret life he was leading in their midst. He stubbed out the butt with the heel of his shoe and walked off along the Strand.

Walsh cut through Embankment and strode purposefully along the north bank of the Thames until he passed Southwark Bridge. The river teemed with activity; boats docked for loading or set out on to the water anew to deliver a cargo. Walsh was heading for a quieter spot, an indent in the riverbank where the water rolled to the left before resuming its relentless journey to the sea. Here you could leave the main road and descend, by way of a steep stone staircase, right down to the water's edge, where no more than a dozen smaller craft were tethered together. The shouts of the boatmen behind him began to recede as he took the stairs down to the quiet towpath and completely disappeared from view.

Walsh's tail was forced into a brisk walk. He had given his subject a good head start to avoid detection but now he would have to make up ground if he was not to lose Walsh. Careful not to break into a run, he increased his pace until he found himself at the steps that led down to the waterline. Mindful of the relative seclusion of this stretch of the river he paused, glancing suspiciously down to the water's edge. The tethered boats were all deserted, the only sound coming from the creaking of old timbers as the boats were pushed up, down and together by the lapping water. There was no sign of Walsh and the man from MI6 frowned then scanned the narrow towpath, which ran along the river. If he followed the waterline carefully, there was a good chance he could still spot Walsh without being seen, as long as he took the first corner cautiously.

Gingerly, he descended the steps and made his way to the corner. He stopped and slowly peered around it. The path did indeed go on for some considerable way but nobody walked it that day. The subject had to have been moving fast to put such distance between them. To do that, he must have had an inkling he was being followed, or why bother to attempt it? There was another possibility that entered the man's head a moment before all lucid thought went from it. Perhaps Walsh had not gone down the towpath at all. He slowly turned around.

A moment earlier, Walsh had stepped silently from the boat on which he had hidden himself. He was now standing less than a yard from the man as he turned. Walsh delivered a crushing blow into the midriff with his right fist. The man crumpled and dropped to the floor. Walsh had hit hard and before he could recover, he grabbed the man's arm and twisted it behind his back.

'Are you the best they can get these days?' asked Walsh, 'tell them to stop following me.' And the man's screams drowned out the sound of his arm snapping.

'Count your blessings,' Walsh told him, 'I could have drowned you in the river.'

The man from MI6 was a pathetic sight all of a sudden, lying on the towpath trying to work out which part of his arm to clasp without causing himself further pain. Walsh surveyed the stricken figure. He seemed older and scared now; a veteran watcher past his prime. Walsh felt no pity. He couldn't afford to. They were both professionals and violence an accepted part of their world. Six would try and stop him from doing his job any way they could; maim him, kill him, betray him to the Germans. If SIS played by those rules they couldn't start crying when he did the same.

The watcher moaned softly to himself as Walsh walked away.

18

'People sleep peaceably in their beds at night
only because rough men stand ready to do
violence on their behalf.'

George Orwell

'Clavelle, I have to say it,' Walsh glanced up from the documents laid neatly on the table in the tiny back room, 'you are an artist.'

'Thank you, 'Arry, I think,' Clavelle replied doubtfully, 'as so often with you the task was impossible,' he pronounced it *am-poss-eeb*, 'but Clavelle, he did it.'

'You don't have to justify your price, Clavelle,' said Walsh, 'it's been agreed.'

Walsh began to assemble the documents together and Clavelle looked concerned.

'The money, it is here?'

Walsh reached into his inside jacket pocket and produced a bulky envelope. He handed it to the Frenchman, who accepted it eagerly.

'Count it here, Clavelle, now, in front of me.'

Walsh scooped up the passes, identity cards and permits and placed them safely in the large outside pocket of his overcoat. Clavelle opened the envelope and let his fingers dance over the notes. When the count was complete, the Frenchman nodded his assent.

'You must be a very important man, 'Arry. Not many can get their hands on such treasure these days.'

Walsh put a firm hand on Clavelle's shoulder in warning, 'Then you had better spend it discreetly. Don't want anybody wondering where you got it from, do we?'

Clavelle made a point of looking round the room, 'As you see, my needs are very simple.'

Both men stood and Walsh made to leave. Then he fixed Clavelle with a look.

'What is it?' asked the Frenchman quizzically.

'I'm waiting for you to tell me.'

'Tell you what, 'Arry?'

'Who has been calling on you?'

'Calling? Nobody calls on Clavelle.' He began to wilt visibly under the merciless gaze.

'You know what I mean; curious people, people with questions; about me, about you.'

'Police?' Clavelle was alarmed at the very prospect.

'Police, perhaps. Not all policemen wear uniforms these days,' Walsh shrugged, 'you tell me. You would tell me, wouldn't you, Clavelle?'

'Oh no, nobody like that, 'Arry, no, I give you my word,' then he remembered the crux of Walsh's question, 'of course I'd tell you, 'Arry, of course. Police make me nervous. Everybody makes Clavelle nervous, except the fool with too much money who buys books. Nobody else comes here, 'Arry, honestly.' He was almost pleading now.

'Not sure I believe you, Clavelle,' and Walsh took a pace towards him, 'you're sweating.' Clavelle was terrified.

''Arry, no, please, there was nobody. I'd tell you. If police came here I'd be gone, away, some place else,' then he added hurriedly, 'but not before I told you. You are my friend.

Like my brother, 'Arry, please.'

'Maybe I believe you, then again maybe I don't, but if you are lying to me, Clavelle, these papers are worthless and so is your life. Last chance to tell me who's been calling on you; very last chance.'

Clavelle was wide-eyed with terror, 'Nobody honestly, 'Arry, just customers, they come in, they buy books, they go, they don't ask Clavelle questions, why would they?' His voice was a high-pitched terrified whimper, 'Please...'

Like Jago, Clavelle had the habit of referring to himself in the third person, as if the crooked personas they both inhabited were merely a disguise, something they adopted for a few hours for professional reasons then put aside at the end of the day. Walsh surveyed Clavelle closely. He reached out his hand, causing the Frenchman to flinch away. Then he patted Clavelle on the cheek. 'Good lad,' he said and left the shop without another word. Clavelle slumped back against the cold stove, putting a shaky hand against it to steady himself.

As Walsh walked off towards Leicester Square he privately regretted having to put the fear of God into Clavelle but it was the only way to ensure the shop, the forger, and Walsh's papers had not all been compromised by Six. Walsh had to be even more on his guard now he knew he was being followed. The injured watcher would of course report back to his superiors. Even if Walsh had managed to attack his pursuer from behind, there would have been no disguising his involvement. Better to be upfront about it then and remind Six who they were dealing with. Though Walsh very much doubted anything official would be done about it, both sides now knew where they stood. The surveillance would be stepped up. From now on Walsh would be followed everywhere. At least it was good practice for France.

There was one other thing he had learned from the day and it brought reassurance. Walsh was still capable of instilling terror and in his line of work that was a very useful talent indeed.

19

*'Underneath the arches, we dream our dreams away
Underneath the arches, on cobblestones I lay.'*

Flanagan & Allen

Flanagan and Allen were waiting for Walsh as he left 64 Baker Street They made no attempt to hide their presence, following him at an even pace, one on either side of the road. Allen was level with Walsh, staring at his subject quite openly, and with undisguised hostility. Flanagan kept a course directly behind Walsh, hanging back a few yards.

Walsh had given all of his watchers names. Flanagan and Allen did not physically resemble the music hall comedians but were alike in one sense. This pair were definitely a double act; you never saw one without the other. If the well-built Allen waited on a street corner as you walked towards it, you could be sure Flanagan, the wiry one, was right behind you, silently following your every footstep.

Flanagan was the dogged little ferret who never tired of the game, happily trailing Walsh all over London for hours, before melting away so somebody else could take a turn.

Allen was very obviously the muscle; exceedingly well built, trained to a peak by the look of him, with narrow eyes and a slight, seemingly permanent smirk on his face, as if he knew something others did not and the knowledge amused him. Allen probably relished the physical side of his work and looked as if he was well practised at it but there was something else. Walsh could see the restlessness, the suppressed impatience, as if all of this walking around behind his target was an unnecessary prelude to the real thing. He was like a big dog tugging at a short chain; too much training and not enough action. When he first spotted Allen, the man had given Walsh a deliberately defiant look, as if to say 'let's see you try and break my arm then'.

Don't doubt I could, if I chose to, thought Walsh.

Walsh was becoming almost used to the continual presence of somebody from MI6 by now. It had been Harold Lloyd's turn to follow him from the doorstep of his home that morning. Walsh's choice of nickname was more apt this time, for the fellow had the same round spectacles, pasty face and nervous countenance as the silent comedian. He also kept a discreet distance behind his subject. Presumably he had heard about the watcher with the broken arm.

Harold Lloyd's shift continued as they both boarded the train, the latter waiting till the very last moment before joining Walsh on the London service, in case he made a dash for it back on to the platform as it pulled away. On arrival in London, he melted away as he always did, to be replaced by a fresh set of watchers from Six; all of whom Walsh took a bitter pleasure in naming. There was 'Clement Attlee' because of his bald head; 'Sweeney Todd', who resembled the kind of East End villain that might carry a cut-throat razor in his boot; and 'Ginger Rogers', who was not a woman but rather a thin little man who followed Walsh with such a light tread he seemed almost to glide as he walked. Others came and went: 'Errol Flynn' with his fussily manicured moustache; and 'The Doctor' because he carried a battered Gladstone bag. Walsh never did learn whether this was part of his cover or if it merely contained his lunch. More often than not though, it was Flanagan and Allen who would be waiting for him in Baker Street, and today was no exception.

It had been this way ever since the confrontation on the towpath. This wasn't covert surveillance of the type MI5 might conduct against suspected foreign spies. These agents were easy to spot. Six were sending Walsh a message. We know you and will follow you till we find out what you are up to and you won't be able to lose us.

Walsh decided the best way to tackle the constant scrutiny was to ignore it, outwardly at least. He would pretend to treat the days leading up to his departure as recreation, while simultaneously working out a way to dump his shadows before the plane to France. The problem was how to successfully lose a whole roster of professionals. It was a task that occupied his mind and eventually a plan came to him.

He had not told Gubbins about his unwanted shadows, in case the senior man was tempted to remove him from the operation. Instead he visited the Baker Street office of Maurice Buckmaster but this time it was not the Colonel he had come to see.

The woman occupying the desk outside Buckmaster's office could still reasonably be described as attractive, if you were not discouraged by a slight hint of the school ma'am. Her gaze was solid and unwavering, her black hair brushed tightly back out of her eyes and pinned firmly in place, as if she despised its impracticality. Vera Atkins was bright, articulate, loyal and famously formidable; best of all she was good at keeping secrets, both for and from her employer, Colonel Buckmaster. Walsh had known Atkins long enough to be used to her lack of preamble.

'Shakespeare again?'

'Why not?' he said.

'Which verse? A bit of *Henry V* perhaps: "Once more unto the breach", and all that?'

Walsh shook his head, 'Too obvious; how about a spot of *Hamlet*: "Oh that this too, too solid flesh would melt, thaw and resolve itself into a dew. Or that the everlasting had not fixed his canon 'gainst self-slaughter".'

'Use that and they will think you have a death wish, as well you know, Harry.'

'You have a point. All right then, what about… "Now are our brows bound with victorious wreaths; our bruised arms hung up for monuments, our stern alarums changed to merry meetings"? Musings on a time of peace after war. That cheerful enough for you?'

'Richard the Third,' she pronounced without hesitation, 'he was an evil bugger too. "I find thee apt" as Hamlet's dad once said.'

'Thank you.' Walsh had the impression she enjoyed their little tussles over the line or two of verse to be used as a code poem. Some went to the cryptographer, Leo Marks, for their poetry. Others, like Walsh, chose a bit of Shakespeare or Keats, Byron or Longfellow as their cipher.

'And the code name this time?' he asked.

'Daisy.'

'What?'

'Daisy, like the flower.'

'Daisy.' There was a long pause as Walsh pondered the code name he had been allocated. He was never one for false machismo; other men might insist on code names like 'Lionheart', 'Eagle' or 'Fist'. Such posturing left him cold but 'Daisy'? There could be only one explanation.

'Price pick that?'

'As a matter of fact…'

'Thought as much; his puny idea of a joke. I'm surprised he didn't plump for 'Pansy'. Well, not wishing to spoil your day,

Vera, but I refuse to go to my probable death with the code name "Daisy". So, either the code name is changed or you find yourself another "Daisy".'

'You really mean that, don't you; you'd actually pull out of a vital operation because of a mildly effeminate code name?'

'It's my final word on the matter.'

Vera Atkins raised her eyebrows. What was the point of arguing with Harry Walsh when he was in this sort of mood? Might as well try and trap lightning in a box.

'I don't know who is more infantile, you or Major Price. What do you suggest then?'

'I don't know,' he thought for a moment, 'how about "Gloucester"?'

'As in "Old Spot", as in "Pig"?'

'No, as in "Duke of"; like Richard before he became "the Third". A much-maligned figure, Richard. Just because he bumped off a couple of infant princes.'

'Gloucester. Fine. Is that all?' And with a stroke of her pen it was done.

'Not quite,' he told her, 'can you get a message to Sam Cooper and Christophe Valvert for me at the finishing school?'

'What message?' she asked, picking up a pencil.

'Tell them we're going early,' he said and she waited for an explanation she might pass on to them. When none was offered she didn't press him. 'I'll give you a time and an RV point. That's all they need to know.'

'All right,' she said, 'in that case I'd better alert the CD too.'

'Why?'

'Because, Walsh, he wants to see you before you leave.'

Walsh slid gingerly out from under the covers, gently lowering them back into place. His wife's face contorted slightly and he held his breath but she did not wake. Instead she rolled over and her breathing became more regular as Walsh slipped quietly from the room.

Walsh pulled on his clothes and left the house through its back door. He doubted Six were watching him twenty-four hours a day. He simply wasn't worth it. Their surveillance was designed to harass and provoke him into making an error and one day it just might, so it was time to go but he had to do this right. When Walsh was ready to disappear it would need to be as if he had stepped off the world.

Walsh padded across the garden in his bare feet, not daring to use a light. There was no moon and Walsh could not see the outhouse but knew it was ahead of him. He kept a straight course towards it, counting his steps till he reached the door. Walsh reached out into the blackness and pressed his palm against the wood then moved it lower till he found the latch. He took almost a minute to ease the outhouse door open, knowing its customary creak could be loud enough to wake the dead on a windless night like this. He cursed himself for failing to oil the door. Finally there was enough of a gap for Walsh to slip inside.

Reaching down, Walsh felt the edge of the toilet seat in front of him and he climbed on to it. With a foot resting unevenly either side of the bowl, he raised an arm, spanning his fingers, and pressed a hand against the ceiling for balance. With his free hand, Walsh reached into his pocket for the screwdriver. He gripped it in his mouth while he ran his fingertips over the smooth wooden ceiling until he eventually found the indent of two screws. Walsh spent uncomfortable minutes gently easing each screw free until he could finally lower the wood they held in place. He then stood on his toes and stretched his arm deep into the recess he had gained access to. His hand dragged over the dusty wooden boards there and found nothing.

A sick feeling swept through Walsh. Six had raided the spot already, they were always one step ahead of him and now it seemed the precious contents of his secret hoard had been lost forever. Walsh told himself not to panic, he stretched further into the recess and his fingertips brushed against something coarse. The rough Hessian material was within his grasp. He had merely pushed it further back than intended. He exhaled in relief.

Walsh was at full stretch and the toilet bowl wobbled alarmingly under his weight. Walsh's arms ached as he stretched further into the recess but his trailing fingers finally gained a grip and he pulled the sack free of its hiding place.

With the door closed tightly behind him, the walk-in-larder was ideal for his purpose. Walsh lit the oil lamp, opened the bag and carefully removed its contents one piece at a time. The first item was wrapped in an old towel and he gently removed the dead weight from its folds. Walsh held the gun up to eye level. He surveyed the dull metal of the Luger for any evidence of deterioration during its long spell in the outhouse. The butt and breech showed no outwards sign of rust. Walsh was thankful he had cleaned and oiled the weapon so thoroughly before putting it away. He'd removed the pistol from a dead officer at Dunkirk. Now he dismantled the Luger, examined each working part and, satisfied with its condition, reassembled the gun, wrapped the towel round it once more and placed the weapon in a khaki holdall. Then he checked the two boxes of 9mm Parabellum ammunition and packed these in tightly next to it.

Walsh picked up a heavy brass knuckle-duster and weighed it in his hand. He slipped it on over his fingers and gripped it tightly, flexing his arm. It too went into the holdall.

Finally, he examined the last item, a little brass box, with the image of an obviously regal woman embossed on it in profile.

An ornate border ran round the lid of the box, containing the national flags and names of Britain's glorious allies in conflict; France, Belgium, Russia, Montenegro, Serbia and of course Japan. Underneath the face of the monarch, the words 'Christmas 1914' were stamped across a partially obscured image of a dreadnought with large ominous-looking guns, ready for action.

Uncle John's little brass box had come back from the Western Front, though he himself did not. The sergeant's pitifully early demise at the age of 22 during the Battle of the Somme was a permanent reminder to Walsh of the soldier's odds. The tin had originally contained sweets and cigarettes; a Christmas box from Queen Mary to each of her gallant lads in the trenches. Upon the death of his father, Walsh was bequeathed the box and precious little else, aside from funeral expenses and a handful of debts too petty to avoid the paying. It was dear to Walsh and he always kept it safe.

He opened the hinged lid and removed its contents. The false papers were still there, in good condition, and had even benefited from months folded away in the outhouse. They seemed more authentic for the ageing. Walsh had used the papers before and, when asked for their return, surprised himself by instinctively claiming they were lost. His superiors may well have doubted this story at the time but took their suspicions no further. The risk was worth it for the extra insurance the papers provided. Walsh kept them in reserve, in case Clavelle's documents ever failed him. He slipped the papers into the holdall.

The box also contained a small wood-handled lock knife. Walsh pressed the release at the base of the knife and the blade was freed. He pressed his fingertip against its point and, reassured by the knife's sharpness, dropped it into the holdall.

There was a final item in the little brass box. Walsh gently removed a tiny black felt jeweller's bag and untied the drawstring, inverting it so the contents dropped on to the larder shelf. At that moment the flame beside him flickered. Four perfect cut diamonds of some value winked back at him in the lamplight.

20

*'A person often meets his destiny on the road
he took to avoid it.'*

Jean de La Fontaine

The neighbours wouldn't thank him and nor would Mary once she was woken by the din but it was the only way to be sure of losing the watchers who had tracked him through the daylight hours. Her mood would not be softened when she read the letter he had left her. He would be leaving before sunrise to return to Arisaig, he had written, and thought it was best this way as he never liked goodbyes. He wondered if that would infuriate her or if she would simply take it all in her stride and whether the thought of either of those possibilities should have bothered him more than they did.

Walsh pulled back the tarpaulin to reveal the motorbike and he wheeled it out of the back gate then climbed on. He couldn't see anyone and strongly doubted that Six would have someone watching his house all night. Their surveillance was meant to be a warning not a twenty-four examination of his every movement but he wanted to be free of them nonetheless so this was the best way.

The Norton's engine roared into life, causing a dog to bark

in protest but he was off and away down the road before anyone in his street could stir.

Gubbins had never seen Harry Walsh off on a mission before; that was a duty usually left to Buckmaster, and on occasion Vera Atkins. If Walsh was particularly unfortunate he would fly out on a night when Price wanted to be seen getting his hands dirty. Most often though, Walsh was left to see himself off and that was much the way he preferred it.

There had been no more word from Vera about the CD wanting a word with him, so he was surprised to find Gubbins sitting in the back of the Humber as it pulled up hours later to collect him by the side of the road. The pick-up point had been prearranged. Gubbins' presence in the car had not.

Walsh handed the keys to the motorbike over to a youthful looking army corporal and ordered him to 'treat it with respect'.

'You don't mind me coming along, Walsh,' said Gubbins. It didn't sound like a question.

Walsh climbed into the Humber. From the corner of his eye he watched as his precious Norton was ridden away in the opposite direction.

The car made its way north and for most of the journey, which covered a little over thirty miles, they travelled in silence then Gubbins suddenly said, 'Buy you a scotch before you go lad,' and he leaned forward to communicate with his driver.

The Humber deposited them at a tiny country pub, the driver waiting in the car outside. There were a handful of fellow drinkers but none paid any attention to Gubbins or Walsh. The place was cosy enough, with large oak beams and a well-tended coal fire that burned brightly, lending the pub the rustic charm of a Christmas card.

Gubbins sipped his scotch thoughtfully. 'I expect you have

been wondering why I chose you for this operation, Walsh?'

'The thought had crossed my mind, sir.'

'Well, I didn't as a matter of fact,' he said, before admitting, 'I am afraid I have not been entirely frank with you.'

Here we go, thought Walsh, another senior officer selling me down the river. It was hardly unexpected but the discreet conversation in the pub, with its atmosphere of the confessional, was a new development.

Gubbins continued, 'When our source told us the Komet would be tested in Normandy we knew this might be our only chance to get to Gaerte. Senior men are well protected so we needed help. We contacted the local Maquis leader, codename Stendhal, to enlist his support for an as yet unspecified operation, in return for weapons and training. If his men can be knocked into shape we think they might just be up to the job.'

Walsh listened patiently. He knew all of this already. There had been much discussion on the role the maquisard would take during the team's briefings. The enigmatic Stendhal was unknown to Walsh but the origin of his code name was not. Stendhal had named himself after the author; a man before his time, a revered French writer and inveterate womaniser. But soldiers were not meant to be readers of books. Better for Walsh if he kept his knowledge of such things to himself. Reading had been one of the few pastimes permitted at his bleak and oppressive school, the one bit of learning they didn't have to beat into him. What impressed him most about Mary when they first met was that she had read more books than he had. Until he realised that was all she did.

'Stendhal's group has no radio,' Gubbins continued, 'communication is slow and difficult. A man must be sent for miles across country to a wireless operator in another area. Word from Stendhal is rare, always to the point and we don't take it lightly. When we requested help with the mission, he sent us the following reply. "Assistance agreed on one condition. The man you send is Harry Walsh, none but Harry. Only Harry will do."'

Gubbins surveyed Walsh for any sign of recognition. 'The next day I came to find you. I assume this is something of a surprise?'

'Yes, sir.' Walsh had never heard of Stendhal before, his group was one of many that had come together in the hills. Walsh knew nothing about their leader. Obviously, Stendhal knew him, however, either by sight or reputation. Walsh had carried out a fair number of missions in France by now, so who knew when and where their paths had crossed?

'So, you don't know the man?'

'Not by that name, no.'

'Does this change things?'

They both knew what Gubbins meant. He feared Walsh might pull out of the operation at the eleventh hour, for there was an obvious possibility in the named request for Walsh. The Maquis leader could be a work of fiction, created by the Germans to trap a specific agent. It would not be the first time an SOE man had fallen straight into the hands of the enemy.

'Possibly,' admitted Walsh and Gubbins looked concerned. As well he might, thought Walsh, since it was clear the CD hadn't told Walsh about Stendhal till the last possible moment and clearly hoped Walsh would press on regardless before letting everyone down. 'I might keep the cyanide in my hand instead of my pocket.'

Gubbins gave him a grim smile, 'Good man. Have another scotch, Walsh, then we'll get you on your way.'

They had two more whiskies in the end 'to keep out the chill' as Gubbins put it, then they got back into the car and drove the last few miles to the safe house where Walsh would be reunited with Sam Cooper and Christophe Valvert. The three men would spend their final hours in a commandeered mansion before boarding the plane for Normandy.

'By the by, Walsh,' said Gubbins as Walsh was about to climb from the vehicle, 'Menzies mentioned you the other day, by name.' That was all Walsh needed; a profile high enough for the head of the British Secret Service to personally know of him. '"Your man Walsh" he kept calling you, as in "your man Walsh had an altercation with one of my watchers the other day". C seemed to think you might have broken the fellow's arm.'

'Really, sir?'

'I told C that his watcher should have minded his own damn business. Follow a chap down a dark alley these days without announcing yourself and you are likely to get hurt. Big boy's rules in our game, right, Walsh?'

'Yes, sir.'

The American greeted Walsh at the door of the rambling old Georgian mansion that had been taken over for the duration of the war. Cooper folded his arms and frowned, 'Where in hell have you been?'

'You sound suspiciously like my wife,' said Walsh. 'I've been looking up some old friends and avoiding some new ones.' Then he asked, 'How was Beaulieu?'

'Very informative,' answered Valvert, 'Sam learned how to fight dirty, just like an Englishman.'

'Everyone knows Englishmen only ever fight fair,' said Walsh.

'So, what happens now, Harry?' asked Sam.

'We get a couple of hours' rest. Later we do the equipment check, then it's the US air force canteen for a meal before we go.'

'A last supper?' asked Valvert.

'After eating what passes for food at Beaulieu, I can't wait,' said Cooper.

'A woman was here before, Harry,' said the Frenchman, 'she was looking for you.'

'A woman?'

'A Miss Atkins,' and Walsh had to hide his disappointment.

'Vera?' First Walsh gets the one-to-one treatment from Gubbins, next Buckmaster sends his personal assistant to see him safely on the plane. This mission was attracting a lot of attention. Hardly the low-key start Walsh had hoped for. 'She is here to give you the once-over, gentlemen, make sure you don't set off with your ration book in a pocket or a picture of a WAAF in your wallet. It happens, you'd be surprised.'

'Nothing surprises me about people and war,' said Valvert.

They followed Harry up several flights of stairs to a loft converted into a temporary barrack, its beds lined up in neat rows either side of the room. 'Looks like we are the only ones here tonight. Should make it easier to get some sleep.' Walsh chose a bed at the end of the room, farthest from the door.

As he lay down, Valvert said, 'You can sleep? I don't know how.'

'I've learned to eat when there's food and sleep when there's time. You'll do it too if you have any sense. You never know when you will get another opportunity.'

'Then I will try,' assented Valvert.

Walsh lay down and closed his eyes. When Valvert had mentioned a woman was looking for him he had instantly thought of Emma Stirling. It was an instinctive yet idiotic notion. Emma did not even know he was on this mission but the thought of her had produced a surge of hope in him. In truth, by now, Emma Stirling had surely tired of his marital status and outmoded sense of honour, and that was as it should be. So why, if he wanted Emma out of his life, had told her as much, did he feel exhilaration at the mere thought of her presence on the base? Because he was a sentimental idiot that's why, acting like a lovelorn schoolboy. Emma was probably out that very night with some chinless wonder from the RAF, a thought that failed to lighten his spirits. Walsh reminded himself he had more pressing concerns than a young girl right now – like survival.

21

'Courage, above all things, is the first quality of a warrior.'

Carl von Clausewitz

Vera was waiting for them on the air base. Their kit was laid out on trestle tables and they went through it methodically. Some of the equipment had been carefully assembled by Elder Wills' men at the Thatched Barn and transported there a day earlier. All of it would be thrown from the plane on its second pass over the drop zone. The civilian clothes were there too, folded and ready, magically altered to make it appear as if they'd been worn for years. An onlooker would assume their wives had 'made do and mended', as befitting a nation under occupation.

Valvert checked and rechecked the radio that would be his sole responsibility in France. Next he turned his attention to his side arm. The weapon was small and light with a .32 calibre round.

'What are you doing with that toy?' asked Cooper as he checked his own Browning Automatic. Cooper preferred the superior stopping power of its .45 calibre ammunition; that and the reassurance of a thirteen-round magazine.

'It's not a toy,' answered Valvert, weighing the gun in his outstretched palm, 'it's a deadly weapon. Also it is small, discreet and easy to hide. Remember that when you are banging away with your cannon as the Germans close in around you.'

Judging by the look that crossed the American's face, Cooper was disconcerted at the notion of Germans getting that close to him without his choosing. Walsh stowed his own side arm, the Luger, along with the rest of the contents of his holdall, including a small bag containing the false papers and the four cut diamonds, into a kit bag that would stay with him during the jump.

'What is it with you and that Kraut weapon, Harry?' asked Cooper.

'A lucky charm. I got out of trouble with this once and kept it. Plus a Luger confuses people over there.'

'I imagine it would,' said Valvert, 'some of the Milice carry them.'

'I've heard of them,' said Cooper, 'French collaborators in Vichy.'

'They were consigned to Vichy France to begin with but moving into occupied territory too now,' explained Walsh, 'all the better to help their German paymasters to destroy the resistance by infiltrating it.'

'Don't they usually wear a uniform? I'd have thought everyone would know who they were.'

'A blue coat, a brown shirt, appropriately enough, and a nice little blue beret,' answered Walsh, 'but you can't always see them coming down the street. They work undercover too, far more effectively than the Germans. They know the terrain, the language, every nuance of the world they inhabit. People are tortured and murdered by them; sometimes they simply disappear.'

'Or are handed over to their friends in the Gestapo,' added Valvert.

'Nice guys,' said Cooper.

'Traitors, I'd shoot all of them,' said Valvert vehemently.

'I'll never understand it. What kind of man would rather fight for the enemy than against them?' asked Cooper.

'The same sort that joined the Nazi party in the early days,' it was Vera Atkins, previously a silent onlooker, who had joined the discussion, 'frustrated minor government officials seeking advancement, former military men with a hatred of communism. They would rather see Hitler in Paris than a communist French leader. Some of them even come from the right of the Catholic Church.'

'The church?' Cooper was disbelieving.

'In Europe the church has always been in politics,' said Vera.

'Don't think all Milice join for political reasons,' said Valvert, 'it's not always about fighting communists. Most of the ones I've seen sign up for pay and extra rations.'

Valvert's temper was up now and Walsh thought it time to change the subject. Cooper did it for him.

'What's this?' asked the American as he opened a small box.

'Cufflinks,' answered Walsh.

'I can see that, Captain Walsh,' he said dryly, 'but why have I been given them?'

'A little SOE tradition. You risk your life in a foreign field for them and they give you a gift to show it's appreciated.'

'Are you serious?'

'Perfectly, it comforts people, apparently.'

'Really?' Cooper regarded the cufflinks closely, 'how very...'

'Quaint?' asked Walsh.

'I was going to say "English". This happen every time?'

Vera Atkins nodded, 'It could be a pen, a hip flask, a lighter; the girls might get a compact. No markings obviously. This time it's cufflinks.'

Cooper placed the box carefully in his kit bag.

'It's meant to be a reminder of home. It can be lonely in the field for weeks or months on end,' Vera explained, 'besides, they do have a practical purpose.'

'Keeping my shirt cuffs together? Unless you are going to tell me they contain cyanide capsules?'

'They're gold, Captain Cooper, which means you can sell them if you have to.'

They did not know when they would get their next meal so they ate the US air force's food heartily. At the quiet table in the servicemen's mess, and on Harry's insistence, they went over it all once more.

'I am a teacher,' announced Valvert with conviction, between mouthfuls of stew, 'of English,' and he wrinkled his nose in disgust, 'such a backward language, don't you think, so lacking in poetry, especially the way Americans strangle it.'

'I strangle it?' asked Cooper. 'You should learn the correct way to pronounce our simpler words before you judge me, Christophe.'

'Yes, but that is not important. It is my second language. You, on the other hand...'

'Don't forget who your allies are, friend. We turn our backs on you and your grandkids will be speaking Kraut.'

'Go on,' prompted Harry, 'the cover story.'

'Of course,' Valvert acquiesced. 'Like I say, I am a teacher. I have recently completed my time in Paris. I am on my way to take up a position in a better school, Catholic of course, with a chance of advancement to, as you English would call it, housemaster.'

'The name and location of this school?'

'Sainte-Marguerite on the Rue Richer in Rouen.'

'And the one in Paris?'

'The Holy Cross & Mary Immaculate.'

'And why are you not on a work detail heading for Germany?'

Valvert frowned and patted his stomach in pretended discomfort, 'Ulcers.'

'Good.' Wash was relieved to see Valvert had at least taken this part of his training seriously, learning his cover story well enough for cursory questioning.

'And what would the Germans discover if they were to look into my fictitious life?' asked Valvert.

'A sympathetic headmaster,' answered Harry, 'who will tell them "yes, there is a Monsieur Limol. He is expected at my school any day now".'

'So you think of it all.'

'We try to.' He turned to the American, 'What about you?'

'Me? I'm from Boston. Okay, maybe not. My name is Jean Dachet. I am a young, promising but rather dull banker from Arras, an arranger of loans. I work for the banking house of "Guerney Felise", who would doubtless verify this?'

Walsh nodded. 'They would.'

'That's reassuring.'

'Go on.'

'I specialise in the granting of loans to factory owners and farmers that support our glorious Franco-German fight against the evils of communism. I am twenty-six years old but yet to find a wife, though I am looking. She must be a good woman of unquestionable moral character with a devout religious upbringing. As long as she's built like Betty Grable.'

'I don't remember that last bit in your cover story,' said Walsh, 'not sure there are too many devout women over there with Grable's legs.'

'Oh, you'd be surprised,' said Valvert softly, as the merest trace of a smile crossed his lips.

'Good, your *legends* sound vaguely plausible. At the very least they should buy some time if you are caught and questioned.'

'By which you mean they will buy others time,' said Valvert

amiably, 'so they may escape before we are killed.'

'Yes,' said Walsh, looking him in the eye, 'that's exactly what I mean.'

There was a moment between them then, as if the magnitude of their undertaking had begun to sink in. Here were three men from three very different nations united against a common evil, about to undertake a mission of enormous importance. All were resolute, yet each carried with him a dark dread that this time he could be the one to lose his life. They had been briefed and re-briefed, trained in every aspect of operational procedure SOE could contemplate; they were proficient in the use of explosives, radio codes and small arms of every type. They had been chosen because they were demonstrably brave, resourceful and patriotic but not gung-ho. A dead hero was no use to anyone. Each of them realised that training and briefings could amount to little once they were actually in France. Walsh and Cooper knew more than most the initial plan rarely survived the opening hours of a mission.

'So, we are finally ready,' pronounced Valvert.

'It seems so.'

'And is that everything?' asked Cooper.

'What do you mean?'

'Oh it's just,' Cooper stretched back in his chair, linking his fingers together and cradling the back of his head in them, 'I have a funny feeling you are not telling us everything, Harry. You disappear for days without an explanation...'

'I had to shake off some unwanted attention. You know how it is, Sam; your FBI aren't always sympathetic to OSS.'

'And you shook off this unwanted attention, obviously. Is there anything else we should know?'

Walsh knew it was pure instinct on Cooper's part but he was impressed by the sixth sense that sent the American's suspicions his way. 'Are you going to give me a speech about trust, Sam, you of all people?'

Cooper held up his hands in concession, a wordless reply that meant 'whatever you say, Harry', though he seemed far from satisfied. After Yugoslavia, Walsh owed the OSS man nothing and his first thought was to ignore Cooper's concerns but, try as he might, the idea bothered him. Gubbins did not have to tell Walsh about Stendhal's message but he had done so. The CD had wrestled with the information and come to the conclusion Walsh had a right to know, even if it hampered the mission. Did Valvert and Cooper not have the same right to be told about the mysterious Maquis leader who had asked for Harry by name? It seemed they did.

22

'Men fear death as children fear to go in the dark.'

Francis Bacon

'Jesus H Christ,' offered Cooper when Walsh had completed his explanation of the enigmatic radio message.

'I don't understand,' said Valvert, sounding like an innocent abroad in his incomprehension, 'what is it?'

Walsh spoke calmly and levelly as he outlined the not outlandish theory they could all be parachuting straight into a German trap.

'Oh,' was all Valvert could offer for a while, until he finally added, 'well nothing can be done about it now and it is not as if we have a choice.'

Sam Cooper fully understood the implications from the outset.

'Thank you for telling me, Harry,' he said angrily as he rose from his seat, 'at least I know to keep my happy pill handy, just in case.' Walsh was struck by their similarity in thinking. Walsh belatedly realised that he and the man from the OSS had far more in common with each other than with most of their fellow countrymen. They were two halves of the same coin, even if neither would want to admit it.

There was an interminable wait for the plane. Walsh was used to the delays but Valvert paced up and down as if he was in a doctor's waiting room instead of a draughty Nissen hut on the edge of the runway.

'You all right?' asked Walsh, the constant movement beginning to irritate him.

'Sure,' said Valvert, 'why shouldn't I be? I'm going home.'

Just then there was a low rumble from outside the Nissen hut. The plane had arrived.

Walsh never lost the sense of being dwarfed by a Halifax, no matter how many times he'd flown in one. He could see Valvert felt the same from the open-mouthed look on his face, as thirty-eight thousand pounds of metal rumbled straight towards them. They waited outside the hut as the twenty-foot-high, seventy-foot-long bomber, with its hundred feet of wingspan, taxied itself into a turn. The Halifax slowed to a complete halt with the engines still running and the hatch opened from the inside to admit them.

Walsh immediately knew there was something wrong. At first he could not quite put his finger on it but the plane was different somehow. The navigator waved them forward and they ignored the noise of the engines and its whirring propellers, walking briskly up to the aircraft to board it one at a time. Walsh was the last to be hauled aboard by the navigator's outstretched hand.

'It doesn't sound right,' Walsh said, feeling a little absurd to be telling this to one of the RAF's finest but he could not ignore his instincts.

The navigator grinned. 'You're a veteran!' he called above the noise, 'this is the new Mark III. We're one of the first with the new engines. Bristol Hercules air-cooled radials!'

Walsh cared little that the Bristol Hercules XVI engine had replaced the Rolls Royce Merlins, nor was he interested in the new Perspex nose and adapted tail of the Mark III Handley Page Hercules bomber. All he knew was that something was different, which meant it was untried and unproven. In his book, this did not bode well.

They sat down in the tiny compartment around the hatch. It was cramped but they were not expecting comfort. Valvert shouted into Walsh's ear, 'I've been thinking about this Maquis leader, Stendhal.' Walsh nodded to indicate he had heard above the din of the engines, 'You suspect he is not a German impostor or you would hardly be on this plane but how do you know you can trust him?'

'How do I know I can trust you?' snapped Walsh and Valvert spoke no more.

There was good reason for his poor mood. Soon Walsh would land in France, with none of his dilemmas resolved. If he were jumping into a trap, Walsh would know soon enough, there would be little they could do except go down fighting. Alternately, if Stendhal was who he claimed to be, Walsh would have to gain the Maquis leader's trust, train then effectively lead his men. Between them they had to recruit more volunteers, avoiding capture or infiltration from SS spies, impostors and traitors along the way. Finally, they would have to devise an assault against crack German troops using an untried citizen's army, which would lead to the death of a top Nazi scientist – a man whose whereabouts and likely daily routine Walsh could, at this point, only guess at. Walsh would have to carry out this task not, in his preferred manner, working alone, but with Sam Cooper, a man he knew and did not trust, and Christophe Valvert, a man he did not know and therefore could not trust. These thoughts and more weighed heavily on his mind as the plane suddenly lurched forward, gradually gathered speed then shot upwards into a clear night sky.

They became used to the altitude at seventeen thousand feet and the chill that went with it. They each had enough layers of clothing under their flying suits to resist the worst of the cold and were as accustomed as they could be to the cramped conditions. Then the plane lurched violently from side to side and dropped suddenly without warning.

'What's happening?' demanded Valvert.

'Probably shaking off a night fighter,' answered Walsh in a voice that was calmer than he felt, for he knew only too well that the Halifax's top speed was 265mph, leaving it seriously disadvantaged if it was chased by an Me 109.

'Oh my God,' muttered Valvert and he turned away to contemplate their fate.

Walsh knew what must be going through Valvert's mind, for he hated the feeling of helplessness when he was a passenger. You could be the most experienced, best trained, naturally gifted soldier on earth and it would count for nothing if the plane you were flying in was shot out of the sky.

Walsh felt his stomach lurch as the pilot took the bomber into a steep dive in what could only be an attempt to elude an enemy. Against a smaller, faster, more manoeuvrable plane the odds were firmly stacked against them. As the Halifax took evasive action, turning this way and that, diving steeply, turning sharply, with engines straining so that they were thrown back against the hard metal of the fuselage, Walsh began to wish he had a god to pray to. Valvert, being more devout, crossed himself repeatedly during the manoeuvres. Minutes passed that seemed like hours and still the evasions continued. Surely it was only a matter of time before white-hot cannon fire ripped the fuselage apart and sent them plummeting into a freezing sea. Then abruptly, miraculously, the frantic manoeuvring ceased. Moments later the smiling face of the co-pilot appeared before them.

'Sorry about the bumpy ride. We had some company back

there. It got a bit sticky for a while.' There was sweat on Flying Officer Taylor's forehead, which betrayed the masterful understatement of his words, 'We think the skipper's lost him.'

Walsh exhaled, 'Then my compliments to the skipper.'

'We'll be a few minutes late at the RV point. Will your contacts wait for you?'

'They will or they won't, we're going anyway,' Walsh assured him.

'Righty-ho, I'll be back when we reach the drop zone.'

They did not have to wait long. The command soon came to attach the static lines and the hatch that covered the modified bomb bay doors swung open. Beneath them they could make out the dark blur of the French countryside, as trees and hills whizzed by below. There was a short delay until Flying Officer Taylor reported the Maquis' signal had been spotted, there were lights up ahead, and a confirming letter of Morse had been flashed with a torch. This was it. It was time to go.

Cooper went first, sitting on the shelf at the forward edge of the hole. He waited and waited for the red light to turn to green and when it finally did he was out of the plane almost before the word 'Go!' from the navigator. Valvert immediately followed, dropping quickly on to the ledge and flinging himself out of the hatch with the navigator's palm on his back to help him on his way. Walsh wasted no time, knowing each squandered second would mean a greater distance between their landing positions. He went through the hatch with the practised ease of one who has made jumps many times before. Then he was out of the plane, body tumbling, waiting and praying for the static line to engage. As always, it was a great relief when it immediately did its job; the chute flared open and his sharp fall was abruptly halted.

Walsh floated slowly down into an inky blackness. To his

left he could still see the yellow flame of the beacon but a crosswind was dragging him further and further away from it. The parachute billowed once more, forcing him violently upwards then down again and off to the right, putting more distance between himself and the RV point. The last thing he needed was to be lost in the woods at night, searching for trigger-happy maquisards, who suspected every cracked twig was an enemy. Got to get to ground as quickly as possible and double back to the reception point.

The ground raced up to meet Walsh and he landed heavily with a grunt, turning an ankle in the process. He lay still for a second, letting his eyes adjust to the dark and listening intently for enemy activity. There were no guttural shouts from German soldiers, and no dogs barking. There was no sound at all in fact and no need for cyanide, for the time being.

Walsh sat up and tugged at his parachute strings, dragging the chute towards him and bunching it together. Then he got to his feet gingerly, testing his sore ankle. No lasting damage; there would be some pain but Walsh was no stranger to that. He set off in the direction of the beacon.

Cooper and Valvert both landed close to the rendezvous point, within yards of the beacon. Valvert landed heavily and immediately lost sight of the American in the blackness. He lay still for a moment allowing the pain of the impact to dissipate. Aside from a mild jarring sensation that ran along his spine he was uninjured. Valvert sat up, unclipped the parachute harnesses and dragged it from his back. He turned around to pull the parachute to him then looked up to find he was staring straight down the barrel of a German rifle.

23

'I believe I am in hell, therefore I am there.'

Arthur Rimbaud

Valvert froze as the cold metal from the Mauser was pressed under his chin and drawn up, forcing him to his feet. Walsh had been right to expect a trap. Why else would he have been greeted at gunpoint? There was movement around him and Valvert squinted, trying to see more through eyes that were not yet accustomed to the gloom. Cooper was being brought towards him, hands high in surrender, by a handful of armed men in an agitated state.

Valvert realised the men were muttering to each other in his native language. He looked closely at the man who was holding him captive. The dark clothing he wore was civilian peasant dress not the grey uniform of the German soldier. The half-dozen fighters making up the reception committee surrounded the newcomers, weapons pointed and ready to fire. They carried an odd assortment of weaponry between them; an obsolete military rifle, an old gun meant for hunting, a captured German machine pistol and the Mauser that had been thrust into Valvert's face. This had to be the maquisards but why were they so agitated and threatening their allies with guns? Were they genuine Maquis or traitors capturing parachutists for German bounty? The armed men encircled them, suspicion in their voices as they spoke to the new arrivals,

'Don't move,' ordered one, followed by 'do as we say.'

Cooper and Valvert complied, standing stock still as they were patted down in a cursory manner. The search seemed to be carried out for the hell of it as nothing was taken from their pockets; they retained their side arms and commando knives along with the false papers.

'Say something,' urged a middle-aged man in a black cap as he prodded Valvert in the ribs with his gun.

'Don't do that!' answered Valvert sharply, and they all stared at him as if he had just landed from the moon and not jumped out of a Halifax. God, they were almost as nervous as he was. The reception committee demanded names so Cooper and Valvert gave the legends assigned to them by Baker Street.

'Who are you here to meet?' asked another man who cloaked his identity with a scarf tied tightly across his face.

'Stendhal,' answered Cooper then added in his most reassuring voice, 'don't you think we should be leaving now, in case anybody else saw the chutes come down.'

The young man he addressed looked barely out of school. 'Come with us,' he said unsurely. Valvert and Cooper trudged ahead of his rifle towards the hedgerows. They were met there by a large, muscular presence; a huge man with a balding head, red face, angry frowning countenance and the crushed nose of a boxer.

'I am Stendhal,' said the man as he took a measure of them. Judging by the look that crossed his face, he was immediately dissatisfied. 'Where is Walsh?' he demanded.

Valvert looked about him – where indeed was Harry? Pushing his face out at the newcomers, Stendhal asked again and this time there was anger in the words, 'I told them it had to be Walsh! No one else!' His voice shattered the calm of the night and Valvert instinctively expected German soldiers to appear at any moment. 'Where is Harry Walsh?'

At that moment, Walsh stepped from the shadows and into the Maquis leader's view. 'Here,' he answered simply as Stendhal's men turned and trained their guns on him, 'and if I was a German soldier I'd have aimed for all the hot air and noise and you'd have a bellyful of bullets now.'

'Harry!' cried Stendhal joyfully, 'they sent you! I knew they would,' and his face broke from its frown into a broad smile. Stendhal's own men watched in bemusement as he marched the few yards between them then scooped the Englishman up in his arms, lifting him clean off his feet in a bear hug. 'Now the war is ours!'

Walsh winced at the grip. Stendhal's strength was formed from hard outdoor work over long periods in all weathers. He had been a fisherman before the Germans turned him into a killer.

Valvert was noticeably relieved, 'So you do know him?'

'Oh yes,' answered Walsh, 'not by this name but I should have guessed when he chose a libertine for an alias.'

'Now that's not fair, Harry,' Stendhal forced a frown, 'the man was a writer of exception and a scourge of the establishment. My real name is known by all here, so I only use Stendhal for the radio.' He held out a coarse hand to Valvert, 'Philippe Montueil.'

The relief Walsh felt outweighed the knowledge that all of Montueil's men already knew his real name thanks to the Maquis leader's exuberance – so much for the secret agent codenamed 'Gloucester'. As usual the first casualty of war was the plan.

Overhead the plane passed by for a second time, shedding its precious cargo of supplies. The parachutes on the ten containers snapped open like umbrellas, one after the other, and floated gently to the ground, some landing in the field in which they stood, the rest coming down beyond the trees.

Montueil gave a low whistle and waved a hand. The men under his command wasted no time in obeying his unspoken order. They scampered off in different directions to collect the containers and bring them in but Montueil looked worried.

'What's wrong, Montueil, not enough?'

'No,' he scratched his head, 'too much. I mean we were not expecting such a bounty, a few rifles maybe, some grenades. How will we get it all away from here?' As soon as he had spoken the words he seemed to have made his decision, ordering some of his men to fetch more carts to transport the containers; others would use what they had to get the equipment to higher ground. A few of the larger items would be buried or hidden in barns. The maquisards moved quickly and never once questioned Montueil's instructions.

Montueil glanced about himself uneasily. 'We must get you away from here now. It's not safe to stay long.'

'Your men are well disciplined,' said Valvert as he watched them load the equipment.

'Some of them; the ones I brought with me tonight,' and Walsh saw the frustration in his eyes when he added, 'others less so, as you will see.'

It took them an hour to reach the Maquis camp and the journey was almost entirely uphill. The camp lay on high ground overlooking the surrounding terrain, a good position, making it hard for anyone to approach it unseen and it was still shrouded in darkness when they arrived. They were greeted by the full complement of the maquisards, around thirty sorry-looking men, some of whom held oil lamps to light their way into the camp. These scruffy, exhausted-looking men peered at the new arrivals with undisguised curiosity and a measure of sullenness.

The Maquis base was a makeshift collection of small shelters made from wood or canvas, some exposed to the elements on one side. Homemade tents were dotted here and there between the larger wooden dwellings. Even in the darkness it was possible to imagine thirty men living here at close quarters, judging by the unsavoury smell that hung about the place.

Montueil wasted no time in ordering the majority of the men away, then he led them to the largest shelter, a three-sided ramshackle wooden building that could have passed for a small hayloft. The embers of a fire still burned here. It was replenished with fresh wood then jabbed at with a stick to coax new flames while Walsh and his companions were urged to sit round it and get warm. Men continued to walk by and stare openly at the newcomers.

'Who have you got here, Montueil? A mixed bag by the look of it.'

'You can imagine. Politically, we have socialists, communists, nationalists and anarchists. You should hear the arguments,' and he shook his head at their lack of accord. 'One or two of my men are crooks, professional thieves who would be in jail if they had not evaded the so-called authorities; then there are soldiers who did not want to give up the fight when our nation surrendered,' he deliberately raised his voice a notch when two younger men walked by and said disparagingly, 'and some are little more than hot-headed young boys who think that war is a game.' Then he concluded, 'Mostly it is men who wanted to avoid the *service du travail obligatoire* in Germany, and who can blame them? This is not paradise but it is better than forced labour in the service of an enemy far from home.' He sighed, 'Leading them is not easy and I sometimes wonder how they will be if we ever have peace. They'll probably kill each other, Harry.'

'Let's worry about that when we have won, shall we?' said the Englishman.

'That is probably best,' conceded Montueil.

'So, how come you know each other?' interjected Cooper.

The two other men exchanged glances and Montueil raised his eyebrows at that. It was Walsh who put it into words, 'That's a long story, Sam,' he said, 'and one for another night.'

Cooper and Walsh were shown to a rickety lean-to that would serve as their shelter until dawn.

'What do you make of it?' asked Cooper as they began to bed down.

'They have few able-bodied men and, till now, very little equipment,' answered Walsh. 'They live like outlaws and spend more time evading the Germans than tormenting them. There is at least one rogue faction in their group, which Montueil is probably losing control of because he has nothing to offer the young ones; meaning no quick victories or easy glory. The camp smells like an unsanitary mess and I've no doubt it will look far worse in the morning. In short, I think this particular branch of the Maquis is so downtrodden it is a miracle they have been able to survive till now.'

Cooper was deflated, 'So we aren't likely to turn them into a force that'll trouble a crack German unit?'

'Of course we are,' Walsh sounded surprised at his pessimism, 'they are good men, Sam, no shortage of courage round here, that's for sure. It's almost exactly as I would have expected it to be in fact. You try living rough for years, being constantly hunted and you might not notice the smell so much. It's a miracle they are here at all and still up for the fight. They will be okay; we just have to take them in hand.'

'Take them in hand?' asked Cooper.

'Starting tomorrow.'

24

'Stir the torpid Frenchman!'

Unofficial instruction given to the SOE,
attributed to Winston Churchill

'It ain't much but it's home,' said Cooper dryly, as he surveyed the camp for the first time in daylight. Living conditions here were grim, with everything caked in a mud churned from the constant action of boots on the same patch of muddied ground. It was difficult to tell where the living quarters, dining area, laundry and latrines began and ended, as the whole thing had been thrown together in such haste. Here and there, items of dripping washing hung from ropes stretched between tents and shelters. 'Looks like the Klondike just after they discovered gold,' and the American shook his head.

'Nothing we can't rectify,' said Walsh.

'I'd rectify it with a large fire.'

There was no sign of Valvert, who did not emerge from the tent he had been given until much later and, when he did, he was grim-faced. Straight away he sought out Walsh and Montueil.

'It's the radio,' he told them, 'at first I thought it was my fault but no, I have stripped and reassembled it twice and still it won't work. It's useless.'

'What can be done?' asked Montueil.

'Nothing with this set. We need another radio. How do you get your messages to London?'

'There is another group. They have a radio,' explained Montueil.

'Then I must go to them right away. I'll contact London and ask them to drop us another set. How far is it from here?'

'A day to walk there and a day back but you cannot go alone. You'll never find them and if you did, they would likely kill you for an impostor. You must go with one of my men.'

Walsh was not happy at losing Valvert from the camp so early in the mission. 'Be careful, Valvert, no risks, okay?'

Valvert nodded dismissively, 'Sure, Harry, don't worry.'

'Just don't get caught.'

He could have added: *And if you do, don't betray us.*

Their first day in the camp passed quickly. The guns had to be unpacked from the crates, the grease removed and all the weapons cleaned. While they worked, Walsh and Cooper quizzed Montueil about German activity in the area and began to build up a picture of life in the area around the camp, down in the little town of Elbeuf and the nearby city of Rouen.

That afternoon, Montueil called a meeting of what he termed the Commune; half a dozen men who acted as the camp's decision makers. They included Alain Triboulet, a former schoolteacher, whose resolutely cheerful disposition they instantly warmed to. He had left a wife and son behind to escape the compulsory work details. 'I look forward to practising my English with you, if you will permit it?' he told Walsh.

'Of course,' said Walsh, noting that Triboulet might just be the one man in camp other than Montueil that he might be able to discuss books with.

Next was Alvar, a Spaniard, who might have been around fifty. His rough tanned skin was leathery and his eyes narrowed into a squint when he spoke, as if the sun shone permanently into them. Alvar explained he had begun his fight against fascism back in his homeland. Now he found himself exiled with the French resistance, still hating the Germans for the help they gave to Franco, determined to exact revenge. Alvar was keen to salute 'my international brothers'.

Other men introduced themselves and finally there was the brooding presence of Hervé Lemonnier; a strong muscular man in his early twenties who scowled at them suspiciously, and made no secret of his distrust. 'We were winning before you came and we will continue to put the fear of God into the Germans long after you have gone,' being a typical example of his opinions, 'so don't try to tell us what to do.'

'Shut up, Lemonnier,' snapped Montueil as wooden mugs of Normandy cider were filled and passed between them. He turned his attention back to his guests, 'I'll drink to your safe arrival, which can never be guaranteed. We've had ambushes and treachery and learned of the deaths of many old friends, which is why my people are edgy. We can trust no one.'

'What's the situation, Montueil?' asked Walsh. 'You've got maybe thirty men here?'

'Thirty-two,' confirmed Montueil, 'that's just my group but there are others all around here, hiding in the hills. There are miles of fields and woodland all around us here so we can see anyone coming. Also, we have men who risk their lives every day by staying put in Elbeuf, the nearest town to here and Rouen, which is twenty kilometres north. They are our eyes and ears, without them we would know nothing.'

'Good,' Walsh nodded, 'they will be very useful.' Then he asked delicately, 'Recent activity?'

'You want the truth, Harry, not too much. We caused them

problems at first, sabotaging everything we could. That was the early days but we had so little equipment and not enough men. Plus, there are traitors everywhere. Soon we became the hunted ones. The Germans, they don't know what mercy is. If you are Maquis then you are a terrorist, so you die. No trial, no appeal, you die. If you help the Maquis it's the same. If you are related to Maquis, still the same. I have lost men, good men, and it is hard to trust the new ones. How do we know where they are really from or who sent them? We have caught traitors.' Montueil seemed to share their shame. 'Those men I kill myself.'

'But the Germans kill quicker than you can,' said Walsh.

'It's true, though if you are very lucky,' and he raised eyebrows at the ironic use of the word, 'they only send you to Le Struthof.'

'What's that?' asked Cooper.

'A camp in Alsace,' said Montueil, 'for the few captured resistance fighters who aren't killed immediately. We don't know much about the place as nobody has ever come back from it.'

'Well,' said Walsh, searching for a crumb of comfort amongst the bad news, 'at least now you have equipment.'

'Yes and I am grateful for it but tell me the nature of this bargain I struck with the British. You need our help with a mission…'

'All in good time,' interrupted Walsh, 'let's see what your men are capable of first and we'll take it from there?'

Montueil nodded doubtfully.

'We are capable of anything, English,' said Lemonnier, 'and don't expect a bargain to stay a bargain when we don't know what you want from us. We might just change our minds.'

Montueil ignored the young man, 'There'll be some food later, though I cannot promise much. The Germans,' and he literally spat into the fire at their mention, 'they steal everything; all of the food, most of the wine, the good stuff at any rate. We eat worse than peasants these days.'

When evening drew near, Walsh was surprised there was no effort made to start the preparation of the meal he had been promised. An explanation came with the appearance of a dot on the horizon that gradually became a figure. The figure was leading a donkey by its reins and, as they came into view, Walsh realised he was looking at a young girl.

'That's Simone,' explained Montueil as the girl drew nearer, 'our saviour.' Simone looked to be around eighteen years old. She was strikingly pretty with olive skin, long, dark hair and a lean, strong frame that showed she was used to outdoor living. 'It is because of her that we eat. She lives on a farm near her mother, they make the food and each night she drags that stubborn old donkey up the hill with two big pots strapped over its hide.' He chuckled, 'Every day I worry that donkey's heart will give out, then we will surely starve.'

Simone reached the edge of the camp and the men all gathered round her. The donkey came to a sudden halt, the two huge lidded pots swinging precariously on its flanks, a little brownish liquid spilling on to the ground. Simone ignored the teasing questions: 'What is it today, Simone, do you have something special for me?' and 'Simone, when are you going to marry me, eh?'

'Idiots,' said the Maquis leader as he regarded his men contemptuously.

'She's a brave girl,' said Walsh 'if the Germans ever stopped her up here…'

'It would be hard to explain,' conceded Montueil quickly, as if he didn't want to entertain such a thought.

That night during dinner, Simone waited patiently for the men to finish their meal, while Montueil held court.

'The Germans treat France like a mine,' he said, 'they empty our country of everything; food, wine, men to work their factories, then leave us barren. Look at this, just look, Harry,' and he tipped his bowl so Harry could see into it. 'We are used to eating cassoulet round here but where is the sausage, the pork, the duck? This is pea soup with a scrap of bacon in it and we are grateful for that, I'm telling you. Don't be angry, Simone, but for you we would eat like pigs but even you cannot weave gold from straw.'

'I'm sorry for you,' Simone said to their guests, 'you are used to better.'

'There are shortages in London too,' and he smiled at the young girl, 'anyway my mother used to make her soup like this, with a ham bone?' The girl nodded. 'It was the most warming thing I'd ever tasted, until today.'

'Thank you,' she said, her face reddening a little.

Montueil laughed, 'Harry is a rare beast, Simone, an Englishman who knows food and perhaps even a little about wine.'

'More than you, you old goat,' chided Walsh.

'Perhaps, but only because your mother was French,' and he turned his attention back to the girl. 'You could do worse in a man, Simone.'

Simone blushed once more and Lemonnier gave her a fierce look, a cloud immediately hanging over him. Walsh noted his jealousy and assumed it was Montueil's intention to cause it.

'Harry's already taken, I'm afraid,' said Cooper with what sounded like relish.

'No! Harry, you have a woman?' Montueil said it with such disbelief you would have thought Walsh had confessed to the ownership of a wooden leg.

'I'm a married man, yes.'

'But how did she ensnare you? Witchcraft? I don't believe it! Harry Walsh married?' Montueil began to laugh at the very notion. 'Can it be true?' and he shook his head at the wonder of it, 'well, she must be special.'

'Then you will leave our women alone,' said Lemonnier and his proprietorial gaze fell on Simone once more.

'I am not your woman, Lemonnier,' and there was clear contempt in her answer.

The men mocked Lemonnier as she left them. He purported not to care but it was only after Simone was gone that he dared answer, 'You will be,' to more jeering from the men.

As Simone made the long walk back to her home she contemplated this Englishman, for she had regarded his arrival with interest. Simone was not sure if he was handsome exactly or if it was the quiet authority he seemed to have over the Maquis that she found so attractive. After all, these same men usually ignored or dismissed her with a bawdy comment yet all but the foolish young ones were energised by the presence of this soldier from London. Simone knew it was her patriotic duty to feed the defenders of her country but the truth was, until now, only Montueil seemed to appreciate her efforts, and here was Harry Walsh comparing her cooking to his own mother's. Captain Walsh had been courteous, you could even say gallant, and he was no stranger to soap, which was more than could be said for the rest of the men. Of course, he was married and there was an end to it. It didn't stop her wondering about him though, as she went on her way. Thoughts never harmed anybody.

It was Walsh's turn to address the commune. 'In the morning I'll show you how to strip, oil and reassemble the weapons.'

'We know how to do that already,' said Lemonnier.

'Then it shouldn't take long. In the afternoon we go up to the high ground where we can't be heard and you'll learn how to use them.'

'You are going to teach me to fire a gun, English?' asked Lemonnier. 'What then? Will you teach Montueil to catch a fish?'

'Let him speak,' ordered Montueil but Lemonnier ignored him.

'Give us the guns and we'll use them. I promise you that,' he said.

'You'll get the guns,' insisted Walsh, 'after you prove to me you *can* use them.'

Lemonnier shook his head. 'This is a waste of time.'

'Maybe, but that's the rule; no training, no weapons.'

Lemonnier was clearly accustomed to getting his way. 'You should take me more seriously, Captain Walsh. I'm the only one round here who has done anything.'

Montueil snorted, 'You? What have you done?'

'I've killed Germans, which is more than you have lately.'

'Killed Germans? Ask him who he has killed, Harry. Go on, ask him.'

'All right, who have you killed, Lemonnier?'

'A German officer.'

'The lowest rank it is possible to be,' added Montueil.

'My men took him when he came out of a café one night.'

'*Your* men?' asked Montueil in disbelief, before sneering, 'They kidnapped a boy, Harry.'

'We took him into the hills and held him there. The whole German army was looking for him by the end.'

'He was barely old enough to use a razor.'

'Shut up, Montueil.' There was hurt pride in the young man's words. Montueil merely glowered at him silently. 'I wanted to burn him alive, poured the petrol over him myself,' Lemonnier said proudly, 'but my men are soft-hearted. They couldn't bear it when he screamed and begged and pissed himself, so I was merciful. We hanged him instead and made sure the Germans knew where to find him,' he concluded the tale as if describing a great victory.

Walsh nodded sagely, 'So, you kidnapped a boy officer, stirred up a massive man hunt, risking the lives of everybody in this camp, then killed him anyway. You'd have been better off shooting him in the street.'

'At least we did something!'

'And what did the Germans do?'

When Lemonnier answered his mouth seemed to go suddenly dry. 'What do you mean?'

'You know what he means,' answered Montueil and he turned to Walsh. 'They chose twenty people at random and shot them in the square. Twenty people dead and all because this one will never listen to me.'

'What would you have me do, eh? Nothing? Sit up here in the hills talking about fighting? I've told you, that's not war!'

'I've told you,' answered Montueil, his voice rising in frustration, 'we wait, until we have the supplies and equipment we need,' and he pointed at Harry, 'until London sends their best man to tell us what to do.'

'Nobody tells me what to do.'

'I can see that,' said Walsh.

'Nobody!' Lemonnier rose to his feet, puffed up to his full size, strong, powerful and full of wounded pride. He was very tall, with a labourer's physique. 'Anybody want to try?' and he looked into the face of each man there. Cooper looked to Walsh, expecting a response but nobody moved or answered the challenge. 'No?' Their acquiescence satisfied Lemonnier, 'I didn't think so,' and he marched away.

'Idiot,' hissed Montueil when Lemonnier was gone, 'now you see what I must tolerate. I should strangle the young pup.'

Then why don't you? thought Cooper. It was as if Montueil had heard his thoughts. 'But he has followers; the young ones. I don't have so many men that I can afford to split the group down the middle.'

Once again Walsh kept his own counsel and Cooper was disconcerted that the young man had been allowed to say his piece and leave without being put firmly in his place. To the American, it smacked of weakness.

25

'A man who is of sound mind is one who keeps the inner madman under lock and key.'

Paul Valéry

The next day a column of maquisards, carrying bundles of weapons and ammunition on their shoulders, snaked its way up towards the higher ground under a slate-grey sky, reaching their destination by mid-afternoon.

As Walsh suspected, they were not as proficient as they needed to be, particularly with the Sten gun. Most of their shots with that weapon were high and wide of the target. He allowed the men several attempts with no particular evidence of improvement, Lemonnier's small band of followers faring no better than the rest. All eyes were on Walsh as he called the men to him. They gathered around him in a semi-circle.

'You have a problem, a big problem,' he told them, 'you are not half as good as you think you are. I'm not questioning your courage and you're keen enough but that won't matter when the Germans are picking you off in a battle. Most of you could not hit a horse's arse from five yards.' One or two of the men laughed self-consciously, some glowered, most just listened silently. Lemonnier's men adopted an insouciant air, as if Walsh was either wrong or could teach them nothing. It was time to assert some authority.

'Yesterday one of your number told me it was a waste of time to train with these weapons,' Lemonnier glared at Walsh who stared straight back at him, 'yet I notice he is no better than the rest of you.'

Walsh could actually see the colour filling Lemonnier's cheeks as he spoke. 'Care for another try, Lemonnier,' and Walsh held out the Sten. The men all turned to look at Lemonnier, who was flushed with embarrassment and anger but hesitant, not sure what to do next. Cooper noted the look of calm on Walsh's face.

'Come on, Lemonnier, take the Sten.'

'I told you before, you don't give me orders, English,' he took a step towards Walsh. 'I did not take orders from the Communists, I don't take them from Montueil,' another step forward, 'and I won't take them from you.'

'But you'll take my weapons?'

'From your dead hands if you choose,' and he reached for the gun.

Walsh spun the Sten around so it was facing Lemonnier butt first. As the young man went to grip it, Walsh put his weight behind a firm shove, which sent the hard metal thumping into Lemonnier's midriff. He let out a crumpled gasp as he took the blow. It sent him backwards and he sagged visibly but did not go down. Instead he straightened and went straight for Walsh, letting out a volley of crude names and curses ahead of the heavy blow he was determined to land.

Walsh threw the Sten to Cooper who caught it easily. The Englishman then took a step back, parried the blow and hit Lemonnier with a sharp jab in the nose that jarred his head back. Straightaway Walsh landed two more jabs to Lemonnier's face but his attacker stayed stubbornly on his feet, blinking at Walsh fiercely as he tried to focus. Walsh was happy for the fight to continue while all the men were watching it. Lemonnier had annoyed him the previous night but there was more to it than that; he was an obstacle that had to be removed if the mission was to succeed. A lesson was needed, a display of authority, and Lemonnier was going to take a beating none of his men would ever forget.

Cooper looked on intently as Lemonnier tried to land a serious blow and Walsh merely stepped away from him. The older man's evasions seemed effortless. It was like watching William Fairbairn toy with a trainee at Beaulieu. Cooper winced inwardly at the memory. The fight was just as one-sided but simpler and more direct, like a boxing match between two mismatched opponents. It was as if he was watching one of those circus prize-fighters that pay out if you can stay on your feet for three rounds against them, thought Cooper. They use your strength and clumsy inexperience against you. You flail wildly and they stab at you, picking their spot with precision, drawing blood, causing pain before gliding away once more.

Cooper lost count of the number of blows Lemonnier had taken. He was reeling now, half blinded from the swelling round his eyes, milling his arms like a small child trying to fight off a bigger boy. All the men had gone silent. The message was clear. Walsh was a professional, whereas Lemonnier was just an overgrown boy with a big mouth. Some of them were probably wondering why they had not done it themselves before now. Even Lemonnier's handful of followers seemed embarrassed by this loss of face. Walsh finished the fight with a tight flurry of punches that left Lemonnier's head lolling uselessly. Then he fell sideways and crashed to the ground unconscious, never again to be taken seriously.

'That's enough training for one day,' announced Walsh, who seemed barely out of breath, 'tomorrow I will show you how to use the explosives. If you listen to me very carefully you might not blow your arms off.' Lemonnier let out a faintly discernible groan. 'You men!' Walsh was addressing Lemonnier's followers and they seemed quite alarmed he could identify them, 'pick him up and carry him back to camp.'

They groaned with the effort required to hoist the huge prone figure aloft but they did not question the Englishman's instructions. Walsh hoped they would grow to hate Lemonnier by the time they'd lugged his heavy frame all the way back to camp. Montueil had witnessed the spectacle without comment but, as the unconscious Lemonnier was carried past him, he gave Walsh a private grin.

'As soon as we've finished the explosives training, we move camp,' Walsh told him.

'Move camp?' asked Montueil, his smile vanishing.

'Surely you don't have to ask me why? The place stinks so bad I'm surprised German patrols can't smell you from Elbeuf.'

'It is true, Harry,' his eyes dropped in shame, 'we live like animals here.'

Walsh put a sympathetic hand upon his shoulder. 'Then tomorrow it all changes and you begin to live like men again.'

As they walked back to camp, Cooper caught up with Walsh. 'Tell me something, Harry, why did you not knock some sense into that knucklehead before?'

'Without an audience?' Walsh asked him and the question was explanation enough.

When they finally reached the camp that evening, Walsh expected Valvert to be waiting for them but there was no sign of him.

'He should be back by now?' he asked Montueil.

'Yes,' agreed the other man, 'he should.'

'Then I suggest you double the guard tonight.' And Walsh wondered what they would do if they had lost a member of their group before they had even fired a shot in anger at the enemy. If Valvert was dead already, this was hardly proof that Jedburgh teams could work in practice. If he had been caught how long could he hold out before betraying them? Walsh wanted to move camp the next day but would that already be too late and if Valvert was still alive but merely delayed somehow, how could he find them if they had already relocated the camp?

Walsh had moved on to trying to find a new way to resolve the predicament of being unable to contact London when there was movement from the other end of the camp. One of the men manning its perimeter had left his post and was walking towards the Englishman. On his left was the man who had escorted Valvert to the other Maquis group, on his right Walsh could make out the diminutive figure of Valvert himself. Relief flooded through him.

Valvert was weary but he confirmed he had located the other group of Maquis, was vouched for by Montueil's man and permitted to send his message to London. A reply was received and an assurance given that a new radio would soon be on its way. Walsh was grateful for that small mercy.

Major Robert Price had been sitting at his desk, trying to decide what excuse he could give to escape a social function involving his wife's extended family, when the message arrived. The cipher clerk knocked gently and walked into the office.

Price muttered something unintelligible to illustrate he had more important things on his mind than the contents of the decoded signal that was handed to him on a slip of paper. The preoccupation with his wife's relatives continued. Even as the clerk left the room and he scanned the words in front of him, Price was still contemplating the extended family to which he owed his property and private income. From day one, the aunts and uncles, nieces and nephews on his wife's side had not taken to Price, considering him both an opportunist and an arriviste, which of course he was, but it still galled him that they failed to even mask their disapproval when he was in the room. For years he had craved acceptance but no longer; they continued to treat him with a form of silent contempt, so he would return the compliment.

Price narrowed his eyes and read the message through once more. No, he had not been deceived, for an opportunity had suddenly presented itself. Of course, the message had not really been intended for the eyes of Major Price. He was out in the cold on the Harry Walsh operation and was damned if he didn't know it. But the cipher clerk had recognised Walsh's code name on Valvert's message. Naturally, though wrongly, he assumed the correct destination for the decoded note was Price instead of Colonel Buckmaster. One of the department's agents needed help; who better to assist Walsh in his hour of need than his immediate superior? It was an understandable lapse of operational security from an overworked operative in a fledgling organisation – an all too regular occurrence for an outfit still finding its feet. Price knew he should really do something about it. Instead he blessed the clerk's error, for it afforded him a perfect opportunity to make life more difficult for Harry 'Golden Boy' Walsh.

Walsh was in Normandy and in need of a new radio, poor cherub. Someone would have to be sent with it of course; now who could Price spare at short notice? He saw an opportunity for mischief. Captain Harry Walsh, always so calm, so unflappable, the man who never lost his head under any circumstance. Well let's see how he handles this. Price smiled to himself. It was time to put a cat among the pigeons.

26

*'If you would be a real seeker after truth, it is necessary
that at least once in your life you doubt, as far
as possible, all things.'*

René Descartes

Sam Cooper lay on a ridge overlooking the valley. In the
far distance the town of Elbeuf shimmered beneath
the sun but it was not the view that held his attention.
Cooper had lain motionless on the hard ground all morning,
watching small dark specks rising from the airfield as the
German fighters flew off on intercept duty. The Royal Air
Force had once manned this same base before the Germans
had overrun France. Hurricanes had flown out of here to
engage the Luftwaffe; now the situation was reversed, with
Messerschmitts scrambled day and night to try and shoot
down relentless waves of Allied bombers.

It had taken half an hour with one of Montueil's guides
to reach his vantage point. Cooper then dismissed the man,
confident he could find his own way back to the camp. He
had decided against using field glasses. They weren't needed
to identify a plane that travelled at the speed of the Komet and
he didn't want to give away his position if sunlight reflected
back off the glass. Now he waited tensely for any sign of the
Komet's presence but none came.

Of course, they could all be the victims of inaccurate intelligence, German plans could have changed or perhaps the Komet was yet to arrive but Cooper couldn't risk leaving here without a sighting. If he did glimpse the plane, he knew Professor Gaerte would not be far from it. And so he stayed.

Cooper waited that whole day with no sign of the Komet. He trudged back to the camp and returned the next day and still there was no sighting of the jet fighter. After three days lying on his stomach he was certain the Komet was not on the base and that was no bad thing. It bought them a little time. Whoever said spying was glamorous, he mused as he brushed the dirt from his clothes? They didn't write about this sort of thing back home in the comics and dime novels.

On his way home at the end of the third day, Cooper climbed an escarpment that overlooked the valley. A dark shape on the horizon had intrigued him. When he finally reached the top, he realised it was a dilapidated old hunting lodge, probably built at the turn of the century. This tiny, derelict wooden building would have slept no more than four keen hunters back then, each looking to make an early start to catch unsuspecting bird life. Now it had fallen into disrepair but still afforded a panoramic view of the surrounding area. This might be just what I'm looking for, thought Sam.

'There's our man.' Montueil was pointing at a shape in the night sky, a little patch of something moving; a gliding, spinning figure coming down to meet them at some speed. The plane that delivered him was already banking away and heading for home.

The parachutist managed to land on both feet, but was dragged along in a stumbling run, before finally toppling over. Walsh had witnessed better landings but seen far worse. The impact wasn't too hard but you could never really be sure with a jump. It was all too easy to break an ankle or put out a knee. Walsh stayed where he was, shielded by the tree line, watching. The parachutist climbed unsteadily to his feet with no apparent harm done. Behind him the radio floated down on a separate chute. He tugged at the strings of his own parachute, struggling to bring the billowing silk under his control while it, in turn, threatened to pull him down once more.

It was time to greet the new arrival. Walsh pulled the cover from the old miner's lamp and held it out in front of him as he stepped into the clearing. He wanted to be seen now. The last thing Walsh needed was to be shot at by a nervous Englishman delivering a radio. Visibility was poor in the darkness but Walsh could just make out the blurred figure. The man froze as he spotted the lamp, doubtless praying Walsh was a friend not a foe. It was a feeling Walsh knew only too well and was perhaps the reason why he risked a call.

'Welcome to France,' he spoke in English, just loud enough for the new man to hear, 'you are safe now,' and he immediately realised how ridiculous that sounded in this land filled with hostile, conquering soldiers.

Still the parachutist did not move. The night was so dark it lent the immobile figure a ghostlike countenance, rendering him almost invisible. Walsh blinked hard and lowered the lantern to avoid its glare. He took in a short, slight figure, clad in a regulation khaki jump suit and skullcap. A balaclava had been added to protect against the cold, it hid the features of the new man, giving him a sinister air.

Finally the apparition moved, advancing on Walsh. There was barely a yard between them when the figure finally stopped and looked him up and down. Then, in one fluid movement the skull cap and balaclava were pulled away.

'Christ on a bike, it's you,' said Emma Stirling with not a little irritation, as her hair fell down around her shoulders, 'I might have bloody well known.'

Emma's mood had not lightened by the time they reached the new camp, two miles from its unsanitary predecessor, and Walsh began to quiz her again about her presence among them. 'I told you,' she snapped, 'I was given an order, that's why I came.' She was speaking as if they were all simple-minded; while Cooper, Valvert, Simone and Montueil sat around her. 'Deliver a radio set to the Maquis, they said, then stay with the group until relieved. That was my order,'

'Stay until relieved?' probed Walsh.

'Yes!' replied Emma, as if he was particularly hard of hearing.

'From Price?'

'From Price.'

'Unbelievable,' and his aggravated tone annoyed her even more. Emma had assumed Harry Walsh had been removed from her life and she would finally be able to move on. She had thought of him often since the night he brought her out of Normandy but, as the days wore on, she told herself it was time to forget this married man who could never leave his wife. Emma loved Harry but knew she could never have him, so Walsh must be consigned to her past. The finality of this enabled her to dare to think of a future without Walsh. Now she faced weeks, possibly months, marooned in a Maquis camp with him, a place so small she could not hope to escape his presence for more than an hour. It was a bitter irony. Price might have caused this situation, deliberately no doubt, but her anger was firmly directed at Walsh. Would she ever be rid of the bloody man?

Sam Cooper watched the interrogation of the new arrival closely. Emma Stirling's answers troubled the American on some vague level. It wasn't the words she used exactly but the tone of her replies that bothered him. Emma seemed exasperated, almost sulky, as she answered Walsh's questions. Cooper had worked with women before and this one was not behaving like an agent. Walsh meanwhile acted like he was scolding a girlfriend about an impetuous purchase. Emma's impatience and Walsh's irritation obviously came from a long-standing intimacy with Harry Walsh, of that Cooper felt sure.

'Who's Price?' the American finally asked.

'My immediate *superior*,' answered Walsh, the last word dripping with sarcasm.

No one spoke for a moment.

'Is there a problem we should be aware of?' enquired the American.

'There's no problem, Sam.' *Just the minor issue of a commanding officer determined to play the mischief-maker.*

'That's right, Captain Cooper, there is no problem. Captain Walsh is none too pleased to see me that's all and the feeling is entirely mutual.' With that Emma rose to leave, 'I'm very tired, I haven't slept much in the past few days. Simone, would you show me the way please?'

As soon as the mortifying appearance of a woman in his camp had been confirmed to him, Montueil had sent for Simone. The fisherman had never been married, his experience of women being confined almost exclusively to other men's wives and he knew little of their domestic requirements. For her part, Simone seemed irked at being asked to leave the men by this older, possibly prettier interloper but she acquiesced, despite her immediate dislike of the woman who seemed so confident with Captain Walsh, to the point of rudeness. Cooper waited till they were out of earshot.

'Correct me if I have misread the situation, Harry, but is there some romantic history between you and Miss Stirling?' Walsh shot him an irritated look. 'I mean I could hardly blame you, she is very easy on the eye, but it would help us all if…' His words tailed away for, in truth, he was not sure how to phrase it. How would it help them all to know if Walsh and Emma Stirling had been paramours? The OSS had not trained Cooper how to handle such matters of the heart. All of a sudden, he felt like a schoolboy who has clumsily trodden on something.

'Goodnight, Sam,' answered Walsh, before he climbed to his feet and trudged morosely away.

'Might as well have said "Mind your own goddamned business, Sam",' offered the American and Montueil nodded slowly in agreement.

Cooper watched Walsh go then he stole a furtive glance back at Emma, who rewarded him with a final tantalising swing of her hips, as she receded into the darkness.

'Can't say I blame him though,' he said and Montueil gave an affirming Gallic grunt.

27

'The resistance of a woman is not always a proof of her virtue, but more frequently of her experience.'

Ninon de Lenclos – French courtesan & author

The following day, Montueil risked a visit to Rouen. When he returned he was a picture of resentment. 'The Germans show no sign the war goes against them. There's to be a grand meal. The local SS gangster will feast every senior military commander and policeman in the area.'

'What's the occasion?' asked Cooper.

Montueil waved his hand dismissively, 'Anniversary of a failed attempt to blow Hitler to pieces before he seized power, in a beer hall. They say he was inches from death.'

'That was an expensive failure,' said Cooper.

'Look what it has cost the world already,' agreed Montueil.

'Makes you wonder whose side he is on,' offered Valvert. 'God I mean.'

'Who is the SS Officer?' asked Walsh.

'A Colonel Tauber.' There was a look of recognition from Walsh. 'Know him, Harry?' asked Montueil.

'We never actually met,' said Walsh evasively.

'Let's hope you don't have the pleasure,' said Cooper.

'So, it's his big night, is it?' asked Walsh.

'One of my contacts has seen the orders.' Montueil was

bitter. 'Three grand chefs to prepare the meal, dozens of assistants and two huge lorry loads of food and wine coming into Rouen from a wholesaler in Elbeuf, the very best of everything they say. The Germans will eat themselves sick that night, on the finest French produce, while we starve out here in the hills.'

'And all the local bigwigs invited to attend, in their fine dress uniforms, with wives, girlfriends, mistresses,' Walsh ruminated.

'Not all three surely?' quipped the American before adding, 'got something in mind Harry?'

'Perhaps,' he turned back to Montueil. 'Must make you pretty angry to hear all this.'

'It does.'

'How'd you like to do something about it?'

'What do you mean?' asked Valvert cautiously.

Walsh shrugged. 'Ruin their evening; give them all a night Tauber won't forget in a hurry.'

'Of course, I'd love to do that, Harry, you know I would, but how can we?' asked Montueil. 'There will be hundreds guarding them. They are expecting officers from the Wehrmacht, the SS, even the German navy has its headquarters at L'École Supérieure de Commerce in Rouen.'

Valvert said, 'You can't be serious, Harry. We won't be able to get within a mile. It can't be done.'

'Yes it can, Christophe, trust me.'

'What about our mission?' asked Cooper.

'The target isn't here yet.' Like the question his answer was suitably vague. 'I say we keep ourselves busy in the meantime.'

'Harry, please,' urged Montueil, 'think about what you are saying. How can we attack a hall in the middle of town when it is guarded as if Hitler himself is in attendance? It isn't possible.'

'Almost anything is possible these days, Montueil, and I say we can ruin their night. Now, are you with me?'

'Of course I am Harry but this is…' Montueil had clearly run out of words to describe the madness in Harry's head.

'Jesus H Christ,' said Cooper as he regarded the Englishman, 'I can tell the cogs are whirring.'

Emma soon learned there was little to do in the evenings but talk. The men would sit around the fire, drinking their local cider or bottles of second-rate wine not already purloined by the Germans. Emma drank sparingly and spoke mostly to Simone who, despite her initial distrust of the new arrival, was eager to hear all about London. Simone had never been anywhere and wanted to go everywhere. Paris would be a good start once this war was finally over and London seemed a world away.

Sam Cooper ambled up to join their conversation and Simone was impressed to learn the number of countries he had visited but Emma was more interested in his homeland. 'What do you miss most, Captain Cooper?' she asked him.

'Me? That's easy, Fenway Park,' and when his answer was greeted with incomprehension he added, 'home of the Boston Red Sox, though they have never won a thing in my lifetime.'

'I'm sorry?' asked Emma in genuine bemusement.

'Baseball,' said Sam, as if it were obvious.

'Sam's American,' said Walsh as he joined them, 'they play each other at sport and call it a "World Series".' He'd been grumpy ever since Emma's sudden appearance. If anything, she felt even more aggrieved, as Walsh had yet to confide the true nature of his mission to her. To think he had once trusted her with their own enormous secret and now he was treating her as if she might secretly be working for Heinrich Himmler.

'You've not seen a Fenway crowd when the Yankees are in

town, Harry, now that's an atmosphere,' Cooper assured him. 'One day my team are gonna win that World Series, then I will die a contented man. But I guess you guys don't have baseball, so you don't know what you're missing,'

'Oh, we have baseball, Sam, I think you'll find we invented the game. Only we call it rounders. Emma probably played it at Roedean.'

'Ignore him, Captain Cooper,' ordered Emma.

'Please, call me Sam.'

'Ignore him, Sam, talk to me instead.'

'All right,' agreed Cooper, 'did you really go to Roedean? I've heard of it.'

'Of course you have,' said Walsh, 'it's the girl's school for the posh and the rich.'

'What do you know about my school?' snapped Emma.

'I know you hated it.'

'Yes, well, maybe I did,' she conceded, 'perhaps I was neither posh enough nor rich enough then,' and she directed the rest of her comments to Cooper. 'I didn't really fit in there. I didn't respond well to the training.'

'Training for what?'

'They were teaching us to be the wives and mothers of entitled men. Oh they didn't say as much but we all knew it really. What else were we destined for?' And she reflected on this, 'But then the war broke out.'

'And you found yourself parachuting into France with a radio set. That's quite a leap, in more ways than one.'

'I had an aptitude for the language,' she explained, 'the one thing I was good at. The talent spotters found me working on translations when the rules changed in '42. Women weren't allowed on frontline duty until then. SOE thought I might be good at this.'

'I'm sure you are.'

'I'm not,' she said, '*sure* I mean but here I am anyway,' said

Emma, not wishing to prolong discussions about her self-doubt. 'So, tell me all about Boston, what's it like?'

'Friendlier than New York, and full of fine people, mostly. We have the best seafood on the east coast. One day, Miss Stirling, you must try the shrimp at the Union Oyster House. That's the oldest restaurant in America.'

'I've been to a pub in Covent Garden older than your entire country,' said Walsh.

'Shut up, grumpy, we are not talking to you,' and Emma made an elaborate point of turning to face Cooper. 'Please, call me Emma. Will you go back there?'

'When the war's over? I'd like nothing better. Live in a brownstone on Beacon Street, get a regular job like a regular guy, walk down to Fenway to take in the game. Yeah that's for me.'

'Except you're not a regular guy though, are you, Sam?' said Walsh. 'Describing this normal life you're never going to have.'

'Sounds like you are talking about yourself there, friend.' And there was a definite edge to their words.

'Does everyone follow baseball in America?' asked Emma quickly. She had no interest in the answer but wanted to distract these two quarrelling ninnies before they came to blows.

'Pretty much. There are two passions in my city; sport and politics, and I'm a typical Bostonian'

'Then I'll look forward to you running for president,' said Walsh sourly.

'Argh, but you're forgetting, I'm Boston-Irish.'

'Which means?' asked Emma.

'Which means America is a long way from accepting a Catholic in the White House.'

'That's no problem, Sam,' said Walsh.

'It isn't?'

'No, just change your religion'

'Just like that, huh?'

'Just tell yourself it's for the good of your country.'

'That what you think of me, Harry? Uncle Sam taps me on the shoulder and all my principles go into the trash can?'

'I never said that, Sam, but it's interesting that you did,' then he added, 'I'm going to stretch my legs, see if the perimeter guards are awake.'

'That man's insufferable,' said Emma when he had gone.

Colonel Tauber was in a lighter mood than usual. Kornatzki even caught his superior giving a little whistle at the end of the recital. 'For a French quartet, I think they've almost mastered the Schumann,' said Tauber as they left the town hall, 'wouldn't you say, Kornatzki?'

'Indeed, sir.'

'It's going to be a fine evening if they play like that. Everybody has accepted, simply everybody, well apart from one or two invitations I sent to Berlin but then one never really expected...' and his words drifted away, for they were not really meant for his deputy.

Tauber's whistling was replaced by a contented humming of Schumann's *Kreisleriana*. The Colonel felt like a man in control of his own destiny. The night would be the triumph he had waited so long for. Tauber had seen less able men rise through the ranks, while he drifted in one unpromising position after another; now, finally there was a chance to break free and move up. The expertly played classical music, the fine wines and elegant dining would all help to propel him up the ranks. If the evening went well, and there was no reason to doubt that it would, Tauber would become an accepted part of the social strata of the region. The Colonel smiled to himself. If the night went with a real bang, word of it might even reach Berlin.

28

'The quarrels of lovers are the renewal of love.'

Jean Racine

The driver of the first lorry took the bend slowly because he had been warned of the steep gradient. Jean had good reason to be cautious. His cargo was precious and its masters unforgiving. He drove the vehicle, which contained the wine, brandy and champagne for the SS Colonel's grand dinner. He knew his life would be as good as forfeit if he went off the road with such a rare and expensive shipment.

Jean had stood nervously by the side of the truck as it was loaded and counted the cases himself, for he had to sign and account for their safe arrival. He was not going to be held responsible if some light-fingered opportunist walked away with a case or two of fine cognac.

As well as their drinks for the evening, Jean's truck was packed to the roof with items that did not require chilled conditions during the short journey from the wholesaler to Rouen; jars of pickles that would accompany the pâté, cherries soaked in kirsch, fresh fruit the like of which had not been seen in the city's shops for many a month. Loaves of bread and baskets of rolls baked that morning completed the load and the smell of freshly baked produce filled his cab with their warm aroma and made his stomach growl. If it had been anyone else's consignment but the German's, Jean would have helped himself to a loaf or two but even that thought terrified him.

The feast was a prodigious one and Jean was responsible for just half of its fare. Behind him, a second lorry was filled with huge blocks of ice slowly sweating away in the daytime heat. Stacked between them were the cheeses and packets of foie gras, boxes of chickens and cuts of lamb; enough to feed the whole city. At least the route was a short one. Before long they would reach Rouen and he could supervise the offloading of his wares. Then he would obtain the necessary signatures and could melt away from the event. He wouldn't want to be one of the poor French waiters forced to serve the hated Germans that evening.

Jean pressed on the brake as he took a second corner, hoping the other driver, whom he did not know from Saint Peter, was awake and would not plough into the back of him. As he rounded the corner, however, all fears of a rear-end shunt went from his mind. There were men in the road and they were armed, aiming their rifles his way. Jean slammed the brake down hard and the other truck driver must have done the same thing for their tiny convoy halted at once. Now the rifles were pointing straight at him and two men advanced on his cab shouting for him to get out. Panicked, he looked beyond them for a possible escape but they had dragged a large length of felled tree out with a chain to block his route. Jean could not go forward, nor could he reverse back up the hill with the other lorry blocking his way. He applied the brake and raised his hands.

Jean was hauled from his cab and instantly replaced there by a gleeful youth who took control of the wheel. An identical fate befell the other driver and Walsh climbed into his cab. Moments later the tree was dragged out of the way and the armed men climbed into the trucks. One of them, a large balding man with huge calloused hands, looked down on them from the second cab.

'Elbeuf is only two miles back the way you came, so get walking but do it slowly because we will know when you get there. Just like we knew when you would reach this spot. Give our regards to Colonel Tauber. Tell him we will enjoy his food and wine.'

'I can't do that,' exclaimed Jean in a panic, 'what if he has me killed?'

Montueil laughed, 'Then we will send our condolences to your wife and family; now get moving.'

Those involved in the raid busied themselves offloading the lorry; box after box was passed from man to man then squirrelled away into a recess of the camp. Other men lit fires and made pots ready for cooking. Montueil was exuberant, his eyes twinkling, arms sawing the air in front of him as he regaled the other men; a fisherman once more, describing the size and quality of the catch.

'The best cheeses! Camembert, Pont l'Évêque and Livarot. Enough for a month!' There were appreciative murmurs at the bounty. 'We found the orders of the chef alongside a copy of his menu, so we know what the pigs were meant to be having for their dinner.' He picked up the waxy paper and read grandly from it, 'Poulet Vallée d'Auge and Pré Salé.' The first was a local chicken dish cooked in a cream sauce; the second, finest lamb specially reared on salt plains around Mont Saint Michel. 'The apples were to be flamed in Calvados and baked in tarts... but not in the colonel's ovens!'

The men all cheered. Then Montueil held up his hands to ensure he had everyone's attention. 'Tonight our beloved Simone will cook for us as always but this time it will be like never before!' The men were in good humour, laughing while Simone blushed ferociously in the background.

Montueil calmed himself, lowering his voice almost deferentially, 'And of course… there is the wine.' There were low chuckles of expectation from men who had lived on the rougher forms of alcohol for a long time, a new cheer followed each wine as Montueil named the cases: 'Pouilly Fumé from the Loire valley, Chassagne Montrachet and Crozes Hermitage, bottles of Armagnac and Calvados and, finally, Dom Pérignon… so they could toast Hitler's survival. Instead we'll drink to the day he is hanged from the Eiffel Tower!'

There were shouts of acclaim from his audience. 'Any man who does not finish three bottles tonight is a traitor!' Unconfined cheering from the men now. 'But the first bottle is Harry's.' Simone handed Montueil a Montrachet and he held it out to Walsh, 'To Captain Harry Walsh, the man who stole the Nazis' dinner!'

Walsh took the bottle from his friend's hand and held it up to his lips. The men started up an excited low murmur and he began to drink. The braying from the maquisards grew louder with each swig and Walsh recognised it as another test of manhood, albeit a good-natured one. Only when he had made respectable inroads towards the middle of the bottle, spilt wine flowing down his chin, did he cease, to cheers and applause from the men.

Montueil was still smiling. 'I would love to see the look on the Colonel's face when he realises none of this feast will reach him! How ever will he explain that to his guests?'

The General stopped to address Tauber on his way out of the town hall. 'So this was the fine dinner you promised me?' He looked at Tauber as if he were a turd. 'I could have eaten better in the sergeants' mess,' and with that he was gone, along with all Tauber's hopes of advancement.

The humiliation burned through the Colonel but he was forced to endure more as a procession of officers left the gathering, damning him with faint praise. 'Interesting choice, mutton,' smirked one, before shaking his head and departing. Their derision was harder to swallow than the tough meat, which was all he'd managed to secure at short notice. Steal would have been a more appropriate word, as his men were sent to every hotel and restaurant in Rouen to commandeer replacements for the treasures taken by the maquisards.

Despite Tauber's best efforts to save the evening from disaster, the hastily improvised meal had not gone well. Though his face had turned to stone, inwardly Tauber was apoplectic. As usual Kornatzki bore the brunt of his fury, after a misguided attempt to calm his superior's panic.

'Perhaps it would be better to postpone,' he'd offered hopefully, 'they will surely understand.'

'Understand!' screamed Tauber, 'what will they understand? That I have no control over the area I am meant to be in charge of! Have you gone mad?'

Hours later, as the procession of senior military men and dignitaries made its way out of the building to discuss his public humiliation with their giggling women folk, Tauber made a vow. He would hunt down those responsible for this outrage and they would pay for it, many times over.

Initially in a good mood, the onset of drunkenness had begun to sour Emma Stirling's view of the world. There was something galling about sitting with the men while they lauded Harry Walsh at every turn, cheering his daring, patting him on the back and raising glass after glass to his health, while he and Emma pretended to be little more than comrades, with no acknowledgement of a shared history, or admission that they had once meant more to each other. Emma felt excluded and more hurt than she would care to admit.

Montueil staggered drunkenly by, clutching another bottle of Montrachet. He slapped Walsh exuberantly on the back with his free hand. 'Why have they not made you a general yet, Harry?'

Walsh laughed, 'We'll all be cold in the grave before that day.'

Cooper, who had drunk as much as anybody but was still very much in control, said, 'Few living men have more experience. At OSS we'd have made you a major, maybe even a colonel.'

'The British Army doesn't work like that, Sam,' said Walsh.

Emma sighed.

'What does that mean?' Walsh asked her.

'Now you are going to tell Sam that only the sons of the landed gentry get promoted above captain.'

'I was not going to say that.' Walsh was becoming irritated by Emma. She had taken on a sneering tone that was starting to grate on him. 'But can you argue that it isn't at least partially true?'

'You should try being a woman in this man's army, Harry, then you would know the meaning of limitations. You know the real reason you don't get anywhere with the brass at Baker Street? You must do.'

'Do I?'

Emma turned to Sam, 'Captain Walsh has a problem with authority. He can't abide anyone telling him what to do; not a man, not a woman, not Winston bloody Churchill.'

Walsh took a deep breath before replying, 'If I ever receive an order directly from Churchill I'll be sure to obey it. I don't remember you being too annoyed the last time I disobeyed one from Price, since it involved getting you out of a big, deep hole full of Germans.'

She ignored that. 'It's not just Price though is it, Harry? They say that since you got back from Dunkirk you don't trust anyone. They say that's why you were sent from your regiment to SOE and why you nearly always work alone.'

'*They* obviously have a lot to say about me.'

'Well, it's true, isn't it? But you're not the only one to come back from Dunkirk. Thousands of other men did and they are not all like you, so what's the big secret?'

'It's no secret, Emma. Dunkirk completed my education. That's all.'

'What happened to you out there Harry?' she pressed him.

'I doubt you'd understand.'

'Why? Because I'm a woman?'

'No, because unless you were there it is almost impossible to explain, and to tell you the truth I don't want to talk about it. It's none of your bloody business.'

'I don't particularly want to talk about it either but I suspect Dunkirk is the reason you never trust anybody you work with, including Sam and including me, so that makes it our business.'

'You can trust Sam if you wish Emma, then see where it gets you.' The American laughed and took another swig from the bottle he was holding. He continued to watch the argument with undisguised amusement. Walsh continued, 'As for me, you're right, I've learned not to trust anybody; at Dunkirk and a dozen other places since. Particularly anyone giving the orders.'

'You mean Price?'

'I mean anybody.'

'But why? I heard they gave you a medal after Dunkirk and promoted you while the battle was still going on.'

'They promoted me for a reason, Emma.'

'Which was?'

Walsh was about to snap now. He opened his mouth to say something then thought better of it and forced himself to calm down before answering, 'Never mind.'

'There you are, you see,' she spoke to Sam, 'he won't tell

anybody anything. He comes with a big bag full of secrets nobody ever gets to know.'

Cooper laughed again.

'What's so bloody funny, Sam?' snapped Emma.

'You two. You are like an old married couple.'

'No, we are not!' Emma protested.

'Yep, an old married couple sitting on your porch, quarrelling over the price of beans. You should hear yourselves.'

Emma got shakily to her feet, her half-drunk bottle of wine swinging loosely in her hand. 'I was sweet on Captain Walsh once, Sam, I admit it, I was,' her words were noticeably slurred, 'though I've no idea what possessed me. The sun must have been in my eyes but a woman can change her mind.'

'Her prerogative,' agreed Cooper, clearly enjoying himself.

'And I've changed mine.'

Emma swayed alarmingly then and immediately stopped talking. She pulled a face as if fighting a sudden feeling of nausea before announcing, with the finality of the resolutely drunk, 'I'm going to bed.'

'Excellent idea,' smirked Sam and he watched Emma's unsteady path back towards her tent. Emma did not even notice as the half-full bottle of wine slipped from her grasp and landed in the grass.

When Emma was gone, Cooper said, 'I'm going to find the lovely Simone, as you've put the only other pretty girl for twenty miles in a foul mood,' he chuckled, 'and you are in big trouble, Harry.'

'Me? Why?'

'Because that girl is clearly still in love with you.' He grinned at Walsh, 'Goodnight, my friend,' and he walked off smiling, taking a swig from his wine bottle as he went.

'Who said we were friends?' Walsh called after him.

29

'I have more memories than if I were a thousand years old.'

Charles Baudelaire

It was crisp and cold, the grass soaked in dew that shone in the silver light of early morning. Emma was not in her tent but she wasn't hard to find. Walsh followed the retching noises to a clump of nearby bushes. She finally finished throwing up as he reached her. Her face was ghostly pale, her eyes filled with tears.

'Oh God, Harry,' she spluttered, 'I'm so sorry. How did I get in that bloody state? I can't remember.'

'Might have had something to do with the three bottles of red wine.'

'Lord, I'm so, so sorry, Harry, I really am.'

'Don't mention it,' he said, though her words still rankled with him. Walsh had expected and been ready for defiance that morning. He'd even prepared a few choice words of his own in advance but Emma's obvious contrition, along with her pitiful state rendered them obsolete.

'No, I mean it. I shouldn't have gone on at you about Dunkirk. You're right. I don't know anything about it and all that stuff about your reputation, that's not true, I don't know why I said it.'

Walsh smiled, 'Actually it is true, well, most of it.'

'No, no, everybody looks up to you. They all think you're fearless.'

'Then they are all wrong,'

'Well, anyway, I'm sorry. I was really very drunk and what I said was unforgivable. I think I was just angry with you,' she looked away then, unable to meet his eye, 'you know, because of us. It was so unprofessional. Sam must think I am a complete flake.'

'No, Sam was highly amused. Look, Emma, it doesn't matter.'

'It does.' She turned back to face him now, looking bereft. Emma Stirling was an easy girl to forgive. She had a quick temper but a kind heart and he could never think badly of her for long. 'Oh God,' she said then and he thought Emma must be cursing her loss of control the night before. Instead her face went paler still and she turned away from him just in time before vomiting hard into the bushes.

'You'll feel better in a moment,' said Walsh trying to stifle his amusement, 'and when you've stopped throwing away a perfectly good dinner, we'll go for a walk. It's time we talked.'

They were sitting at the top of the hill, side by side and silent, the entire valley stretched out beneath them, while he tried to find the words. He finally admitted, 'I don't know where to begin.'

Emma shrugged, 'Begin, as they say, at the beginning.'

Begin at the beginning, thought Walsh, and where would that be? Just after he led the bayonet charge?

Falteringly he began, 'I heard it all later, from a fellow lieutenant who was in on the discussion, but I could have guessed most of it,' he paused for a moment before continuing, 'the battalion was preparing to fall back. The whole bloody army was in disarray at that point. The German advance seemed unstoppable. The general and the colonels were trying to choose a company to fight a rearguard action in our sector, to allow the rest of the men to be evacuated out of Dunkirk.

'It wasn't just a question of choosing a hundred or so men to fight to the last man. That could be done with barely a moment's thought. No, the tricky bit was selecting the officers who'd stay behind and lead those men, to fight and die with them. I know a man; a fellow junior officer who was in that room with the top brass and there was braying indignation at some of the names offered up. Lots of "can't order him to stay behind. I've known his father for years" that sort of thing.'

Emma recognised his all too realistic impression of an outraged senior army officer.

'And so they continued, discounting those with social connections or an inability to do the job. They needed a captain at least and it seemed there was no suitable candidate.'

'Except you.'

'I was a humble lieutenant.'

'But I thought... oh,' and the penny finally dropped.

'Exactly.'

'They promoted you so they could leave you behind?'

'Yes, all of a sudden it seemed I was the right man for the rank after all. All I was required to do was salute them, hold the line and die quietly with the minimum of fuss once they were all aboard the ships and away, making the supreme sacrifice for the honour of the regiment. It was bad timing on my part. The day before, I led a bayonet charge to retake a gap in the line. A battlefield promotion was my reward they said, but I knew differently.'

'If that's true then it's shocking but are you certain?'

'Oh yes, apparently at one point the General asked if I was anybody at all. I can remember the reply word for word "I have it on good authority he's the son of a commercial traveller".'

'Oh God.'

'I bet they all wondered how I got my commission in the first place. I was sent for, praised for my outstanding contribution to the defence of the line, then hurriedly promoted to captain. Almost in the same breath I was "volunteered" to stay behind and fight, until the last man if need be, to cover the regrettable but necessary evacuation of the battalion. The Colonel was very decent about it,' he added dryly, 'got his batman to sew the new rank on to my battledress for me there and then. He didn't think I'd have time to do it myself and would have hated me to die inappropriately attired. Then he gave me a section of perimeter to hold and wished me "Godspeed".'

Describing long-suppressed events to Emma made the memories fresh again. Harry found he could vividly recall the chaos of that day now. As he emerged from battalion HQ, the rest of his outfit was moving west as swiftly as the battalion's remaining shred of dignity would allow, the wounded piled into trucks, the able-bodied marching under their own steam along roads clogged by fleeing civilians and burned-out vehicles. Bullets were fired into the radiators of abandoned trucks while the engines were still running, so the Germans could have no prospect of using them, following an arrival considered imminent.

Walsh had to trudge against the tide as he walked past line after line of exhausted men. And who had been first to greet him? As always, it was Lieutenant Tom Danby.

'Harry, is it true? Do I have to salute you?' And he grinned at Walsh, his white teeth a stark contrast to the mud and smoke that stained his face. The grin stayed in place until Walsh broke the news.

'They're leaving us behind, Tom.'

But Emma did not need to know about Tom Danby. She waited

patiently for Walsh to continue then finally asked, 'How did you get away, Harry? I mean, if you were meant to fight to the last man and you didn't desert?'

'No, Emma, I did not desert.' He was aghast at the notion.

'Sorry,' she flushed, 'that was a stupid thing to say. Still, it must have been tempting, given the circumstances.'

'I just did it differently, that's all. At first we spread out along the perimeter we'd been given but it was too wide and there were far too many gaps. I reckoned we could hold the German armour and infantry for a few hours at the very best before we were completely wiped out. But there was an alternative.'

'Go on,' she urged.

'We advanced.'

'You advanced?' Emma was shocked. 'While the whole British Army was retreating, you advanced?'

'Well, moved forward at any rate. We took the fight to them. I split our forces and hit them in little groups as they approached key points we identified. We blew up a bridge, held a road at a narrow stretch, we turned a static line of regular soldiers into a guerrilla army and it worked, for a while. But I made one mistake that came back to haunt me when I eventually got back to my regiment.'

'What was that?'

'I sent some of the men home. Didn't think I needed all of them for that kind of warfare. I kept some volunteers but the rest drew lots. Forty of them got back to the beaches and away.'

Walsh had ordered one of his sergeants to coordinate the withdrawal, getting them to leave in small groups during the night, their feet bound with bandages and torn blankets, so the Germans did not hear the sound of men marching over broken glass that littered the town.

'I bet your colonel blew a fuse.'

'He did but I assumed I'd be dead by the time he found

out. I didn't expect to survive, which was the basic flaw in my plan.'

'What happened?'

'We did all right, to begin with. We held up the German advance far longer than anybody could reasonably have expected and inflicted a lot of casualties. Then, inevitably, we were caught in the open, trapped, and it got bloody,' Walsh looked down at the ground, 'close quarters stuff, bayonets, all that.'

Walsh could feel the familiar ringing in his ears, as the blood began to rush to his head and the creeping sense of panic returned, triggered by the memory of the desperate battle to escape. Even if he had wanted to, there was no way to describe the reality of such a fight to Emma. It was too close, too frenzied and Walsh had been right in the middle of it, adrenalin, fear and blood all coursing through his veins at once.

As the German fire came down on them, Walsh roared at his men to move forward. His heart was pounding and his breath came out in snorts as he powered forward. The bullets missed their moving targets at first. Walsh's men returned fire and continued to sprint forward, desperate to get out of the open killing ground around them, but the German rifle fire grew more accurate and Walsh's men were inevitably cut down.

All about them was confusion; one of Walsh's men cried out but there was no time to look round let alone stop. Got to keep moving, to break away. They reached a line of enemy soldiers by a farmhouse who seemed surprised these men had not fallen with their comrades. Walsh raised his rifle and shot a man in the face then went further into the melee. He shot a man in the chest then the chaos was all around him. There was a blur of movement ahead as shapes crossed his path and he fought frantically to get through and beyond them, parrying blows, stabbing with the bayonet, sinking it into unprotected flesh then moving on. One of his sergeants was hit and a grenade exploded nearby, deafening Walsh. Ears ringing, unsure if he had been hit by the shrapnel because of adrenalin, he was dimly aware the man who had just killed his sergeant was turning a rifle towards him. Walsh slammed his bayonet into the German's stomach; even among the carnage he would never forget the look of complete surprise on the dying man's face as he twisted the bayonet and pulled it free.

He shot another man and ran forward once more. All about him khaki and grey shapes were engaged in vicious hand-to-hand fighting of the bloodiest and most desperate kind. There were screams from wounded or dying men and roars from their attackers as soldiers from both sides did their best to kill each other. Walsh knew he must keep moving or die.

He shot his way through, immediately coming face to face with a German captain who had dropped an empty rifle and was now reaching for his pistol but Walsh was on him before he could take it from its holster. The captain realised he was lost and had just enough time to say the single English word, 'Don't' before Walsh cut him down where he stood. Walsh scooped up the captain's Luger and jammed it into his belt.

There was movement behind him and Walsh spun to aim his rifle but it was two of his own men. At that moment the shooting abruptly ceased. It was only then Walsh realised they'd done it. A handful of them had broken through.

The remainder of the German force was falling back to regroup, perhaps taken aback by the fierceness of resistance. More than half of Walsh's force lay dead or dying, in close proximity to the German fatalities they were responsible for, and the remaining men he commanded found it hard to believe they weren't among them.

The elation was short-lived. Behind him, propped unnaturally up against a thicket, like a drunk who has passed out, was the wretched figure of Tom Danby; his eyes lifeless, a large maroon patch on the khaki fatigues where the burst from a machine pistol hit him full in the chest.

There was no time even to close his best friend's eyes let alone bury him, so Walsh, moving dumbly, hurried the survivors along.

'Harry? Are you alright?' asked Emma, when he had been silent for a full minute.

'Yes,' he said in a manner that brooked no contradiction, 'let's go.'

As they walked back to the camp Walsh explained, 'I sleep-walked through the rest of it. There were hardly any of us left and all the boats were long since departed. Eventually I gave my final order. "It's every man for himself. Good luck and off you go."

'I stayed for a while to cover them, sniping at anything that moved with a bolt-action Enfield, which was all I had left, fully expecting to die as soon as a handful of men found the courage to rush my position, but no assault came. I gave my men twenty minutes start and found I was still alive. Eventually I fell back and that's all there is to tell.'

'But how did you get out if all the boats had already left?'

'That's another long story, Emma.'

'Which you are not going to tell me.'

'Come on, let's get some breakfast.'

'Oh, I don't think so, Harry.'

Walsh had hoped the nauseating idea of food would discourage further questions.

30

'Sigh no more, ladies, sigh no more
Men were deceivers ever
One foot in sea, and one on shore
To one thing constant never.'

William Shakespeare, *Much Ado About Nothing*

Walsh lay awake that night remembering. By recounting his experiences to Emma, he had reopened the Pandora's box of his suppressed memories and now he was unable to replace the lid. It had got him to thinking. How had he become so trapped? What had made his younger self walk into this life so thoughtlessly? The answers to these questions and more could all be traced back to the nightmare of Dunkirk.

A few short weeks after his escape from France, Walsh had found himself walking out into the chill of an uncommonly cold afternoon to find Mary. The Danbys had a long garden to the rear of their house. Here, partially shielded by a birch tree, on a white wooden bench built for two, sat Mary Danby, eighteen years old, beautiful, innocent and profoundly damaged, shattered by a brother's loss.

Mary wore a thin dress despite the chill, which she seemed unaware of and sat slightly stooped, an opened book in her palms. Walsh was not sure if she was actually reading or whether the book was a prop to insulate her from the outside world. He had thought about the words he would use but, now that they were face to face, he had no idea what he was going to say to her.

In the end he settled for a simple, 'Hello, Mary,' spoken softly, so as not to make her start.

'Harry,' she looked up at him, 'have you been with mother and father?'

'Yes, but I wanted to see you. I'm so sorry.'

'You said you'd bring him back to me, you promised,' she reminded him and the words were agony for Walsh. He had promised it true enough and been a fool for doing so. *I'll look after him, Mary*, he'd said, *I'll bring your brother safely back to you.* It was the sort of thing people said in war, to calm those left behind. Harry Walsh had looked into those beautiful brown eyes and would have promised her anything at that point. He'd meant it too, at the time, even though it was no more in his power to give her that than to hand her the moon. What's more, he'd promised it to the one girl in England who would take his words literally. Mary still believed men went off to war like the knights in Malory's *Le Morte D'Arthur*, that they could make things happen through pure hearts and by their force of will. What a damned fool he'd been. It was one more mistake to add to all the others he'd made.

'I know,' he said, 'and I tried.'

She stifled tears, then nodded firmly, 'I know you did.'

'It's cold out here, Mary,' Walsh spoke like he was reasoning with a child, 'don't you think it's time to come inside now?' It was as if his words had broken a spell. She rose to her feet to follow him and Walsh instinctively took her ice-cold hand in his. Mary gripped it tightly as if she might suddenly fall.

But she did not want to go inside so, leaving her by the

door, he went to fetch her coat. They walked for hours; the army officer and the beautiful girl and Walsh remembered how he had promised her brother he would take Mary to the 'flicks' one day, to see a film and 'bring her out of herself' as Tom had delicately put it.

'She's young,' Tom had said, 'and a little fragile. I do worry about Mary but I know you'll look after her, so it would be all right.'

Yes, I'll look after her, thought Walsh, if I do nothing else I can do that much at least and in his mind he swore it silently to Tom Danby.

They linked arms and received approving looks from a handful of Mary's neighbours. After all, the poor young girl had recently lost a brother, now it seemed she had a fine and handsome suitor, and a captain to boot. They all dearly hoped nothing bad would happen to him.

Twelve months later they were married, with a fitting symmetry that pleased everyone around them. It was more than six months before Walsh realised he had made a terrible mistake and a full year before he would fully admit it, even to himself.

The Maquisard commune was in session again. The men were buoyant, flushed with pride following the seizure of Tauber's supplies and eager to relive the moment when he was deprived of them.

'Well, stealing the enemy's food was a good start but it is not going to win us the war,' Harry reminded them.

'So what is it to be next then?' asked Valvert.

'I think a number of things,' said Harry and he outlined his plans. Havoc was what he had promised Menzies and that was exactly what he was going to deliver.

The next night, as darkness fell, small groups of maquisards left the camp quietly in different directions.

Montueil took men and explosives; Cooper and Valvert dressed in workmen's clothes and set off for the rail yard; Emma, Walsh and a handful of men walked half the night to reach a bridge that spanned the river. Earlier, Walsh had taken the chastened and bruised figure of Hervé Lemonnier quietly to one side and showed the young man that he had recently knocked out how to use the Welrod then he gave him an important job to do. Lemonnier seemed surprised to be entrusted with the work but promised Walsh that he would succeed or die trying.

Cooper and Valvert slipped into the railway sidings at Rouen, eluding a solitary German sentry, just as the French civilian maintenance crew took its break from the night shift. Each man carried a metal can and they moved in a stooping half run, careful not to crunch the shingle underfoot.

Valvert was nervous but determined, more afraid of letting anyone down than he was of being captured. At any moment he expected to hear the bellowed challenge of a sentry. If it came, he still did not know whether he would surrender, try to run – though it would be hopeless – or stand and fight till the end.

Every noise was magnified as they crossed the dark yard; each new sound made the two men freeze then peer about them in the gloom of the depot. It seemed to take an age but finally they reached their target, a line of flatbed, rail freight cars.

Cooper spoke in a hissed whisper, 'Start at the other end and meet me in the middle. Make sure you spread it thickly into every axle bearing.'

Miles from Rouen, Montueil's men were in position, lying on their bellies, spread out on either side of the railway track under cover of the tall grass. If a train came or a German patrol reached this isolated spot then word would be passed down, man to man, with a series of waved signals until it reached Montueil. He would then stop what he was doing and slide back into the cover of the bushes.

Even so, Montueil felt exposed out here on his knees at the edge of the track. The night was lighter than he would have liked, the moon against him, and the job could hardly be hurried. Montueil had the small torch Walsh had given him. From time to time he risked switching it on to check his handiwork before snapping it quickly off again.

Montueil considered himself a confident man but tonight he was sweating like never before and his mouth was as dry as sand. He had never handled plastic explosives, or PE as Walsh called it, before. There had been time for just a couple of demonstrations. Montueil could tell some of his men were nervous at the prospect of actually detonating the explosives themselves. As the leader, he had reluctantly volunteered himself for the task, which seemed to greatly amuse Walsh.

'RHIP, Montueil, RHIP?'

'What?'

'Rank Has Its Privileges, my friend,' explained Walsh and Montueil had failed to see the joke.

He wasn't sure how long it had taken him to attach the plastic explosive to the track but the job was almost complete. Now he took the long, thin cigar-shaped time pencil from its case and gently introduced the detonator to the PE. All the while he remembered Walsh's careful warning. The time pencil could be affected by a number of external factors such as age, heat or moisture, and he should not rely on the accuracy of the timings. Montueil set detonation for forty-five minutes and prayed this would not actually give him forty-five seconds. He gave a signal to his men and they retreated back into the woods, visible relief on the nearest faces.

They made their way home and, less than half an hour later, there was a massive explosion that tore out a sizeable section of track and could be heard for miles. Montueil checked the time on his watch, scowled and shook his head. Harry was right about the time pencil. The detonation had been nearly twenty minutes early. At least he had been warned.

Emma watched as Harry scaled the iron stanchion of the bridge. She allowed herself to consider the gruesome possibility that at any moment he could slip, fall and plummet to his death far below. It was a superstition. She felt that if she entertained the horrible notion of Walsh's death head-on then it would never actually happen. Her thoughts immediately turned to Mary. If he did die out here, would they make Emma go and tell his wife, because they might reason a woman might do that so much better than a man? For the first time she wondered what Mrs Harry Walsh was really like and whether she might actually be able to read the guilt on Emma's face. Then she reprimanded herself for such foolish thoughts. Emma reminded herself firmly that they were in the middle of a sabotage mission and she should concentrate on this and this alone. She trained her eyes on the empty road ahead of her, which cut through the hills and ran all the way down to the bridge, scanning it for any sign of the Germans. Not a soul stirred.

Walsh was making steady progress. He'd ruled out a descent from the top of the bridge, as the overhanging angle was not in his favour and the Germans had been inconsiderate enough to place barbed wire and sandbags in his way. Easier to climb from the foot of the bridge and try not to think about the drop if he fell, for he knew he would never survive it. The Maquis had suspended a long rope from the top of the bridge right down to the foot of the riverbank. Walsh used this to climb as far as one of the iron stanchions that supported each corner of the bridge. He told himself this should be no more nerve-racking than the numerous cliff climbs he had completed during his commando training when he first joined SOE.

Walsh reached the stanchion and was able to stand on it. He was just edging along the curved girder he had chosen to plant the charges when he heard Emma's whistle. Walsh froze, for the prearranged signal could mean only one thing – a vehicle, a person or, worst of all, a patrol was approaching the bridge. He lay perfectly still upon the curved girder. As he did so, Walsh inadvertently looked down and caught a glimpse of the moonlit bank next to the dark flickering waters of the river far below him. It made him feel giddy and he clung harder to the girder, hoping his luck would hold out. Let it be a lone vehicle, or a couple of bored soldiers on their way back from a brothel on foot, drunk and with no inclination to peer too closely at a new rope hanging over a sandbagged bridge.

He could hear the low rumbling of an engine now, followed by its grating groan of protestation as the driver tried and failed to find a lower gear on his descent. The sound became more even as the lorry drove on to the bridge and began to slow down. Walsh knew if the driver stopped and got out he was completely trapped.

Walsh listened intently. There was a squeaking sound and a rattle from the chassis as the lorry drove by. The driver pressed the throttle, allowing it to accelerate over the wider section of the bridge right above Walsh's head. The bridge rumbled under the weight of the truck and the girder he clung to vibrated beneath him, but a moment later it was gone. Walsh realised he had not let out a breath while the lorry passed and his arms had gripped the girder so tightly they ached from the effort.

Walsh knew he had to get the job done. He reached behind him into the sack on his shoulder. He retrieved a small canvas bag with a fuse coming from one side and a detonator hanging out of the other. This seemingly innocuous package contained enough plastic explosive to destroy the stanchion, rip through the concrete above it and send the bridge crashing down into the river below, or so he hoped. Walsh just had to set the charge and make sure he climbed back down again before it went off and buried him under the rubble. He primed the explosive and once he was satisfied he began his descent.

As he climbed carefully down the rope, with a sheer drop directly beneath him, Walsh told himself that if he survived the war he would never do another dangerous thing as long as he lived. He grimly pondered the safest, most boring job he could possibly take; bank manager, schoolteacher, insurance salesman, anything but soldier.

When the bridge finally blew, they were far enough from it to evade the first Germans on the scene but still close enough to hear the blast that ripped up through the concrete, propelling huge fragments of rock and metal high into the air and tearing a gap in the bridge that was yards wide.

Lemonnier was smoking nervously at the end of the alleyway that led into a side street at the edge of the town of Elbeuf, a little over twenty kilometres from Rouen. The glow of his cigarette was an unnecessary risk that might give his presence away to a passing patrol and the English soldier would probably have berated him for it but Lemonnier badly needed a smoke to calm his nerves. This was the first time he had ever had to kill someone who could actually fight back or run, and he had to make his move at exactly the right time.

They knew the routine Neuvetaille followed each night. The baker, a known informer to the State Police with friends in the dreaded Milice, left his wife at the same time each evening for a neighbourhood bar whose terrace overlooked the left bank of the Seine. There he would sit alone enjoying three perhaps four glasses of wine and a pastis or two before ambling back home in a fug of alcohol.

When the Maquisard commune drew up their list of targets, it included the road bridge, the rail track, the rolling stock and Neuvetaille the hated informer. Alvar had suggested they send a message on the folly of collaboration with the enemy. Lemonnier had hardly spoken during these meetings since the beating he had taken from Walsh, but it was he who suggested Neuvetaille – for his arrogance, his swagger and his assumption that nothing bad could ever happen to him while he was a friend of the occupier. They had all looked to Walsh for a decision. Would it be acceptable to gun down an unarmed civilian in the street to show others the fate that could befall a traitor? Perhaps this would offend his English sensibilities? Walsh took his time before answering. They expected dissent. However, he merely asked, 'are you sure this man helps the enemy?'

Triboulet replied on their behalf, 'Certain, Harry, he is known for it. He sells the Germans their bread and gives them information on his customers. Jews have been rounded up and information supplied on the resistance, he is not even discreet about it.'

The schoolteacher's testimony was enough for Walsh. 'Then he should die,' he said quietly and that was the end of the matter.

Lemonnier had not expected to be given the job. Yet, for some reason, Walsh had trusted him with one of the key actions of the night. He now found himself perversely seeking to regain the approval of a man who had publicly humiliated him.

Lemonnier stubbed out his cigarette and stepped further

back into the shadows for Neuvetaille was coming at last. The baker was walking unsteadily along the street towards him. Lemonnier weighed the Welrod's length in his hand once more then repositioned it under his long, dark raincoat. He waited till Neuvetaille had almost reached his house then moved off at walking pace to meet him in the middle of his street.

Neuvetaille took his keys from his pocket, dropped them on to the ground and let out a groan of exertion as he bent to pick them up. He walked awkwardly up the five steep steps to his home and was about to put the keys in the lock when he heard his name being called. Puzzled, Neuvetaille slowly turned to find himself looking down into the face of an obviously scared young man staring intently back at him.

'What is it?' asked Neuvetaille when Lemonnier offered no further explanation. It was then he realised the youth was holding what appeared to be a short length of drainpipe and he pointed at the baker. Fearing assault, Neuvetaille tried to turn to let himself in but, before he could, there was a soft popping sound and the bullet from the Welrod caught him plum in the chest.

Lemonnier watched in fascination as Neuvetaille's eyes bulged and his hand went straight to the wound. One of his knees gave way and the baker tumbled heavily down the stone steps towards his killer. Lemonnier had to jump back out of the way as the body rolled on to the pavement beside him.

The killer was rooted to the spot, unable to move or do anything except stare into the shocked face of the man he had just executed. He had done it and he'd done it right, he had made this man's wife a widow and turned his children into orphans, ended his life and all his hopes for the future with a single squeeze of the trigger, so why was he not now running down the road?

'Move, idiot,' Lemonnier actually found himself saying the

words out loud and it finally broke the spell. Walsh had told him to walk calmly from the body to avoid suspicion but the English soldier was more used to killing than he was. The young man did not stop running until he was at least three blocks from the traitor's body.

31

*'One can be the master of what one does,
but never of what one feels.'*

Gustave Flaubert

Colonel Tauber awoke the next morning to a series of alarming bulletins. A bridge across the river had been destroyed, causing a diversion of some twenty miles; the rail track was damaged also, in need of an expensive, time-consuming repair; and the locomotives earmarked to transport the tanks of the 2nd SS Panzer Division to the Eastern Front had all mysteriously seized up in the night. The cause of this baffling mechanical condition was yet to be determined, for the railway mechanics in Rouen were not familiar with carborundum grease, an abrasive formula designed by the Thatched Barn for just such a purpose.

As if all this were not enough, a prized informer had been gunned down in the streets of Elbeuf on his return from an evening drink. Suspiciously, not a soul had heard the shot that left this baker bleeding to death on the pavement, which surely pointed to a conspiracy of silence.

Tauber was embarrassed and this caused an impotent fury.

'What in God's name is going on?' he demanded of Kornatzki. 'A month ago no one could blow his nose in this region without me knowing about it, now, overnight, we have seemingly descended into anarchy. I'll not have it! Send patrols out into the country and get those lazy swine from the Milice to start sniffing around. Find out who is behind all this and do it now! When they do catch the men behind this, Kornatzki, we will show no mercy. The whole country will learn their fate. Now get on with it!'

And when Kornatzki did not immediately move, 'Why are you still here?'

'That's not everything, I'm afraid,' he said timidly, 'it's the professor from Berlin. He has arrived.'

Tauber could not believe his own luck, 'But, he's…'

'A week early,' Kornatzki confirmed, 'and I'm afraid he wants to see you immediately. It's about the arrangements for his stay.'

'What about them?'

'I regret to inform you the professor will not accept our suggestion of living on the air base. Instead he is demanding to stay at the hotel.'

'But it's for his own security? Did you not explain this?'

'I did, Standartenführer, but he was adamant that security was your… *our* responsibility and must suit his requirements,' he hesitated then continued, 'and he has further demands.'

'Demands?' Tauber's anger was growing. 'Well, I'll say one thing for him,' he threw that morning's reports back onto his desk, 'his timing is impeccable!'

'I hear Tauber is not happy,' said Montueil, 'there was a lot of shouting at his headquarters,' before adding, 'they need civilian workers there for administration.'

'And one of them is sympathetic to our cause?'

Montueil shrugged as if that were of little importance. 'She is my cousin.'

'Here's to family,' said Cooper.

Montueil smiled then. 'It is all anybody is talking about

in the town, the night when quiet resistance became open defiance. There is not a man, woman or child who did not silently cheer inside when they learned of our exploits. What do you have planned for us now Harry?'

'All in good time, my friend; let the Gestapo and the Wehrmacht chase some shadows for a day or two. Then we will make our next move.'

'Very well but my men enjoy this work and they believe in themselves once more, so please, I beg you, do not keep them idle for long.'

'Don't worry, they'll get plenty of chances to prove themselves.'

'One other thing,' Montueil said it as if he had almost forgotten, 'I have a man at the best hotel in Rouen. He sends me a message. The Germans have thrown everybody out, even some of their own senior men kicked from their rooms to make way for an important guest, a scientist and his team, who will be working on the air base.' Cooper and Walsh exchanged a look. 'It seems like this professor you asked us about has finally arrived.'

'Thank your contact. Tell him any information on the professor will be most welcome,' said Walsh, 'it's lucky you had a man there Montueil.'

'Harry, please, a hotel in Rouen permanently filled with senior German officers and you are surprised I have a contact there? More than one my friend, more than one, how could you ever doubt me?'

'My apologies,' said Walsh, 'please ask them to keep a close eye on the scientist for me. What he does, where he goes, when and with whom?'

'Sure, Harry, whatever you say.'

Days passed without incident or, frustratingly for Walsh, any news on the professor or his daily routine at the hotel. Walsh could do little while he waited but arrange further training sessions for the men of the Maquis to improve their hand-to-hand combat skills and improve their familiarity with the various explosive devices he had brought with him. 'Pay attention,' he would urge them, 'and you might not lose an arm.'

As time slowly passed, Walsh was beginning to doubt whether Montueil's much vaunted contacts at the professor's hotel would ever amount to anything. Then the Maquis leader finally approached him with news.

'It's my man at the hotel in Rouen, I'll call him Romain, it's better you don't know his real name. He has information on the scientist, this Professor Gaerte.'

'Good,' Walsh was reassured Montueil was taking security so seriously, 'what did he tell you?'

'All I know is he has news but it is very dangerous for him. He won't write anything down and cannot risk coming here but he is prepared to meet you, Harry, in a room at another hotel, the Europa on the Rue L'Eglise. He will make himself known to you there.'

Sam Cooper overheard this, 'That's risky, don't you think?'

'Everything we do is risky,' commented Walsh, then he turned back to Montueil. 'Tell your man I'll meet him.'

Montueil arranged for Walsh to join one of Simone's labourers, as he took produce into Rouen in the farm's little green van. That morning they drove into the capital of Normandy, a city that had once been the centre of an Anglo-Norman empire but was now ruled over by Nazis and their collaborating French officials. Simone's worker took a back route to avoid a known roadblock then drove deep into the city, past the ancient cathedral and along the banks of the Seine. He dropped Walsh at the humble hotel chosen for the rendezvous.

Walsh checked in and there was a moment's unease when

he presented Clavelle's papers but they passed the scrutiny of the disinterested middle-aged woman on the front desk. He asked for a particular room, which Romain had given him via Montueil, explaining he had stayed there before and liked the view of the square from its window. The woman was happy enough to accommodate him and it meant Romain could come directly to his room, attracting less suspicion.

Walsh was shown to a spartan room at the rear. Its solitary window allowed a little daylight to illuminate the faded wallpaper. The room was clean but quite bare save for a good-sized bed, a small wardrobe and tiny chest of drawers. The only decoration came from a bland landscape painting, depicting a ploughman in his field, and a notice pinned to the door outlining the hotel's regulations, chief among them the absence of guests after a certain hour and the need to keep the water level in the bath to a minimum.

Walsh had expected a shared bathroom some way along a corridor, so he was pleasantly surprised to find a small door that led to a tiny bathroom for his sole use. Six weeks ago he might have considered the room basic but, after cold damp nights in the camp, it now seemed impossibly luxurious. Walsh still had hours before his meeting with Montueil's man. He drew a warm bath to scrub away the grime of the camp then fell on to the soft mattress and was asleep almost immediately.

Montueil approached them while they ate. He was grim-faced. 'There is a problem.' As always he addressed Cooper and Valvert directly but Emma, because of her sex, was ignored. She was well used to such treatment by now on both sides of the Channel but it still galled her. Why ever did men assume they always knew best when there was a mountain of evidence to the contrary?

'Harry is waiting for my man at the hotel but I have received a message. The plan has changed. He wishes to meet Harry away from the hotel, at a café, somewhere more public where he can see everyone and not today. It may sound foolish to you but he is worried about security and has good cause. We have lost many people since the struggle began so I cannot ask him to stick to the plan. He will simply not comply.'

'Then give me the name of the café and the time and I will get a message to Harry,' said Emma. They all looked at her. 'Well, it will be less suspicious if I go to his hotel than if it were one of you, wouldn't it?' She had them there. If Emma were seen entering Harry's room, most onlookers would assume it was an everyday instance of adultery, the married man and his mistress in the discreet hotel room, and Emma had played that role before. Even these days, it wasn't necessary to report an extra marital affair to the Gestapo. Emma could see the look on their eyes as the men all arrived at the same conclusion at roughly the same time. If a man were seen to enter the hotel room of another it would be little consolation to them both if passers-by assumed the assignation was sexual.

'Okay, good idea,' conceded Montueil hastily.

The time for the appointment had long since passed so Walsh finally ventured out. He would stay one more night at the hotel in case his contact was unavoidably detained but after that he would return to the camp. It was too risky to stay any longer. Hopefully Montueil's man would follow the agreed fall-back plan and visit his room at the same time twenty-four hours later.

For now, Walsh was determined to salvage something from the considerable risk he was taking by his presence in the city. A look at the professor's hotel would be a start. He hurried past it in the manner of a worker who is late home for a dinner being prepared by an unsympathetic spouse. Without gazing directly upon the building, Walsh took in the elaborate carved entranceway of the Hotel Meurice with its permanent armed sentry, and he spotted the second man who stood back in the shadows of the main door. Above the entrance were three more floors. Each room had its own shuttered window and balcony. Behind one of these windows was the man he had come to kill, presumably resting after a long day working on one of the Führer's miracle weapons.

It felt alien to be out on the streets of Rouen so brazenly after his time in the Maquis camp. Walsh had his papers of course and his cover story was well rehearsed. He was a vendor of wines, excluded from compulsory work service because of asthma, taking what was left once the Germans had plundered the best of course, then selling it on to the hotels that welcomed the occupiers. He knew his cover well for it had been his father's occupation before the war.

Walsh senior had crossed the Channel often, had met Harry's mother on the French side of the water and brought her back to England with him. Walsh could only imagine his father's happiness, as distant now as it was short-lived – the beautiful French wife, the young son, then the cancer that took that wife from him, leaving him with a permanent, sad reminder of her in Harry's boyish face.

The rest was all too predictable. 'Remember Harry,' his father would tell him as he raised his glass, 'wine is a good servant but a poor master.' Edward Walsh would fail to heed his own advice. Somehow he would just about manage to hold things together during daylight hours but there was never an evening when he did not test a sizeable quantity of the product he bought and sold. When he inevitably joined his wife, ten years almost to the day after the disease that took her, it was clear the main cause of his death was alcohol. What Edward Walsh really died of might romantically be described as a broken heart, exacerbated by an overburdened liver.

Walsh had borne witness to and understood his father's

loneliness and despair. It was one of the reasons for adopting his old life as a cover story, for it was the only thing that now remained of the man.

Walsh returned to the hotel, hoping his contact hadn't tried to visit him during his short absence. He walked along the corridor till he reached his room then turned and glanced back the way he had come but there was no sign of anyone. Walsh placed his hand on the doorknob but did not open the door. Instead, he pressed his ear against the wood. Was there a sound, a movement from within, or was it just the swish of curtain against an opened window?

Walsh took the Luger from his belt and placed it down at his side where it could be quickly hidden once more. He didn't want to point a gun at a member of the hotel cleaning staff. Walsh turned the doorknob gently then pushed the door hard. It swung noiselessly open. There was no one in the room and he almost relaxed but immediately sensed a presence in the bathroom. Someone was in there, he knew it. Walsh gently closed the outer door and approached the bathroom cautiously. Its door was closed but the latch not fully engaged. It could be a chambermaid silently going about her business but he would take no chances. Walsh raised his boot and gave the door a firm kick. As it flung open he went straight into the room, raised his gun then stopped in his tracks. Emma Stirling started and just managed to stifle the scream before it could alert others, her hand darting to her mouth. Emma was lying in a shallow bath, the regulation couple of inches of water permitted by the hotel management failing to mask much of her nakedness.

'Christ, Harry,' she managed in an alarmed whisper that would have been a loud exclamation if they had been anywhere but occupied territory. Her arms moved instinctively to cover her breasts and she squeezed her legs tightly together. 'You scared the life out of me.'

'What are you doing here?' he asked idiotically, knowing he should tear his gaze away from her but finding he was unable to.

Emma suddenly felt priggish disguising her nakedness from a man who had once been her lover and she lowered her arms, hiding nothing from him now. 'I brought you a message from Montueil,' she said defiantly. Paradoxically in her naked state, Emma felt more in control than the obviously distracted man before her. 'When I saw the bath I couldn't resist it.' Walsh was clearly discomfited by her nudity and he was hardly acting like a gentleman, standing there, staring at her and making no move to leave. 'Didn't think you'd mind.'

'I don't.'

'It's all right, Harry, you've seen it all before,' Emma was starting to enjoy herself now, there was something deliciously naughty about this and it was reassuring that she could still distract him.

'Not recently,' Walsh said quietly before he could think of a better response. Then he seemed to wake from his trance, 'I'll leave you to your bath.'

'It's all right,' she said, 'I'm done,' and she rose, water running from her hips and trickling down over her bare legs. Emma held the bath for support and lifted her leg over the side as she climbed from the tub. Standing on the bath mat, Emma looked about her with exaggerated nonchalance. She reached for the smallest towel in the bathroom and raised her arms to unhurriedly dry her hair, leaving her body entirely on show. Walsh stood dumbly by, not knowing what to say or do.

'You can have my water, if you like,' she said, as she walked towards him.

Walsh moved out of her way and caught the sweet smell of Emma Stirling as she brushed past him. He instinctively turned to watch as her naked rear swayed towards the bedroom. When he turned back he caught his reflection in the mirror as he wrestled with what remained of his conscience. He had tried to bury his feelings for Emma Stirling, lord knows he had tried, but there was surely only so much a man could take.

'Bugger it,' he told his reflection softly, 'you'll probably be dead in a week.'

And with that he turned and went to her.

As was often the way of these things, it was the work of an informant that led them to the hotel that morning. Combret, the leader of the local Milice, had seen it a hundred times before. A sweating, frightened individual who claimed he was acting to save a loved one. The informant denied money was a factor but took it just the same. They always did. The man had been scared right enough, more so than normal and Combret had used his fear against him. When a man knows his treachery will cost him his life if it is discovered, he is easy to own. Though the informant did not realise it, Combret could go back to this creature time and again. Work for me or be turned in to your own group for bloody retribution. Whatever the informant's motivation that day, the intelligence he provided was priceless. Apparently an Englishman was staying at the Hotel Europa.

32

'Conscience is our unerring judge, until we finally stifle it.'

Honoré de Balzac

Morning sunlight streamed through a gap in the curtains onto Emma's face.

She stirred in his arms, stretched like a cat and looked up at Walsh, who smiled down at her.

'I was beginning to wonder what I had to do to get your attention these days, Harry.'

'That did it all right.'

'Glad you finally noticed me.'

'I never stopped noticing you.'

They lay in silence for a while until Emma said, 'Know when I first noticed you?' Walsh correctly assumed she did not expect an answer, 'When you spoke to us at Arisaig – on how to handle life in the field. The regular instructor gave you quite a build-up before you arrived; you didn't hear that bit did you?'

'No.'

'A "remarkable man" he called you, somebody we should listen to very carefully, a brave man who has been in and out of France for years. He said you went into occupied territory so early there wasn't a training program to follow and you practically invented what he called "field craft". By the time you walked into the room we were all completely in awe. None of us knew if we could survive one mission and here was a veteran of so many. You made quite an impression.'

'I had no idea why Price sent me there or what I was going to talk to you about until I began.'

'He probably just wanted to be rid of you for a few weeks.'

'I imagine so.'

'But you did talk to us, Harry, without notes as I recall, and everything you said made such sense. You scared me to death because I wouldn't have thought of any of it. We'd spent weeks being taught by men who had probably never left England. Oh, some of it was good but a lot of it was tosh I'd forgotten before I'd even left the lecture room. But not from you, we were hanging on your every word. Everything from how to jump out of a Halifax without breaking your nose on the lip of the hatch to how to put a whole factory out of action.'

Walsh smiled. 'So you were paying attention.'

'Oh, I was. I noticed you all right, Harry Walsh, and you noticed me, eventually.'

Walsh could be more frank now. 'I noticed you right from the beginning.'

'No you didn't but it's nice of you to pretend you did. The first time you noticed me was when they gave us all the night off to go into town and I walked into that dingy little pub on my own. Lucy had a cold remember, and I was about to turn round and go right out again, when you came waltzing through the front door.'

'Timing is everything.'

'And do you remember the first thing you said to me?'

'No.'

'Liar, it was so good you must have used it before, probably often, but I didn't care. You said, "Darling, I've been looking for you everywhere, please come home. The children miss you." I think it was the first time I'd laughed since I arrived at that bloody awful place. The looks the men gave us as you escorted me out of there!'

'They thought you were a bad mother but I knew the real truth, you just had poor taste in pubs. I felt duty bound to take you somewhere better.'

'Well, it can't have been that bad, you went there.'

'What if I said I only walked in because I saw you go inside? What if I told you I'd trailed you from the railway station? How would that make you feel about me?'

'I don't believe you.'

'It is part of an instructor's job to follow potential agents into town and see how they act when they have had a few drinks. Will they behave indiscreetly, compromise themselves; tell the landlord they are agents about to be parachuted into occupied France? You'd be surprised how some people are once they've had a sniff of the barmaid's apron.'

'Oh I see, so you tailed me there, did you? But why march up to me straight away before I ordered a drink?'

'Because I told you, I noticed you right from the beginning, Emma. You were sitting in the second row of the lecture hall, listening a little more intently than the others and you caught my eye.'

'Second row?' she frowned, 'I may have been. Go on, I'm half convinced.'

'I noticed your brown eyes and your long, dark hair was tied back,' and he smiled, 'oh yes and you wore green as I recall.'

She laughed. 'It was khaki and we all wore it. Plus the eyes and the hair don't count when you are here with me now. That hardly constitutes a memory.'

'True but the eyes do count and they are why I tailed you to the pub and broke every regulation in the book that night, and a few more later.'

'My God, maybe you are telling the truth. I'm amazed and very flattered. And there was me thinking I was just another conquest for you to boast about in the officer's mess, Captain Walsh. Don't frown like that, Harry, I'm joking. I did wonder if my complete lack of resistance might have given you second thoughts about me though.'

'You resisted, for a while.'

'Two evenings in the pub as I remember; my mother would have been mortified, but I didn't care. I'd already convinced myself there was no way I would survive France so I was damned if I was going over there as pure as the driven snow. War changes things, Harry, we both thought that as I recall.'

'Yes, we did.' Walsh became serious then, 'Emma, I'm sorry I couldn't see you again after Arisaig.'

'You did see me once – to let me down gently? I thought it was quite noble of you really under the circumstances. It was all a bit too close to home for you in London, wasn't it?'

'Yes.'

'I was under no illusions, Harry, well maybe a few but they were entirely of my own making. You were honest from the start. "I'm married" you said "and always will be." You didn't exactly lead me on, I could never say that.'

'No.'

'But people do divorce you know, this is 1943 after all and the whole world is turned upside down. A man can leave his wife and it barely warrants a raised eye brow these days, perhaps only a paragraph in the paper.'

'But not me.'

'Why is that, Harry? Why can you never bring yourself to even think about leaving her when you are clearly unhappy? You have strong feelings for me, I know you do but when you stopped seeing me it was like you were slamming a door in my face.'

'I'm sorry.'

'Don't be, it's all right. I'd just like to know.'

'Because I made a promise,' Walsh felt unable to add anything to the inadequate words. Emma seemed unwilling to risk the newfound accord between them and she too fell silent. 'I have to go and meet Montueil's contact or I'll be late,' he climbed from the bed and began to dress, 'but I will be back, Emma.'

'Then I'll be here waiting, Harry.'

Even if he had not had a description of the clothes Romain was wearing, Walsh could have picked him out in the café. He sat alone, nervously drumming his fingers against a knee and nodding his head almost imperceptibly, as if there was music in the room that only he could hear.

'Romain, it has been such a long time,' said Walsh.

'Yes, indeed,' spluttered Romain as he shook hands. It was as if he had forgotten the script he himself had insisted upon to begin their encounter, the fake introduction designed to ensure no impostor could ever take Walsh's place. 'I have been working too hard to see my dear old friends, please forgive me.'

They ordered coffee from a disinterested girl. The café was virtually empty and Romain had chosen his seat well for the empty tables around them afforded privacy. The coffee arrived and the girl retreated, which was the signal for Romain to come straight to the point.

'Montueil trusts you, so I will trust you. He tells me you need to hear about the professor who stays in our hotel?'

'That's right,'

'I can't stay long, it's too dangerous to be seen with you. You have until I finish this cup of coffee for your questions then I leave, so speak fast.'

'It's very easy, tell me everything he does; what time he wakes up and when he goes to bed, does he eat breakfast, what time does he leave the hotel and when does he return?'

Romain nodded. 'What is his room number and where is it? Describe the room.'

'Sure.'

'Where does he take his meals, does he leave the hotel or stay in at night, how many guards does he have and where are they?'

'Okay.'

'Who does he spend his time with; soldiers, friends, other scientists? Does he have visitors?'

Romain snorted, letting out a little laugh, then he looked down at his coffee and stirred it self-consciously.

'What?'

'Visitors, yes, there have already been visitors.' For some reason Romain seemed to find this amusing.

Combret was pleased with himself. There had been no Englishman at the Hotel Europa that morning as they burst through the door but there was a pretty young girl. They took her away for questioning and found the girl spoke perfect French. It was flawless in fact with no trace of an accent, so good it just had to be her second language. There was no slang or patois, no mispronounced vowel sound or out-of-place small talk, no fashionable phrase picked up from a governess or maid that showed itself, as it would, under the stress of protracted interrogation. Evie Soyen was too good to be true. In other words she was a fake.

What Englishman? There was no Englishman. Evie had booked the room in a man's name because her father had told her men would be less likely to bother her. What rubbish, though he could understand why men would want to bother her. He himself would not be averse to bothering Evie Soyen, whoever she was, but he knew the Gestapo insisted on receiving its captives intact and undamaged, they preferred to do the harming themselves. Let the Germans damage the girl then. What did it matter? Combret had just done a very good day's work.

As for the girl, from the moment she had slept in the Englishman's bed she was doomed.

33

'This love will undo us all.'
William Shakespeare, *Troilus & Cressida*

Walsh returned to the Europa in time to see Emma led from the building. He was standing on the opposite pavement when she was bundled into the car by two men in plain clothes. One of them was barking orders at the other and Walsh could tell they were French not German, so it was the Milice not the Gestapo which offered some hope. At least he was in a position to try and help Emma if he could just work out how. If he had returned from his appointment with Romain two minutes earlier, he would have been in that car too and unable to do anything.

Walsh was meant to return to the camp that day, picked up by the same labourer in the little green van. When he made his rendezvous with the driver he was relieved to see that Montueil was with him. 'I wanted to make sure everything was all right,' he told Harry.

'It's not all right,' Walsh told him, 'Emma has been taken. The Milice arrested her at the hotel.'

'But how could they know she was there?' asked Montueil.

'I don't know,' Walsh admitted, though he had a pretty good idea.

'It must be Combret, a real shit,' then he conceded, 'the

Milice is bad but the Gestapo would have been worse.'

'What will the Milice do?' asked Walsh.

'Take her to one of their houses, interrogate her and, when they are done, give her to the Germans.'

It was the merest glimmer of hope. 'Then I have to get to Emma before they hand her over.'

'Harry, it may be too late, they might already have given her up.'

Walsh knew that was entirely possible but he couldn't give up on Emma, not yet. 'They would want to hand her over with a story, a confession, wouldn't they? Who she is, where she's from, who she is working with?' Walsh knew he sounded as if he was trying to convince himself but there was a logic to this. 'A suspicious woman is one thing but for the Milice to really please their masters they'd want to hand over a self-confessed enemy agent, signed, sealed and delivered. And that might give us a little time.'

'I hope you are right, Harry.' Montueil did not add anything. He didn't have to. Once Emma was in the hands of the Germans there would be no saving her.

'Tell me about this Combret,' urged Walsh.

'What do you want to know?'

'Everything.'

Combret walked into the dark drawing room of his cold and draughty home. He sighed. It had been a long day and the housekeeper had allowed the fire to die out again. He turned on the light and started. Walsh was sitting in his favourite armchair, pointing the Luger straight at him. Despite the fear in his heart he understood immediately.

'You have come to kill me?'

Walsh shook his head. 'I've come to show you how easy it would be to kill you,' said Walsh, 'the rest is up to you.'

'I have a choice?' Combret was attempting to hide his

nervousness, 'May I?' and he slowly turned his palm to pat a pocket.

'Make sure you light it very slowly.'

With exaggerated caution, Combret took the pack from his pocket. He removed a cigarette and lit it with a shaking hand. Walsh noticed the lighter was gold. Montueil had said Combret worshipped only money. The Milice man took a long drag on the cigarette, his eyes never leaving Walsh's.

'The peasants round here have been threatening my life for years.'

'But I'm a professional. If I tell you I'm going to kill you, it will happen.'

Combret nodded slowly, 'Oh, I believe you, Englishman. You are English I assume and so is the girl? You did say there was a choice? Perhaps a more satisfactory outcome for both of us?'

'Release her.'

'That I cannot do.'

'Then you die tonight.'

'I see.'

Walsh immediately changed tack, 'They can't win this war, the Germans. You must know that. Since Stalingrad, with America on our side, you understand there's no way.' Walsh took Combret's silence as grudging acceptance. 'Between us we will defeat them. It's just a question of time.'

'Perhaps, in five, ten years. Who knows? Maybe instead they will beat you and the Americans after all.'

'Five, ten years, possibly a lot sooner than that. Then where will you be, Combret? A hunted man, a criminal, a fugitive hiding from his own countrymen. I wonder what they will do to all of the traitors when it's over. Hang you in the town square I should expect, in front of everybody. They'll bring the children to watch, make a day of it.'

Combret snorted, 'That day is a long way off, English.'

'It could be a lot closer than you think, unless you are clever, unless you have something to fall back on, more than just Deutschmarks or Francs. They'll be worthless, won't even get you out of the country.'

Combret was listening now. 'What are you thinking of?'

'The goodwill of the allies you helped along the way, testimony from commissioned officers in Her Majesty's armed forces that you occasionally worked for us, turned a blind eye when it was needed, saved a life from time to time.'

'Oh sure, you'd do that for me. You'd save me from the mob despite my so-called crimes. As soon as I sent for you, you'd forget I existed. You'd say bad luck and he got what was coming to him, he deserved the noose. You would not stand up for me in the courtroom when so many others stood against me.'

'I would. For her life I would, for the girl. Just bring me the girl. I'd give you my word here and now and I take my word seriously.'

Walsh knew he'd overplayed it but he couldn't help himself. What would Price have said? 'I rather think you've over-egged the pudding there,' and for once he'd have been right.

Combret smiled his understanding, 'So it's love. And I thought you were just screwing her till your war is over and you run back home to your wife. Oh, you don't need a wedding ring; you have the married look about you.' Combret seemed more relaxed suddenly, as if he understood the strength of his hand. 'She doesn't though. Wonder if she thinks you'll leave. Do you think Evie, or whatever her name is, dreams of becoming the next Mrs English?'

'Be quiet.'

'I'm just wondering what she is thinking, that's all. Maybe she doesn't know what you and I know, that we men never leave. We have our fun and go home. Isn't that how it always works? She'll get tired of longing for you eventually, waiting for her own home and children. When she starts to get older you'll, how can I put this, reluctantly set her free? She'll probably love you even more for that, if you handle it right, even though you'll be very glad to see the back of her by then.'

'Shut up.'

'Except that is not how it will happen because she has an appointment with the Gestapo in the morning and she is going to keep it.'

Walsh crossed the floor with frightening speed, grabbed the older man's shoulder, forced him to stand rigidly upright and landed a crashing blow into Combret's stomach with the fist that still held the Luger. The Milice man let out a huge gasp and would have dropped to the floor if Walsh had not held him there. Walsh steered Combret into an armchair and dropped him unceremoniously into it. It was more than two minutes before Walsh deemed him sufficiently recovered to continue.

'I knew appealing to your better nature would be a mistake, you don't have one, but your sense of self-preservation alone should convert you to my way of thinking. If it doesn't then perhaps this will.'

Combret winced, expecting another blow. He was still in severe pain. He'd been assaulted by someone who knew exactly what they were doing. Never had he been struck with such force and there was anger behind the blow, as well as professional expertise. He lamely held up a hand to parry the next punch. Instead he felt the light sensation of a small velvet bag as it was dropped into his lap. Puzzled, Combret drew back the string, opened it and spread the contents into his outstretched palm. His mouth widened at the sight, for he was now holding four perfect diamonds.

'They are yours when you bring me the girl,' explained Walsh while Combret gaped at this treasure.

Combret sat up now. He was almost recovered. He'd been

transfixed by the huge diamonds and asked Walsh, 'Where did you get them?'

'Traded them and I'll trade them again to you once I have the girl.' He made Combret put the gems in the velvet bag and hand them back.

'Bring her to the stone quarry outside town in two hours. Come alone.'

'It's not possible,'

'Oh you'd be surprised what's possible when your life depends on it.'

'But the Gestapo are expecting her in the morning.'

'What are they expecting? A young female suspect, so that is what you will give them.'

'Who?'

'I don't care. Someone else.'

'You want me to hand over an innocent girl to take her place? Is that what you are saying?'

'Don't try to pretend you are outraged, Combret. You'll do what you have to do to cover yourself with the Germans. Whether you pick an innocent girl or a genuine suspect is entirely your concern. Just bring me the girl.'

'Ruthless bastard aren't you, English?' Combret sounded impressed.

'The stone quarry, with the girl but otherwise alone. If you bring anybody with you, anyone at all, they will be killed and so will you. That's another promise by the way so there can be no misunderstanding later. Mercy is a quality in short supply these days and I won't be wasting any of it on you. You understand?'

'Of course. And the diamonds?'

'When you hand over the girl, I hand over the diamonds.'

'Then you kill me, yes?' he sneered.

'No, like I said, I take an oath seriously.'

'I hope you do, English.'

'Normally, killing you would be easy. I wouldn't go so far as to say I'd enjoy it but it wouldn't trouble me. But tonight all I want is the girl. Bring her, unharmed. The diamonds are yours and you get to live. Maybe next time we meet it will be different.'

Maybe it will, thought Combret, maybe it will. 'I agree.'

'Good, now get up and turn around. I need to search you.'

Combret stood and Walsh turned him round till he faced the fireplace. 'Put your hands on the mantel, palms down.' Combret complied and Walsh kicked his legs wider till he was in a star shape, his head down, feet level with his hands, palms pressed on to the mantelpiece either side of the antique clock as it began to strike the quarter hour.

'Now don't move.' Combret could hear Walsh's voice but not see him now. Tell me, Combret, because I'm curious. What is it that turns a man like you into a traitor? Is it greed, simply the money or are you going to say there is a more noble reason for selling your soul to the Germans?'

'I'll tell you, English, but I doubt you will understand. Your country has not been invaded like ours and no, I don't mean the Germans. We were invaded years ago, France died long before 1940. The nation I knew as a boy had already disappeared. My country was being fought over by radicals and communists while the Jews bankrolled them both. The only shame I feel is the embarrassment that we could not put our own house in order. Imagine having to get the Germans to rid our country of the communists, the queers and the Jews. They do our dirty work for us. Perhaps you are a Jew lover or a friend of Joseph Stalin and you think everybody should just travel along together regardless of their race. Is that it? Do you still think you would like your country so much if it was not an island? Who would you side with if England were the dumping ground for every socialist and so-called freethinker in Europe?'

Walsh did not respond.

'What would you do then, eh, English? Tell me that.'

Still no reply. Combret waited a moment for he did not want to be hit again. He kept his hands and feet where they were but slowly, cautiously, turned his head, only to find he had been addressing an empty room, for the Englishman was gone.

34

'A man who has been in danger, when he comes out of it forgets his fears, and sometimes he forgets his promises.'

Euripides

'Where is the girl now?' Combret was grim-faced and serious. There was something else there – anger? But not directed at his right-hand man. Whatever had transpired between Combret and the mysterious Englishman it had left his leader eager for blood and he had gone straight to the Milice HQ, a building which they had taken over almost gleefully since it had once been the headquarters of the local communist party.

'Locked in the cellar,' answered Bruno.

'Good,' Combret had learned to keep prisoners from the Gestapo until he was ready to hand them over. It made matters less complicated if he decided it was better for someone to simply disappear. Only Bruno and Combret had taken Emma from the hotel, which simplified matters. This girl was a precious commodity and now he would make the most of her.

Bruno Genoud had not been given all of the details, nor did he need them. Bruno was not a thinker but he had enough faith in Combret to comply with his wishes. It had always been this way, ever since Combret first took the illiterate, heavy-set country boy under his wing. Bruno was a peasant, with an agrarian view of the world, which made him instinctively agree with Combret's right-wing politics. Who were the communists but land grabbers and murderers? Who were the Jews but communists by another name? Bruno wasn't particularly fond of the Germans but they were here now. It was an unavoidable fact. There was no disputing their control over France. Better to work with them then and stop the communist hordes swarming in from the east. Besides, under what other regime would there be an elevated position for such a simple man as Bruno. Combret made use of his muscle, his loyalty and simple view of the world to good effect. Bruno repaid him by hurting the people he was instructed to hurt; nearly all of them Jews or communists, or sympathisers of Jews and communists, which amounted to the same thing, and by not asking too many questions. Not asking any questions at all in point of fact.

'Bring your rifle,' ordered Combret and he explained what he had in mind, before adding, 'normally I'd ask the Germans to send their soldiers but the Englishman would see them coming. He won't see you though, Bruno, you're too good for that. Be invisible,' he urged the younger man, 'just make sure you don't miss, that's all.'

Bruno was deeply offended by the notion. He was a hunter, always had been, ever since his father had first taken him into the woods as a little boy and taught him how to aim a rifle. If the target was in range Bruno could not miss.

'And where will you be?' Bruno asked Combret.

'Baiting the trap.'

Emma was blind and scared, her remaining senses heightened by the loss of her sight. Muted sounds took on a far greater significance as she strained to make sense of them. The blindfold caused her to blunder into objects her captors did not bother to warn her about as they dragged her along. Where were they taking her?

They had removed Emma from the locked cellar, binding her hands tightly out in front of her before applying the blindfold. Now they rested meekly on her lap as the car sped along. The blindfold was too tight and the rope chafed at her wrists but she was otherwise unharmed, though she felt sure this condition was unlikely to last. As soon as the car began to move she was gripped by a terrible fear this would be the final day of her short life, for she could see no other reason for their journey.

Emma had been readying herself for an appointment with the Gestapo that had been promised for the following morning. At least there might be a slim chance she could talk her way out of trouble. Emma had gone through her cover story over and over in her head. She would use the aggressive tone of the wronged innocent. They had made a ridiculous mistake and must release her immediately. This had given Emma a grain of hope. But the Milice had changed their mind about handing her over and she knew they had a reputation for making people simply disappear. Emma was beginning to reach a tearful despair. She was almost glad of the blindfold so they could not witness her distress.

She knew she was heading out of town from the upward tilt of the vehicle, which set her back more firmly into the rear seat. She was now more sure than ever that she would be killed and her body buried in the woods where it would never be found. Emma had tried not to think about death but the stark reality of it was staring her in the face. The Milice had done this kind of thing before to their own countrymen so why not her? One young girl, who cannot easily be proven to be a spy or a saboteur, might become an inconvenience. How undeniably expedient for the Milice to simply rid themselves of this nuisance with a bullet in the back of the head?

It occurred to Emma to tell them everything then; who she was, how she had been sent by London to assist the maquisards, their names, descriptions and location. Anything to avoid this lonely, pitiful fate hundreds of miles from her home and family, with no one ever knowing what became of her. Emma forced herself to fight the increasing sense of hopelessness and despair. She told herself she was not dead yet, that she owed it to the others, including Harry, especially Harry, to stay silent for as long as possible, right to the end if need be. She forced herself to stay alert, concentrate on the journey and take her chance if it came.

Both men were in the car with her. She knew that for she could smell the man next to her. It was the same stale, unwashed and sweaty odour she had come to associate with Bruno, her chief tormentor who possessed a bulk large enough to make the seat they shared sag slightly, as its springs buckled underneath him. Bruno it was who underlined Combret's threats of violence by his muscular presence, his idea of amusement to make repeated mention of Emma's handover to the Gestapo then draw his chubby finger slowly across his throat, while making a clicking sound to indicate her doom. Emma guessed Combret was driving and that it would be Bruno who would do the dirty work when it came to it.

The car was climbing again, the road steeper now. She could feel her head being forced gently backwards as it began a long ascent and there were tight bends. Then finally the car began to slow. The driver was trying to ease the brakes as gently as possible until it came to a total halt. The rear passenger door was opened and closed and Emma felt the chill of the night air and this, coupled with a gradual easing on the rear seat springs, meant Bruno must have left the vehicle. The car idled for a while, its engine ticking over but Emma could tell it wasn't moving. What was Combret waiting for? Minutes passed though Emma could not be sure how many, until the car finally moved away then continued its slow and steady journey up the hill. What in hell was going on?

Walsh was waiting for Combret as the Milice man drove into the disused quarry. He kept out of sight to begin with but left a lantern burning in the centre of the clearing and Combret moved towards it, halted the car, got out and went to the rear of the vehicle. Wasting no time, he dragged Emma roughly from the car, ensuring he was behind and to one side of her. He pressed a revolver into her torso as his eyes darted from left to right.

'Where are you, English?' he called into the darkness, the strain showing in his voice. 'Show yourself.'

For a moment Walsh made no move. Instead he took his time, taking in the scene. Emma was standing so stiffly she could have been posing for the school photograph at Roedean. She seemed unharmed, though of course he couldn't tell what she had been through just by looking at her. Walsh told himself he would kill Combret if he'd touched her, regardless of the deal they had struck.

The skittish Combret was not so calm now. Walsh calculated the distance between them and his hiding place in the undergrowth, keeping a wary eye out for anyone the Milice man might have brought with him. Though he did not trust Combret, Walsh had gambled the man's love for money and fear of retribution would outweigh his keenness to impress the Gestapo. Only when he was sure Combret was entirely alone, did Walsh walk into the clearing, the Luger held out in front of him.

'Drop the gun, Combret.'

'Harry?' Emma called before she could stop herself. Walsh winced. In her surprise and relief she had used his real name once more.

'Harry is it?' asked Combret.

'I said drop the gun.'

'Why would I do that? I did what you asked. I brought the girl. Now you give me the diamonds and I go.'

'No arguments, Combret,' and he carefully aimed the gun at the Milice leader's face. 'If you want to leave here alive you place the revolver on the floor in front of you and move back.'

Combret would never normally have conceded his advantage so readily but it was not part of his plan to shoot the Englishman. Bruno would do that for him, and so he surrendered his weapon. With a show of reluctance, Combret held his arm out to the side to give Walsh a clear view of the revolver then he bent his knees and slowly lowered himself to place the weapon on the ground. He then dragged Emma backwards with him.

'Now you come out where I can see you clearly,' ordered Combret and Harry walked into the light.

Any moment now, thought Combret, Bruno will cut him down. Thanks to the lantern, he will have a clear shot. The Englishman would stand no more chance than the deer that succumbed to Bruno's rifle the last time they hunted together.

'You have the diamonds?'

'I have the diamonds.'

Then I will take them from your still warm carcass, thought Combret. His vengeful fury at the man who'd invaded the privacy of his home was beginning to reach its zenith.

'So how will we do this,' he was stalling the Englishman, waiting for the beautiful moment when the shot rang out and Walsh fell to the ground. Then the diamonds would be his and in the morning the girl would keep her appointment with the Gestapo.

'It's very simple. You let go of the girl and she walks towards me,' said Walsh, 'when I am happy she is unharmed, I give you the diamonds and you leave, without your pistol naturally.'

'Why not the other way around?' What in hell was keeping Bruno? He'd had ample time to get into position. Why didn't he fire, damn him? 'You give me the diamonds then I give you the girl.'

'Because it's my show, Combret. You do as I tell you.'

'Very well,' Combret assented. He wanted to scream 'Now, do it now, shoot him, Bruno!' at the top of his voice, for he had almost run out of stalling tactics.

'Then you let me go, eh?' and still no shot came.

'Then I let you go.' Walsh was beginning to sound impatient.

Just then there was a rustling from the bushes at the far end of the clearing and a grim-faced Sam Cooper emerged, holding a familiar object, Bruno's hunting rifle. Combret's heart began to thump hard in his chest.

'He had a friend waiting for you,' Sam told Walsh, 'with this,' and he dropped the rifle onto the ground.

'No friend of mine was here.' Combret's voice was high, instantly betraying his guilt and rising sense of panic.

The American turned to him, 'Then you won't mind that I cut his throat.'

Combret turned ghostly pale in the lamplight. Of course, Walsh knew he could never trust the Milice, which is why the maquisards had been watching his car as it approached then Sam had gone hunting in the night. Walsh sighed in the manner one might when a child has been naughty, 'I told you what would happen if you did not come alone,' and he raised the Luger once more.

Combret held up his hands in the manner of a surrender. 'No, wait,' then Emma wriggled free and stepped away from him so she could no longer be used as a shield, 'sure, sure, yes, but,' Combret was rambling, trying to find the right words as he backed away from Walsh, 'it's not...'

Walsh walked towards him, quickly closing the distance

between them. Combret's eyes flew towards the pistol in Walsh's hand and he backed away fearfully.

'No, wait a moment, let's talk...'

'There's nothing left to talk about.'

'I can help you,' pleaded Combret, 'I can give you information... I can...' but he seemed at a loss now to explain just what it was he could do for them and Walsh was still coming. Instead Combret settled on the single word, 'please'.

Walsh ignored the cornered man and adjusted his aim to administer the final shots.

'Wait, don't! Not like this, not out here... please.'

Emma jumped as the loud crack-crack of two bullets broke the silence of the night. Even with the blindfold, Emma knew Harry had just employed the double-tap method used by SOE to send two rounds, one straight after the other, into his target and she realised Combret was gone.

Emma did not see the Milice man's body fall almost backwards, as the bullets took Combret in the centre of his chest. He was dead almost as soon as he hit the ground.

'Harry!' cried Emma, unable to bear the darkness and uncertainty any longer. Harry walked towards her and pulled the blindfold away from her eyes. Then he used his knife to cut Emma free from her bonds and embraced her.

As he did so, a dozen curious maquisards, who had been completely hidden from view, slowly emerged from the bushes to survey the corpse of the stricken Combret, a man considered almost untouchable because of his position, who had been lured out into the night then clinically despatched at the hand of their ruthless new leader; and he had succeeded in rescuing the girl into the bargain, which meant two miracles in one night from Captain Walsh.

One of the maquisards spat on Combret's face as Harry led Emma away but not before she took one last look at the body. The maquisards would dispose of Combret and the foolish

Bruno. Their bodies would be buried deep in the woods, somewhere they could never be found. Emma shuddered at their fate, because she had been convinced of an identical one for herself that night. It had been a grim and hard day. Better them than me, she thought, as Harry led her safely away.

35

*'It is more shameful to distrust one's friends
than to be deceived by them.'*

Duc de La Rochefoucauld

That same night Walsh moved in to Emma Stirling's tent. The Maquis accepted this for it was nobody's business but their own. The next morning, just after first light, Walsh and Montueil walked up the hill together away from the camp so they could not be heard.

'Who could have done such a thing, Montueil?' asked Walsh.

'I have been thinking about nothing else, Harry, over and over in my mind, but I cannot believe any one of us could betray you.'

'And yet someone did or how could the Milice know I was at the Hotel Europa?'

Montueil shook his head slowly. The big man seemed tired all of a sudden and looked every one of his years.

'Who knew about it?' asked Walsh.

'Only the ones who were there when we talked of it.' He counted each name on his fingers, 'Alvar, Triboulet, Lemonnier, Valvert, Cooper, Simone, Emma, you, me.'

'Nine other people knew I'd be at the Europa, apart from your man at the hotel. Let's discount you and me, shall we?'

'I'm glad you feel that way, my friend.'

'Emma is hardly likely to place herself in such danger and has no reason to betray me so...'

'Okay, from the men I know, Alvar's hatred of the Germans has lasted through two wars in two different countries; Triboulet abandoned his family to fight with us and never flinched, I cannot see either of them running to tell the Germans anything except "go to hell".'

'Lemonnier then?'

'Harry, I know he is a hothead, one might even term him a fool and he has reason to resent you for knocking him on his back in front of everyone, plus I think he is jealous that Simone looks up to you...'

'But?'

'But really, I cannot believe it, can you? He may not see you as a friend but help the Germans by giving them your head? I simply cannot accept he would do this thing. He hates them even more than me I think, if it is possible to measure hatred. And you gave him the job to silence the baker, which was a clever move, it kept him close.'

'So none of those three, which leaves Valvert and Cooper?' conceded Walsh.

'Can you trust the American?'

Walsh paused. Would anything be gained by telling Montueil about Yugoslavia? He decided not.

'The truth is I don't fully trust anyone. I can't afford to.'

'And Valvert? What did you know of him before this mission?'

'Nothing but that is quite normal.'

'So, you don't know him at all,' concluded Montueil, 'and he does have a radio, takes it with him up to the high ground to get a better signal but no one ever goes with him, nobody hears what he transmits or to whom.'

Walsh had to concede Montueil had a point. 'True, but

there is another possibility we have overlooked.'

'And what is that?'

'Your man in the hotel. Who did he tell about the Englishman he was going to meet; a trusted friend? Did he boast about it to his lover? Is there a relative who worries he is risking his neck like this? Did he get sloppy? Can he truly be trusted? Perhaps the Germans own him.'

'I'd love to tell you all of that is impossible, Harry, but you know I can't. Maybe one of our trusted group told someone else and that trust was betrayed; perhaps the woman you mentioned on the hotel desk did not like the look of you or maybe she was suspicious of Emma. Who knows, we could talk about this all day and never work out the truth. How many of us really know any one at all, Harry? We are all of us a secret.'

'So what do we do now?' asked Walsh.

'Prevail, my friend,' said Montueil.

An hour later, Walsh watched the convoy from a distance through field glasses. It rumbled swiftly along the road, throwing up clouds of dust on either side. He was flat on his belly next to Cooper as they counted the professor's personal bodyguard.

'Two cars?' asked Cooper of the staff vehicles sandwiched between the troop lorries and flanked by motorcycle outriders.

'One is probably a decoy. Either that or there's Luftwaffe top brass accompanying the professor to the airfield every day.'

'Then we hit both cars,' said Cooper.

'The only way to be sure,' agreed Walsh.

The convoy rumbled past while they both silently contemplated the difficulty of attacking a well-drilled, battle-hardened unit with a ragged bunch of half-trained partisans. Causing a little havoc was one thing, conducting a successful assassination on Gaerte was looking like a much more daunting mission.

'We could use some of those fancy explosives of yours, blow the trees down to block the road behind and ahead of them,' suggested Cooper.

'Maybe,' admitted Walsh and he almost added *and then what* but thought better of it. Would it be the Germans who were trapped by an ambush like that or the Maquis if they were overwhelmed?

Perhaps Cooper was thinking the same thing for he asked, 'Are you sure we couldn't get to him at the hotel?'

'Not according to Montueil's man. Gaerte's security detail is made up of Leibstandarte SS; elite, battle-hardened troops specially ordered there by Colonel Tauber. They have men outside every door and more inside. No one gets in unless they are known staff. There are no other residents in the hotel except the group of scientists, their bodyguards and officers. Guards are on duty in the hotel reception, in the kitchens and on every landing. There is a guard outside Gaerte's room twenty-four hours a day, even when the professor is at the air base, so there's no opportunity to get into his room and plant explosives, hide in there and wait for him, or conceal weapons to use later. We can rule out all of that. The cooking of his meals is supervised and the chef tastes everything before it reaches his plate. The food is then delivered to him by one of his own men, so poisons cannot reach him. He never ventures from the hotel at night, nor does he leave the air base during the day. The only way to get to him is to attack the convoy on its way to or from the air base.'

Cooper digested the information then sighed at the seeming hopelessness of their situation, 'You know, when I first signed up, I believed God, luck and training would get me through this war.'

'And now?' asked Walsh without looking up from the field glasses.

'Just luck.'

'Blasphemer,' chided Walsh, 'never underestimate the value of training.'

Cooper laughed, 'So what do you believe in, Harry?'

'Men, mortars and machine guns,' replied Walsh without hesitation.

'Well, we have some men,' acknowledged Cooper doubtfully, 'and a couple of machine guns.'

'Here's to luck then,' and he handed Cooper the plain silver hip flask, 'go on, I think we've earned the right.'

Cooper took a drink and winced, 'God, what is that?'

'Calvados, to keep out the cold.'

'I think I'd rather be cold,' and he handed the flask back to Walsh who had a swig himself then took one last look at the convoy before it disappeared from view in the distance. He turned back to Cooper.

'Assuming the lorries are full, what are we looking at? Platoon strength?'

'I'd say so,' said Cooper, 'with motorcycle outriders and maybe a couple of personal bodyguards in the two cars.'

'We might still outnumber them,' said Walsh, 'slightly.'

'I'll grant you that but these guys are the elite. If they are veterans pulled from the front line for this detail their trigger fingers'll be damn itchy. How many of our guys is each one of those veteran soldiers worth in a firefight?'

'You're right,' conceded Walsh, 'the odds are not good.'

Cooper nodded in agreement. 'You about ready to tell them what they are getting themselves in to?' he asked quietly.

'I think so.'

Walsh finally delivered the news of their mission to the Maquisard commune in an unflinching manner and without any form of false optimism concerning the likelihood of its success. He wanted each man understand the situation. It was received less positively than even he could have anticipated. There was stony silence at first but then an opinion was finally offered up and it was a forcible one.

'My God, we'll all be slaughtered!' Coming as it did from Montueil, the leader and optimist of the group, Walsh realised this was probably as good as it was going to get. His brief, factual account of the need for the attack on Gaerte's convoy had not been persuasive enough.

'Not necessarily...' countered Walsh but he wasn't permitted to continue.

'It's a crazy idea,' interrupted Alvar. 'I know, I've seen it,' he said before adding, 'I've done it! Attack a convoy with rifles and Sten guns, they shoot back with heavy machine guns. They'll cut us to pieces.'

'Ordinarily we wouldn't risk it,' said Cooper, 'but it has to be a full assault or nothing. Otherwise we won't get the Professor.'

'And what of the reprisals,' asked Alvar, 'do you really think the Germans won't massacre civilians if we kill their famous professor?'

'No,' admitted Walsh, 'I'd say there is a strong chance of reprisals against the civilian population.'

'And you want us to go ahead and assassinate him anyway?' asked Montueil. 'Do you realise what you are asking these men to do, Harry?'

'I think so, yes.'

'I'm not sure you do,' their leader told him, 'you don't have family in the town.'

It was Lemonnier's turn to speak, 'Almost every man here has a mother, sister or wife in Elbeuf or Rouen. Some have children. They could all be shipped to a camp or shot in the square. Are you seriously asking us to risk that?'

'Yes, I am. You risk it every day already by your participation in the Maquis. This increases the risk, I'll grant you, but it's the only way.'

'Then you ask too much!' shouted Montueil.

Walsh allowed Montueil's fury to abate. 'Perhaps, but we have to kill this man, one way or another.'

'Because of his miracle plane?' asked Triboulet, who was calmer than his comrades.

'Yes,' said Walsh.

'Could it really prevent an invasion?' pressed the school teacher.

'It could, unless we stall it.'

'Then we have no choice,' concluded the teacher.

'No,' said Walsh, 'none whatsoever.'

And I have no choice either, thought Walsh than to trust you all, though I can see by the looks on your faces right now that you no longer want to follow me and I'm almost certain one of you betrayed me to the Milice. How else could they know I was at the hotel that day? But who could have done it?

Walsh would tread more carefully from now on. He had no choice but to inform the Maquisard commune of his intention to kill the professor, he could hardly do it alone after all. But he would not betray the detail of his plan just yet. The date, timing and method of the attack would stay with him until the last moment, when it was impossible for anybody to leave the camp and tip off the Germans.

Gaerte approved of her. The young whore's flesh was pleasingly firm, her naked skin turned golden by the light from the bedroom's lamp. This was one aspect of the professor's status he had become happily used to; a steady flow of young women. His wife was safely back in Germany so she could never hear about this and his elevated position ensured he would never want for female company at the end of a long and demanding day. Women were discreetly procured for him on demand.

The girl was dressing and was mercifully mute. He hated it if they tried to talk afterwards. Gaerte would never engage any girl for a second visit if she was talkative. In fact he preferred variety, rarely requesting the same girl twice, considering each one to be a personal conquest. Gaerte preferred them young, pliant and swift to leave once the act was over. Aside from beauty, that was all he desired of a woman. Gaerte had enjoyed watching this long-limbed brunette undress. She had been a welcome interlude after a frustrating day wrestling with the never-ending problem of the Komet's fighting weight.

Gaerte's new idea was to make the plane land in a powerless descent with the engine turned off, a white-knuckled pilot sliding it down in a steep glide, praying he would land softly enough to keep the volatile mix of fuel from igniting around him. That day's experiments had proved only partially successful, the plane had not exploded but it did dip dramatically to one side on landing and a wing had been damaged, which meant more cost, further delay and one of only two serviceable prototypes out of action until it could be repaired.

So far not a single enemy pilot had been engaged and Gaerte had no spectacular kills to boast of in his reports to Goering but he was convinced the glider principle could work on landing. If he could just squeeze a few more seconds from the fuel mix and reduce the weight still further he was certain the flight time would increase. The pilots would then gain precious extra moments in the air to locate incoming targets and the kills would follow. No one failed to be impressed by the speed of the Komet or its manoeuvrability in the air. If Gaerte could just keep it in the skies for a little longer, the hard part would then be keeping score of the downed Allied pilots.

Kornatzki reported no breakthrough regarding the mysterious disappearance of the Milice leader. Combret had simply vanished. Tauber suspected he lacked confidence in the outcome of the war and was attempting to flee the country to save his own skin. He instructed Kornatzki to alert the border guards then continued to quiz his second in command on Combret's recent movements.

'The man operated in such secrecy,' admitted Kornatzki, 'even his own men didn't know what he was up to most of the time. He often worked alone or with that big peasant body guard. No one knows anything about the night he left, though one of his men said he saw a Maquis informant a couple of days ago.'

'An informant?' Tauber became animated, 'from within the Maquis? Do you have the name?'

'Not yet, Standartenführer, but I am investigating.'

'You're investigating?' Tauber was unimpressed. He couldn't contain his interest. He scraped back his chair and rose to his feet. 'Get the name from Combret's men,' he ordered, 'make sure they understand where their loyalties lie, sweat them, frighten them, make them give it up. Do it now. When you have the name get them to arrange a meeting with the informant and we will take the man off their hands. My God, this could be the breakthrough we've been looking for.'

36

*'As long as people believe in absurdities
they will continue to commit atrocities.'*

Voltaire

Walsh opened his eyes just as the earliest dawn light peeped through the flap of the tent. Emma was still asleep beside him and his first thought was the lack of any pressing need to leave the warmth of her side. Then he noticed something, a sound or more accurately the lack of a sound. Walsh realised he had woken because of the complete silence. Usually he awoke around the same time each morning, roused by the beginnings of a dawn chorus. Today there was nothing. Walsh waited but still no sound came from outside. What could have scared the birds away from the camp?

Quietly, without disturbing Emma, Walsh crawled towards the tent flap and parted it very slightly, just enough for him to see a sizeable portion of the camp. The shock hit him like a blow. A German soldier was walking silently through the camp, crouched low, his Schmeisser MP40 machine-pistol at the ready. Walsh spotted a second just behind him, then a third. The Germans were in the camp, infiltrating the Maquisard lair, aiming to kill or capture everyone there.

Fear took a grip on Walsh then, his heart raced and his

chest began to heave. At first he was frozen, convinced he could no longer breathe, as the panic gripped him but Walsh knew he had to act if they were to have any chance of survival. Behind him Emma murmured and rolled over. Realising he had stirred, she opened her eyes, sat up, blinked at him and was about to speak but he shot her a look and pressed a finger to his lips. She understood immediately and froze. Walsh crawled back to her, grabbed his bag, retrieved the commando knife with its large serrated blade and pressed its handle into her hand. He spoke quietly yet urgently.

'Soldiers, outside, in the camp, we can't go out this way, cut through the back of the tent, do it now.' Emma was stunned but she nodded and took the knife. She stabbed its razor sharp point through the canvas then moved the blade quietly downwards in a sawing action until a long slit began to appear. Satisfied with her progress, Walsh took the Luger, crawled back to the front of the tent, pulled the flap aside aimed and fired twice. Walsh reasoned this was as good a way as any to alert the camp to the presence of the Germans. The crack of the pistol was louder in the silence of the morning.

The two nearest men, including the soldier with the MP40, fell to the floor, fatally wounded from Walsh's shots. He immediately ducked back into the tent. The others, shocked by the unseen assault on their fallen comrades, abandoned stealth and began to call to each other. Some returned fire, blazing wildly, unsure of the direction of Walsh's bullets. Others sent indiscriminate bursts into the nearest tents and shelters. Walsh saw panicked and bleary-eyed maquisards begin to emerge from their shelters. Some were cut down before they realised what was happening. Walsh realised there were too many soldiers to make any kind of fight of it. They had to run.

Wash turned back in time to see Emma disappearing through the hole in the tent. He stuffed the pistol into his belt, grabbed his bag on the way and scrambled after her. Emma seized his arm and hauled Walsh through the gap and they were off and running, hurtling through the long damp grass at the rear of the camp, desperate to reach the protection of the woods. Behind them the camp erupted with noise, bursts of gunfire drowned out the desperate cries of dying men. The Maquis were being slaughtered and there was nothing Walsh could do about it. He did not need to look behind him to realise that this was a full assault. Walsh realised if the Germans had done this properly there would be no escape for any of them. The door would already be slammed shut.

'Head for the high ground,' shouted Walsh but she was already going that way and they scrambled up the hill together. It was so steep Emma's palms hit the ground in front of her as she stumbled upwards. Walsh expected them to be cut down at any moment but no shots found them. Were the Germans too busy fighting their way through the camp? They rounded a clump of trees, hoping to use them for cover, and almost collided with two German soldiers running into the camp from the opposite direction to outflank the Maquis. Both had their bayonets fixed. The nearest made a stab at Walsh who jumped back to evade the bayonet. On the second lunge he stepped to one side, grabbed the end of the rifle on the follow-through and pulled hard, throwing his attacker off balance. The soldier stumbled and Walsh hit him viciously in the face with the butt of his own rifle, knocking him cold.

From the corner of his eye, the second man loomed upon him. It was too late to evade the blow, too late to do anything except take a bayonet in the belly. Walsh had a moment of realisation that it was all over, he was going to die here in this French field. Then there was a loud crack and the second soldier fell forward onto the grass and lay motionless.

Emma was standing stock-still, a shocked expression on her face, the Browning Automatic still pointing straight out in front of her, as if she half expected the dead German to rise again and she would have to shoot him once more.

'Thanks,' he said, the inadequate word all he had time for. Walsh spun Emma round to face the opposite direction and gave her a push to help her on her way. There was no time to reflect on his narrow escape or they would be killed where they stood. They pressed on up the hill, the sound of gunfire and men screaming behind them spurring them on. Emma was wild-eyed and Walsh realised this was probably the first time she had ever killed anyone.

It took the Germans less than fifteen minutes to overrun the whole camp; now there was an eerie silence as the storm subsided; no more gunfire or screaming, just a few barked orders from the officers to shatter the calm. Walsh pressed his finger to his lips and Emma nodded. They crawled slowly forward until they reached the edge of the ridge high above the camp, their position affording them a perfect view of the devastation far below them.

They had been lucky. Though they were not yet entirely free of danger, Walsh's swift reaction to the assault got them though the cordon of soldiers before it closed tightly around the camp. Walsh had risked an occasional backwards glance as they climbed, checking for pursuers, but none came. Instead there was only the horrifying spectacle of the camp being overrun by the soldiers. They had a bird's eye view as the Maquis vainly tried to engage or evade their attackers. He witnessed the last act of one man, as the poor desperate soul tried to run and was cut down. Others were rounded up at the point of a bayonet and forced to their knees, their hands bound behind them before they were hauled up and marched away while the killings went on around them.

Now from their vantage point, Walsh and Emma could see bodies strewn between the tents and small shelters, and witnessed a similar number of captured maquisards being loaded on to a truck for questioning. Torture then transportation to the notorious camp at Le Struthof would follow.

It was then that Walsh noticed the second line of prisoners, for not all of the captured men were being taken away. To one side were a dozen helpless figures kneeling in the mud, hands tied behind their backs, heads bowed, being watched over by soldiers who were laughing and joking. Walsh reached into his bag and pulled out binoculars then looked again. To one side of the group was a figure Walsh instantly recognised. Colonel Tauber was holding a pistol. It was going to be an execution.

Walsh trained his field glasses on the line of captured men, desperate to find out who had been chosen to die? Tauber moved behind the line of men and the first shot from his pistol rang out then straight after it there was another. Two men fell forwards. It was impossible to identify the sprawled figures now lying face down in the mud.

Tauber was clearly relishing his work and he wasted no time in taking aim at the third in line. It was the fourth that caught Walsh's attention and his heart sank. Next to die would be a tall, tanned, swarthy man who was holding his head up as high as he could, unbowed, determined to show defiance even in death.

'Jesus,' gasped Walsh.

'What?'

'It's Alvar.'

'Oh no,' and as Emma spoke there was a puff of smoke from Tauber's gun and Alvar was gone.

'That bastard,' said Walsh, 'if I have the chance I swear I'll...'

'Who else?' asked Emma urgently and Walsh trailed his field glasses down the line. He recognised each man there and experienced a grim jolt of recognition in every face; a word remembered, a gesture, a joke shared in one of a hundred interactions from weeks in the same camp together. All of these men would die, right in front of his eyes and Walsh was powerless to help any of them. He had almost reached the end of the line, gaining some hope from the faces that were missing, though he knew they might already be dead or taken away in the lorry. He had not seen Sam Cooper or Montueil, Triboulet the schoolteacher, nor Lemonnier; and Simone would never have been at the camp so early. He knew she would hear the gunshots from her farm, and that was just as well, or she might have walked straight into a German ambush. Then Walsh's eye fell on the last man in the line and he realised the cowed figure was Christophe Valvert.

Tauber had not yet reached Valvert, there were still two or three to die before it was his turn but he would not have to wait long. Walsh scanned the ground around him, desperately searching for a way for Valvert to make a break for it but he already knew it was hopeless. There were soldiers all around him, chatting and laughing as the men were killed. One even appeared to be filming the act. They were proud of themselves.

'They've got Christophe too,' said Walsh.

'Oh God,' gasped Emma.

Tauber despatched the last man but one in the line then he reached the lone figure of Valvert, whose head had been bowed the whole time, as if in prayer or merely desperation. And then a strange thing happened; Valvert raised his head, turned to face the man who was about to kill him and said something. Tauber stopped, lowered his gun for a second and leaned forward incredulously. Valvert spoke once more and something passed between them. Valvert was talking and Tauber listening intently. The exchange did not last long but whatever was said it had an immediate effect on the Nazi. Tauber suddenly flew into a rage and aimed a clumsy kick at Valvert's head. The bound Frenchman fell on to his side and Tauber lashed out at him again, kicking him twice more before suddenly remembering he had a gun in his hand. In his fury he sent bullet after bullet into Valvert's body, which twitched and jerked as each round found its mark.

Walsh could not help but be moved by the defiance Valvert showed. 'Good for you, Christophe,' he said quietly.

'What happened?' asked Emma.

'I'm not sure but Valvert said something to that Nazi colonel just before he was shot. Whatever it was, it got the bastard worked up into a right old rage.'

'Oh,' was all Emma offered in reply. She had not witnessed and perhaps could not fully appreciate Valvert's defiance in the face of an absolute evil like Tauber but Walsh could not think of a finer way to face death. To turn towards the man who thinks he has won, the Nazi who is about to kill you, then tell him where to go. He only hoped he would possess the same courage himself when his own time came.

The informant was weeping. Kornatzki knew this even though his view through the narrow hatch of the cell door was hampered by the gloom. He knew it even though no sound came from the hunched figure whose face was obscured by his hands; Kornatzki could tell from the silent convulsions that racked the man's body that he was sobbing uncontrollably. He left the informant alone for a time before returning, this time with the Colonel. By then the sobbing had ceased but the man appeared no less wretched for it. Was this the look Judas had before he hanged himself, Kornatzki wondered?

'I don't know why you have been weeping,' said Tauber, showing even less understanding of the human condition than Kornatzki would have credited him with, 'you are perfectly safe.'

'What have I done?' Kornatzki felt the choked words were

aimed more at the man's maker than Colonel Tauber.

'You have acted sensibly to remove terrorists from the world and saved your life into the bargain.'

'I did not do it for my own life.'

'No, of course not, it wasn't to save your skin and it certainly wasn't because of the money we paid you.' Tauber permitted himself a sly little smile, 'it was for your family, wasn't it? Well let's just say the rest is a bonus then, shall we?'

'What are you going to do with me?' and fresh tears fell, 'you said you would…'

'We promised you salvation,' Tauber lifted a chair from the centre of the room and sat down in front of his informant, 'and you shall have it. We were careful to keep you separate from the men we brought in. One at a time they will leave for Le Struthof, never knowing who in their number was wise enough to cooperate with us. I have seen Le Struthof and I would not recommend it even for a day, much less a year. They work men to death there. You should rejoice, for you will never know what it is like. Instead you will soon be a free man.'

The prospect gave the informant fresh alarm. 'I can't go back out there, you've got to protect me. If anybody suspects…' And he could not bring himself to describe his likely fate.

'Don't worry. In a day or two we will raise an alarm and start a manhunt. One of the men captured during the raid on the maquisards will have managed a daring escape. No one will know you left the camp long before the raid on it. Hell, I'll even send patrols out with dogs looking for you and all the while you'll be safe in here. The patrols will cease but the town will know there is a fugitive out there who has eluded us. Everyone will be praying for you. I am sure it will be good for their morale, don't you think?' This prompted a new bout of weeping.

'There are others like you working for us within the so

called "resistance movement". We will arrange to have you taken in by another band of maquisards. You will infiltrate them and report everything back to us.'

Kornatzki could see the informant was shocked to the core. The poor fool thought he would merely have to live out the rest of his days with one unspeakable act of betrayal on his conscience, not realising his living hell had only just begun.

'I can't do this again, I can't.'

'But you must,' Tauber said it so reasonably, as if he were making a perfectly fair bargain, 'if you wish to stay safe.'

'No, no, I can't do it, I won't. I did it this one time because the Englishman would have got us all killed anyway and civilians too, but I can't do it again.'

'Mmm, very well,' Tauber murmured the words gently as if his suggestion for a drink in the local café had been politely declined due to a prior engagement, 'if you really feel you cannot provide this small service then it is as well you tell us now,' he made as if to leave and Kornatzki followed. 'I think I will arrange for all of your comrades to come together in the holding cell to say goodbye to you before they leave for Le Struthof. I'll explain you won't be joining them and the reason why but don't worry, I feel certain they will understand. They will surely forgive you once you explain your motives. After all, they are family men too. We'll leave you to think about it for a while, shall we?'

And they left the ashen-faced traitor to consider his options.

37

*'God created man and, finding him not sufficiently
alone, gave him a companion to make him feel
his solitude more keenly.'*

Paul Valéry

They walked a long way in silence, alone with their thoughts. So many good men killed that day, thought Walsh, and others captured, which meant as good as dead, and all for what? A bridge destroyed, a rail line damaged, a traitor killed. It seemed such a puny bargain now.

For her part, Emma kept returning to the moment when she had pulled the trigger and killed the young soldier. The move had been instinctive. She was protecting Harry and somewhere deep within her there was elation, for she had most definitely saved his life. But for Emma Stirling, the legendary Harry Walsh would be dead. He had saved her life twice before; once when he rescued her from an impostor's trap and again as he bargained her from the Milice, and it felt good to repay him. It made her less the junior and unequal partner. But there would always be a small part of her that would regret the act, and it left her wondering about the man she had killed. She hoped he had been an unflinching Nazi zealot or did she merely shoot a scared, young man, conscripted into the army through no choice of his own. Did he have a sweetheart, a sister? Was there a mother somewhere waiting for the telegram?

She told herself it was wrong to think this way. Even she could see the soldiers that attacked the maquisards were hardened SS, and she really had been left with no choice; it was either him or Harry, so she forced further thoughts of the soldier from her mind and trudged on in silence.

'Where are we going?'

'It's not far now,' said Walsh. 'Sam found an old hunting lodge when he was scouting the air base. We agreed we'd use it for a rendezvous if anything went badly wrong.'

'Who knows about this?'

'Not many,' he admitted, 'I didn't think that was wise. Only Sam, Valvert and Montueil. If any of us were caught we agreed the lodge was the one thing we'd never give up. We should be safe there.'

Emma was angry, 'And were you ever going to tell me about this place?'

'No need,' he said dismissively, 'I wasn't planning on leaving you.'

They reached the lodge by mid-afternoon and, exhausted, sat down outside it to wait, not knowing when, or even if, Cooper or Montueil would come.

'Who did it, Harry? Who betrayed us?'

'I don't know, I really don't.' He could have given Emma a list of suspects, but the names seemed scarcely credible. Walsh felt guilty for ever doubting Valvert; his suspicions based on little more than the poor man's habit of keeping himself to himself. Someone had betrayed them though, that much was certain. 'I'll find out,' he assured her, 'and when I do I'll kill the bastard myself.'

They waited at the old lodge all afternoon and into the evening but no one came.

'Do you think they're...' asked Emma, as the darkness closed round them.

'I don't know,' snapped Walsh, 'but there's no point in leaving now. There are tins of food in my bag and we can sleep on the floor of the lodge. This is as good a place as any, until we know where we stand.'

'All right,' agreed Emma, though it seemed pretty clear to her they stood alone.

Tauber leaned forward over his desk, eager for an update.

'What progress on the search for the Englishman?' he asked of Kornatzki.

'There are patrols out everywhere and I'm conducting house-to-house searches in Rouen and Elbeuf in case he is being sheltered there. There are still five unaccounted for, assuming our informant is telling us the truth, including the Englishman, an American and a girl.'

'An American and a girl?' Tauber tutted, as if to say whatever next. 'I can't imagine how an elite Schutzstaffel assault team could allow anybody to escape from a surprise attack when they were all still in their beds, let alone a woman. We knew everything, the site of the camp, the location of the lookouts, all killed silently before they could raise the alarm, and still they let the Englishman escape. It's shoddy, simply shoddy.'

Kornatzki was grateful someone else was on the receiving end of his master's scorn for a change. 'We will redouble our efforts, Colonel.' It was the kind of meaningless, unquantifiable phrase Kornatzki often employed when he wished to buy some time.

'Do so, but the Englishman will be long gone by now. All he can do is run, that's all he ever does; run away.' Tauber rose from his desk and picked up his leather attaché case. He gave a self-satisfied little smile. 'I am going to see the professor this morning to tell him how I foiled a British plot on his life.

That ought to make him appreciate us a little more, don't you think?'

Cooper had chosen the location well, for the lodge afforded an uninterrupted view of the valley below, and Walsh spotted the figure long before she reached them. There was no need to take cover because the new arrival was Simone.

Walsh wondered how she could have known about the lodge. The answer came in her breathless explanation. 'Sam sent me to find you. He didn't know whether you were alive or dead but he said, if you made it out of the camp, you'd be here.'

'Where is he?' asked Emma.

'Hidden in an old barn on the edge of our land. It's not safe to hide him in the house. Our workers know he's there but they won't tell.'

'That's the only good news we've had, Simone,' said Emma, 'we thought Sam must be dead. Have you heard about anyone else?'

But Walsh cut across her, 'Why didn't Sam come himself?' he asked, 'is he hurt?'

Simone nodded. 'He's been shot,' she said, 'he managed to get to us then he collapsed.'

'How bad is it?'

She seemed to hesitate, 'It's bad but we think my mother got the doctor to him in time. He is a friend of our family for many years and will not betray us. He took the bullet out of Sam's side.'

'Can he be moved?'

'The doctor says no, not yet. He must rest and I will care for him.'

'That's good of you, Simone,' said Emma and Walsh thought he detected something hidden behind Emma's words but he wasn't sure what it was.

'Can we see him?' asked Walsh.

'Perhaps, it might be possible,' she hesitated, 'tonight maybe, once it gets dark.'

'Tonight then,' said Walsh in a tone that brooked no argument.

Sam Cooper was almost unrecognisable; his face a ghostly white and his hair matted to his forehead by sweat. He was too weak to even raise a hand in greeting when they scaled the ladder to see him. Simone had done her best to make him comfortable in the roof of the old barn, preparing a bed of sorts, with blankets set down on straw. He was completely hidden from view on the ground floor. She had been careful to leave ancient cobwebs in place by the front of the alcove so, when the ladder was removed it looked like little more than a tiny ledge that must have been undisturbed for years. The rest of the barn was in a dilapidated state with holes in its roof and broken panels in its walls. If the German patrols did make it out as far as the edge of Simone's farm, they would hopefully be fooled into thinking no one had set foot in here in years but Walsh knew that a determined search would uncover their friend. Sam needed to heal quickly so he could be moved. Looking down at the American now, Walsh knew that prospect was unlikely.

Simone had explained that when Sam collapsed on her doorstep the trusted farm workers had wheeled him out to the old barn on a cart then carried him as gently as they could into the upper part of the barn. Walsh could only imagine the agony of that journey. Despite their care, Cooper had passed out through a combination of intense pain and blood loss. Simone stayed with him while the doctor went to work, until he finally woke and begged her to fetch Walsh.

Simone's mother had been trying to feed the American some

soup when they arrived but he was too ill to take any. She gave up and left them to talk.

'Harry,' he managed, 'good to see you. No flowers?'

Walsh shrugged, 'Didn't pass a cemetery.'

Cooper laughed then winced in pain.

'Sorry,' said Walsh.

'My own fault,' said Cooper, 'keep forgetting I've been shot. Ain't that the thing? In agony most of the time, and when I'm not, I forget and move and...' he winced again, no further explanation was needed.

'Well, you'll live,' said Walsh brusquely, 'I've seen men a lot worse than you and they were back in action in no time. You're a lucky man.'

'I do know it,' said Cooper grimly, 'just don't feel it yet,' Simone offered him water and Cooper sipped it gratefully, 'but we both know I won't be back in action for a while yet.'

'I'd say you have the best nurse in France,' said Emma brightly, searching for something positive to offer Sam, who was whiter than a corpse.

'That's a fact,' and he gazed at the French girl as if she was his own personal guardian angel. 'Simone saved my life. When the shooting started, well I just ran. I'm not proud of myself but they were on us so fast I couldn't do anything else.'

'That's exactly how it was for us,' admitted Walsh.

'I managed to get one of them but the bastard shot me before I sent him to hell. I was bleeding and I doubt there was anywhere else I could have gone but here. Simone got me to the barn and patched me up. The doctor came later and took the bullet but without her I'd have bled to death for sure.' The effort needed to speak was tiring him and he let his head fall back on the pillow.

'We should let him sleep,' said Simone.

'You're right,' said Walsh, 'can we stay here tonight, Simone?'

She shrugged. 'What difference will two more make? The Germans can only shoot me once.'

They slept in the lower part of the barn so as not to disturb Cooper. Emma asked quietly, 'Do you think he'll recover?'

'I don't know, Emma, he doesn't look good, but Sam's young and strong and he's a stubborn bastard.'

'Like you, you mean?' countered Emma.

'Sam is nothing like me.'

'More than you'll ever admit.'

'He's right about one thing though,' said Walsh, 'Simone kept him alive this long.'

'Well, she would,' said Emma matter-of-factly.

'What do you mean by that?' he asked.

'Young Simone is in love with our Sam, can't you tell?'

'Really?' He could not hide his surprise.

'Isn't it obvious?'

'Not to me,' said Walsh and he wondered what secret, unspoken language women dealt in that made it so.

Next morning Sam Cooper didn't look any better but at least he was strong enough to hold a conversation without passing out in mid-sentence.

'Do me this favour, Harry,' he grimaced, 'when you find out who did it, don't show them any of that English mercy.'

'There's no danger of that.'

'Too many good men dead,' added Cooper, 'and I almost joined 'em. What bugs me the most is we never did find out if they could have taken that convoy. It wouldn't have been easy but I'd have liked to have given it a try all the same. Instead, you get to tell London the bad news: Professor Gaerte lives and breathes and this mission is over.'

Walsh could not fault Cooper's appraisal, his plans had been wrecked by the attack on the camp; the maquisards were all either dead or captured and he had to assume the Germans knew about their plot to assassinate Gaerte. They would be scouring Rouen and the countryside around it for survivors, which meant Walsh would be hard pressed even to get safely away from here. Colonel Tauber had won the day. It had been eating away at Walsh – the thought of Tauber lording it with his superiors, boasting about the massacre of the maquisards and revelling in the interrogation of good men like Montueil. The more he thought about this injustice the more the rage began to build within him.

'Who said it's over?' asked Walsh defiantly and Emma stared at him.

38

'We owe to the Middle Ages the two worst inventions of humanity – romantic love and gunpowder.'

André Maurois

Only when they were reasonably convinced Sam Cooper was unlikely to die imminently from his wounds, did Emma and Walsh leave the American and return to the isolation of the hunting lodge. They slept together in the ruined building but made sure no trace of their presence could be found there during daylight hours. Their meagre possessions were stored in just two bags, so it was easy to run at the slightest hint of an approaching patrol and from their vantage point they could see everything for miles around. Simone brought food and regular news of the doctor's bulletins on Sam Cooper's steady progress. It seemed he was recovering and Walsh could now detect the relief in Simone's eyes.

The frenzy of patrols into the countryside and the house-to-house searches in Rouen and Elbeuf gradually began to subside. The SS were pleased enough with themselves for destroying the local Maquis group. If an Englishman, his girl and an American had escaped the net, along with one or two lowly foot soldiers from the partisans then it was a pity, but it would not ruin their self-congratulation. The foreign agents were likely to be miles away by now, they would reason; terrified fugitives, desperately trying to flee the country. Only a fool would stay in the area but then Walsh had been called a fool often enough before, usually by his own commanding officers.

'You've been quiet,' Emma told him.

'Have I?'

'For days.'

They were lying on the floor of the hunting lodge, not sleeping, staring up at a pregnant moon that was clearly visible through a hole in the dilapidated roof.

'I've been thinking it all through, where we went wrong, the people we lost; Montueil, Triboulet, Alvar, Lemonnier, the others, poor Christophe. It leaves a bad taste in my mouth.'

'Is that all?'

'What else is there?'

'What did you mean the other day when you told Sam it wasn't over?'

Walsh paused before answering, 'Just that.' He picked up a stick and started to scratch random lines into the dirt with it, avoiding her gaze. 'I meant I hadn't given up; that maybe I could still think of a way to get to Gaerte.'

'It sounded to me as if you already had.'

'Perhaps.'

'But it's dangerous?'

He looked her directly in the eye then and nodded slowly.

'So what's your big plan?'

'It was something Montueil's contact at the hotel told me when I met him in the café. I didn't think much of it at the time and we had the Milice to contend with.'

'But he gave you an idea.'

He nodded again but stayed silent. Emma watched Walsh as he continued to use the stick to draw shapes in the dirt to distract himself. She waited for him to to speak again and when she could take no more of the silence, she said it for him.

'And it involves me otherwise you would have gone off and done it by now.' Walsh did not contradict her, 'But you can't keep thinking like that. There's no "us" when we are on a mission, and we have to kill Gaerte. If we don't, this war could drag on for years. If there is a chance we can get to him, any chance at all, then you must tell me.'

'Even if it means dying, Emma?'

'Yes.'

39

'In my view women were very much better than men for the work. Women as you must know, have a far greater capacity for cool and lonely courage than men.'

Captain Selwyn Jepson, SOE Recruiter

Harry Walsh was not feeling proud of himself. How could he be? First he went to Simone to tell her that Sam Cooper must be moved, whether she deemed him well enough to travel or not. Walsh knew what they were about to attempt would have the Germans swarming all over every inch of countryside that they'd neglected so far and there was a better than even chance that this time they would find Sam.

Simone took the news without complaint. She told Walsh of her plan to spirit Sam away to a different Maquis group miles from there. 'I made contact with them and they have already agreed to take us when that day comes,' she informed him.

'Us?'

'I'm going with Sam. I won't stay here on the farm and wait for the Germans to take me in. Someone will mention my name eventually.' It was a possibility that had crossed Walsh's mind. 'We'll just have to go sooner than I planned.'

Simone explained how she would take the little, green truck

that normally ferried the farm's produce to market and use it to transport Sam to higher ground. They would walk the rest of the way to the camp. If they took it slowly, Simone felt sure Sam could make it.

'Before you leave,' asked Walsh, 'can I use the van?'

'Yes,' she told him, 'what do you need it for?'

Walsh answered her with silence and a grim smile. Simone understood. 'I don't need to know,' she admitted, 'and I probably don't want to know.'

'You'll get it back,' he promised, 'I just have to make a little visit to Rouen.'

Simone's truck would help Walsh to commit his next shameful act; the kidnap and terrorising of a blameless middle-aged Frenchwoman.

Romain's face was a picture. It would perhaps have been amusing under different circumstances but there was nothing funny about Walsh's situation or the risks he had taken to come into the city, evading the German checkpoints and passing patrols. He'd left Simone's truck parked on a side street then went the rest of the way on foot until he reached the café Romain visited; the same one they had met in before when Walsh had begun to plan a mission involving the now destroyed Maquis force. The café overlooked the rear of the hotel where the man worked so Walsh waited there and was able to witness him leave at the end of the day but he did not enter the café. Walsh drained his drink and followed Romain down the street and increased his pace till he could catch up with the man without drawing too much attention to him by running.

'Romain,' he called and when the man did not hear or chose not to turn, Walsh reached out a hand and placed it on his shoulder. The startled man spun round and a look of panic greeted the presence of Walsh.

'What are you doing?' he hissed at Walsh, 'are you crazy?' He shrugged off the other man's hand.

Walsh was thankful there was no one else in range to hear those words. 'I've got the money you lent me, Romain,' he said brightly in a tone that was louder than his companion's.

'I can't do this,' Romain whispered and his eyes darted from side to side in case they were being watched.

'Let me buy you a drink then to thank you,' said Walsh with a forced smile. Then he lowered his voice and placed a hand firmly back on Romain's shoulder, 'I need to speak to you about the professor. It won't take long.'

'But they're all dead,' his tone was disbelieving, as if he couldn't understand why Walsh would still be interested in the German professor.

'Yes,' said Walsh firmly, 'they are. We were betrayed by someone.' There was menace in his voice. 'So, help me now and perhaps I will be able to convince myself it wasn't you.'

It was fortunate for Walsh that Madame Dechabert, like many who worked in her trade, chose to keep her occupation and her private life distinctly separate.

The plump, middle-aged lady who lived alone in the cottage near the village school house let it be known that she lived off investments but did not fully disclose the nature of them to her neighbours. Instead she allowed a vague understanding that her money came from property in town and that this property could be rented, for the right price.

Madame Dechabert considered this to be a half-truth; the brothel was property after all and both its rooms and her girls could be rented out by the night or, more commonly, by the hour. There was nothing to be gained from revealing the truth, however, unless she actively wished to be shunned in the village and called out by the Catholic priest from his pulpit for her debauchery. This was not hypocrisy on her part but simply an awareness of the double standards most people held about her profession. Madame Dechabert was a brothel keeper and though most people in her country knew that these places existed and were largely tolerated by the authorities as something many people wanted or needed, she also realised her standing in her own community would be severely imperilled if anyone knew she personally provided such a service.

When Harry Walsh had first questioned Montueil's contact at the hotel, Romain, he had learned a great deal about the condition of Professor Gaerte's residence there, including his preferred form of entertainment and who had been entrusted with organising it. At that stage, the information didn't seem to be of much use to him. After all, he was planning to kill the man not blackmail him but he listened nonetheless to the tales of women being regularly procured for the scientist. His more recent visit, which had so alarmed Romain, was needed to get the details of who provided these women and where they came from. It was then he learned of Madame Dechabert's role in proceedings and, being a thorough man, he had listened further to Romain's description of her double life, as both brothel keeper and quietly respectable resident of a village just outside Rouen.

During the long days following the slaughter of the Maquis and Sam's tortuously slow recovery from his wound, somehow the germ of an idea had been planted in Walsh's mind. Now he had a name: Madame Dechabert; and a place: her village. All he needed now was an exact address and this was eventually procured with the help of Simone, who simply let a number of close and trusted souls know it was required. Within two days, discreet enquiries had been made and the exact location of the brothel owner's cottage had been confirmed.

Just like the Milice leader, Combret, Madame Cecile Dechabert returned home one evening to find Walsh sitting calmly in her living room. When the shocked woman saw him, he placed a finger to his lips then gestured with his gun, beckoning her to leave her home by the rear door. She looked terrified but she went quietly enough.

Emma kept a pistol trained on Madame Dechabert as Walsh drove them deep into the countryside. The two women were hidden in the back of the green van. Madame Dechabert had been instructed to say nothing and in fear she complied.

Only when they were miles outside the city did Walsh halt the truck and climb into the back with them to commence an explanation. He began by informing the terrified brothel keeper that she would die unless she told him everything about the German professor, the girls she sent him, and exactly what he did with them once they were inside his hotel room. Initially, he sensed she was still too scared of the Germans to cooperate, so Walsh produced his knife and threatened to cut her throat unless she changed her mind. He must have been convincing for she immediately told him everything. Sometimes Walsh wished there was a more potent weapon than fear but, if it did exist, he was yet to become aware of it.

'One of Gaerte's men made the first approach,' she told him, 'he requested "a lady's company" for the Professor. That's how it began. Now he is a regular client.'

'How often do you send him a girl?'

'Every two days. There was one last night so he is expecting another tomorrow.'

'Who chooses them?'

'I do and it's not so easy, as the professor prefers new ones and I am running out of suitable companions. Some are reluctant. They may be whores but they are still patriots,' she told Walsh defiantly, 'as am I. Do you think I like sending my girls there but what choice do I have? None.'

'I don't doubt it,' he said.

Madam Dechabert explained that her girls did not live in her bordello, so it wasn't necessary to summon them there for the job. Instead she would despatch a messenger to a girl's apartment. She would then be required to show up punctually and perform satisfactorily. Because the guards were expecting a girl they were none too concerned when one duly arrived, even if they had never seen her before. They were aware of the professor's need for variety. There was no code word, all they had to say was that Madame Dechabert had sent them. They would then be escorted to Gaerte's landing, whereupon the guard on his door would search the girl before admitting her. The sessions with Gaerte would last between half an hour and an hour and were not especially taxing.

'Sometimes he will pretend to punish them, you know,' and she illustrated her point with a smacking motion against her own thigh. 'He likes to play the headmaster,' and Madame Dechabert shrugged, as if she had long ago given up trying to comprehend men, 'mostly he just wants to screw them and send them on their way. Sometimes he's asleep before they are even dressed. That is all I can tell you about him.'

Walsh thought for a while and when he finally spoke she listened intently.

'Have you chosen the girl for tomorrow?'

'Yes.'

'And has she received her message?'

'Not yet.'

'There will be no message.'

Madame Dechabert nodded then immediately glanced at Emma who avoided her eye. Walsh continued. She would not be returning to the brothel that evening or the next. Madame Dechabert would write a note, explaining that a relative had been taken suddenly and seriously ill and she would not be back for a couple of days. Walsh would arrange for the note to be pushed through the door in the middle of the night.

'My mother is still alive, by the grace of God,' she suggested.

'Good, cooperate with me and you will see her again soon. The worst you will have is one uncomfortable night in the woods.'

'It will not be the first time I have slept in a field. I am not so grand,' then she frowned 'but what will the Germans do when they know I helped you?'

'They won't know. You were forced. I'll leave you tied up. A message will be delivered stating exactly where the collaborating bitch-whore can be found.' Madame Dechabert nodded in support of this plan. 'They will find you terrified but largely unharmed,' she raised her eyebrows in disbelief, 'the members of the Maquis do not murder women,' Walsh continued, 'usually. Besides, we kept you alive for a reason. When you are questioned by Colonel Tauber, as you will be, I want you to give him a message.'

'Is that it?' He nodded. She thought for a moment then looked about her at the isolated location, 'I don't really have a choice, do I?'

Walsh showed her the pistol, 'It's either that or I kill you now. I can't let you leave.'

'I see,' she said, 'and the professor, what are you going to do?'

Walsh smiled, 'I'm going to send him a message as well.'

40

'It's no use saying, "We are doing our best."
You have got to succeed in doing what is necessary.'

Winston Churchill

A little over twenty-four hours later, Emma set off for her
rendezvous with the professor, in clothes borrowed
from Simone and her mother and altered to give her a
more burlesque appearance; the skirt considerably shortened,
a precious pair of silk stockings loaned, garish make-up
applied and the top two buttons of her blouse left undone.
After terrorising Madame Dechabert and tying her to a tree,
this was another reason Walsh was feeling far from proud of
himself. He knew he was sending the woman he loved into
mortal peril and there was a strong likelihood he might never
see Emma again.

Simone drove the little green truck into Rouen. Her cargo
included a consignment of fruit and vegetables, which could
be accounted for as produce to be sold on a market stall the
next morning, and Emma, whose presence would be much
harder to explain. For that reason and to avoid the inevitable
German checkpoints, Simone drew the truck to the side of
the road a couple of kilometres from the edge of town and
let Emma out. She kissed the English woman on both cheeks

and whispered 'bonne chance' then got back into the truck immediately and drove off towards town, leaving Emma on her own to make her way slowly and cautiously into Rouen on foot.

Watching Simone's truck rattle round a corner and disappear from view, Emma had never felt more alone.

There was a uniformed guard on the front door of the professor's hotel. Emma approached him and he regarded her with suspicion till she became irrationally convinced he could read her nationality and true intentions just by looking at her face and was about to raise his rifle. 'Madame Dechabert sent me,' she managed, 'for the Herr Professor.'

The soldier looked at Emma dispassionately for a moment then stepped wordlessly to one side to admit her. As she walked into the hotel Emma Stirling told herself to get a grip and not to let the terror she was feeling weaken her judgement. She knew just how easy it would be to betray herself at the critical moment. One wrong word or gesture that made her appear out of place, a look that caused suspicion; any one of these would be enough to condemn her.

Emma had been briefed on the layout of the hotel and now she walked through the large open lounge towards the ornately carved wooden staircase that led to the first floor, her eyes fixed firmly ahead so she did not have to return the gaze of the handful of SS officers drinking in the hotel's lounge. They immediately stopped talking as she entered the hotel and she sensed their eyes upon her. This was not a new sensation for Emma but it was the first time that adoring gazes had come from a room full of enemy officers, all of whom assumed her to be a whore. It made her feel even more nervous to realise how vulnerable she was here; a woman from an occupied land in a hotel filled with its conquerors, who now regarded her with the carelessness they would reserve for someone who had slept with countless men for money. Any officer-class chivalry these men might retain for wives and sweethearts would surely not extend to her and as they watched her like dogs eying a bone, she realised the only thing that might save her from brutal treatment was their fear of upsetting the important Nazi scientist she was about to meet.

The only sound in the lounge came from the heels of Emma's shoes, which clicked as she took each self-conscious step across the ancient wooden floorboards that creaked under her weight.

Eventually, when she was no more than a couple of steps from the staircase and the German officers were some way behind her now, one of them spoke. The shock of his loud voice made Emma freeze instantly before she realised he had spoken in German and not to her. He must have made a lewd joke about her because his comment was followed by braying laughter from the other men.

Move, Emma, she told herself firmly but found she was still rooted to the spot in fear, unable to obey her thoughts, *move damn it!*

With a supreme effort of will Emma put one foot in front of the other and stepped on to the staircase then she kept going, as the sound of the laughter died away to be replaced by distracted conversation from the men.

Madame Dechabert's girls were always given the Professor's room number but Emma didn't need it. Gaerte's room was the only one on the first floor that had a guard standing outside it. The soldier was a big man and he seemed alert, snapping his head to one side to look at Emma. He visibly straightened and took a step towards her but his face softened when he took her in and his gaze told her that he understood the reason for her presence.

'Mademoiselle,' he greeted her with a tiny bow.

'I am here to see the Herr Professor,' she repeated, since this approach had worked with the guard on the main door.

The sentry had a little French, perhaps enough for an occupier to get by. 'Of course,' he managed politely, even though she was a whore, 'one moment,' and he held out his arms to indicate that she should allow him to search her. Emma complied, stretching out her own arms, and the guard took his time. First, he ran both of his hands all the way along one of Emma's outstretched arms, squeezing and patting her through her clothes as he went then he tackled the other arm. Next, he examined her hat and pressed gently against it, even though it would surely be impossible to hide a gun or a knife there, and he let his fingers trail through her hair as if she might be hiding a poisoned hair pin. He paused for a moment before letting his hands move lower and their eyes met, he was close enough for her to smell the tobacco on his breath.

'Forgive me,' he said a little nervously then he let his palms travel from her shoulders and right across then underneath her breasts, which, even allowing for the terror of the moment, made Emma want to slap him hard across the face but then she reminded herself that she was a whore, who was used to being pawed like a lump of meat, so instead she gave him a disapproving look, which implied she knew he was allowing himself to handle the goods without paying for them and he flushed a little. He paused momentarily at her navel, as if he was contemplating where his duty began and decorum ended, the palm of his hand now rested against the top of her skirt and his eyes narrowed slightly. Perhaps he remembered then that she was a whore not a lady and Emma felt his hand press more firmly against her, fingertips slipping beneath the waistband of her skirt. She knew it was about to slide further.

'Stop or the professor shall hear of it.'

The soldier froze, his hand halting just inside the waistband of her skirt and their eyes locked once more. Emma stared back at him defiantly and, for a moment, she was convinced he was about to degrade her for the sake of it or perhaps as a punishment for her resistance but his fear of the professor must have been more powerful than his anger at being told what to do by a whore. He silently withdrew his hand and turned towards the professor's door.

Gaerte was in his bathroom when the knock came; it made him start and he realised he was excited. He paused in front of the mirror to check his appearance, even though the girl was already paid for and it hardly mattered but he still liked to think of each one as a conquest. Gaerte ran a hand through a disobedient clump of hair, pinning it to his forehead then walked back into the bedroom before calling, 'Yes.'

The SS guard insisted on letting the girl in himself. It was an intrusion, an impudence that highlighted the man's low-rank vulgarity, though it was not an indiscretion Gaerte would find easy to complain about to the man's superior officer. How does one describe a lack of decorum concerning the manner in which a whore is indiscreetly let into one's bedroom?

Gaerte's irritation was soon forgotten once he got a good look at the girl. She was young, slender and strikingly pretty with a natural look, eschewing the gaudy make-up so common to members of her profession, with just a touch too much red lipstick to give her away. Her hair was pinned back and partially hidden under a hat. She might have looked almost like a lady if it were not for the excessively tight skirt that clung to her like a jealous lover, its hem inches too high above the knee for respectability.

Gaerte dismissed the guard with a nod, leaving the two of them alone in his room. The girl seemed a little nervous. He was used to that. Gaerte's status rendered them all the same; young, beautiful but scared and he preferred not to put them at their ease. She called him 'Herr Professor'. He dipped his head slightly, going along with the sham, pretending she was a lady.

She adopted the firm tone of the schoolmistress then, 'You will please make yourself comfortable on the bed while I prepare,' and she walked towards his bathroom. She did not ask his permission and he could have reprimanded her for the presumption but he suspected some of her clients enjoyed being spoken to in this manner and, if truth be known, so did he. Having his every whim blindly catered for without question by terrified subordinates meant that being addressed by an equal was a very rare occurrence for Gaerte these days. Being ordered about by this female was a refreshing change. It excited him to play the helpless one for a moment.

He would indulge her then for her beauty alone. He acquiesced, stripping completely then lying brazenly face up on the bed, not bothering to cover himself or his excitement while he waited for her to return.

She was gone a while but not so long for a woman and he had time to let his mind wander to the latest breakthrough he had made with the Komet. That very morning, the idea had come to Gaerte to use two separate combustion chambers. Like many of the best scientific breakthroughs this one was deceptively simple; one could be used at high power to get the plane through the air and into its first climb, the second would be engaged at lower power, as the Komet flew level looking for targets. Gaerte was already predicting an increase in intercept time of as much as eight minutes. This was the significant breakthrough he had been seeking; all it required was a few more weeks and the Komet would be truly battle ready. The bountiful rewards afforded a hero of the Third Reich were finally within his grasp.

Gaerte's private bathroom was small but the facilities far grander than the functional versions in Harry Walsh's humble hotel room when Emma had visited him, a lifetime ago in a more innocent time; before she had killed a man while witnessing a massacre. Everything in this tiny room was made of marble, glass and gold, and spoke of money and power but Emma had no time to take it in all in. She knew she had to move quickly. She removed her hat then swiftly unbuttoned the blouse and let it fall to the floor. She took off the skirt then felt for the loose thread at the back of the waistband. If the soldier had been more intent on doing his job correctly instead of groping Emma for his own gratification, he might have noticed it and if he had felt along the rear of the skirt's waistband he may even have discovered a foreign object there. The thin wire of the garrotte would usually have had a handle on either side but Emma could not have hoped to conceal it like that, so instead there was a loop tied in either end that was just wide enough to insert two fingers and it was lagged with material to protect them from the wire. Would she have enough strength to strangle Gaerte with it? In truth, she had no idea. Could she even kill a man with her bare hands like this? Shooting the soldier had been bad enough but she had done that to save Harry and hadn't been close enough to smell the man. Not like this.

Emma folded the slim wire and hid it in the back of the French knickers she wore. She then took a moment to look at herself in the mirror, as she tried to will herself some courage. She told herself that this terrible thing had to be done and must be done exactly as Walsh had instructed her; otherwise the guard outside would kill her or she would be taken prisoner and the Gestapo would torture her to death. Emma knew she could not falter. *Courage*, she whispered the word to herself in the mirror as if saying it aloud was enough, *courage*.

41

'Demoralise the enemy from within by surprise, terror, sabotage, assassination. This is the war of the future.'

Adolf Hitler

When the girl emerged, she was dressed only in her underwear, a clichéd concoction of bordello items that included the regulation suspender belt and stockings. Her hair was down now and she looked even more desirable. He was going to enjoy this. She seemed a little taken aback by his unashamed state, which surprised him, but she became instantly business like.

'Do you like what you see, Herr Professor?' she asked in a tone she must have considered coquettish.

'Perhaps,' he replied, not wanting to give her the satisfaction of knowing how exciting he found her, though that must have been obvious enough.

'Then you will please turn over and we will start with a relaxing massage,' Gaerte was disappointed. He preferred not to waste time on such things. She must have seen this in his face, for the girl quickly added, 'only for a short while and it's a very special massage. I promise you've never had one like this before,' and again there was something in the way she said it that made him willingly compliant.

Gaerte rolled over, placed his face and forearms on the

pillow and immediately felt robbed of the spectacle of this shapely girl. He wanted to watch as she removed what remained of her clothes and would insist on that in fact.

He felt the edge of the mattress sag a little as her delicate weight was added to it. She crawled gently towards him. He felt the smooth skin of her legs brush against the inside of his and he parted them to allow her to move closer. Then she dipped her head and let her hair fall onto his back. She teased him with it, running the strands sensuously back and forth across his flesh. She was right. He had never experienced anything like this before. The girl climbed further still and then she was straddling his back. Her hands were on his shoulders now, kneading the knots from his back and neck. It felt glorious and he was glad he had allowed her to be the dominant one. Then she stopped and removed her hands for a moment to give him more instruction.

'Please hold your head back just a little, Professor,' her voice was low and was there just a trace of nervousness there? Was it too much to expect that she might be excited too, intoxicated by the thought of his power? Was her fear perhaps turning into arousal? There was such a thin line between those emotions. God this was good, he wanted it to last forever and willingly obeyed, tilting his head up and back.

Emma moved fast, the garrotte was already in her hands and she made it into a loose loop, lifted it up and over Gaerte's head then down until it's sharp wire brushed against his throat. Before he realised what was happening, Emma tugged the wire back then pulled each end with all her might and the wire closed tightly around Gaerte's throat. He let out a choked gasp but the garrotte stifled even that sound, which was the reason Walsh had chosen the weapon.

He had shown Emma how to use the garrotte. She had watched intently and practised, knowing she could afford no mistakes. Gaerte could not be permitted to fight her off, cry out and raise the alarm. Emma knew she had one opportunity to kill him and this was it. By now, Gaerte's arms were failing at his sides and he was desperately trying to buck his hips in an attempt to unseat Emma. She'd expected the struggle and she steadied herself – her left knee firmly on the mattress and she moved her right knee suddenly, planting it hard into the small of the professor's back. It acted as a counter to all her strength, as she pulled on the wire, which closed tighter and tighter around the professor's neck. Gaerte was still thrashing like a wounded animal. Emma's hands ached with the force required and she realised she might not be able to hold on much longer.

Just when she thought she might lack the strength to finish it, Gaerte suddenly went rigid and the life abruptly ebbed from his body. His arms went limp and his head lolled forward onto the pillow. Emma pulled the wire tight one last time to be certain he was finished. She met no resistance. Only when she was absolutely sure he was gone, did she finally allow herself to loosen her grip. There was a low gasping sound. At first she thought Gaerte might still be alive but it was just his final breath being expelled from his airway.

Emma slid from the bed and slumped to the floor. It was not just physical exhaustion she was feeling now but the stark realisation of having ended a man's life with her bare hands. The garrotte had been a wise choice, a length of wire that was easy enough to conceal under her clothes. Harry had been right; the plan was dangerous but it worked. Professor Gaerte, one of the finest scientific minds of the Third Reich was dead, murdered at Emma's hands. There was no pleasant way to describe it. Emma Stirling was now an assassin.

She waited in his room for half an hour. Every instinct Emma had told her to get out of there immediately, to run and keep on running but she knew she must not listen to this panicked inner voice. Harry had warned her against it, instructed her to wait, so there was nothing out of the ordinary that might alert the Germans. If she left now, earlier than the other girls, the guard might become suspicious and want to check on the professor. And so she stayed.

Emma washed her hands repeatedly but the indentation marks from the garrotte still showed clearly on her palms. What I did probably saved the lives of thousands, she told herself. This is war, she reasoned, and no time to develop a conscience. Still, once Emma returned to the room, she could not tear her gaze from the bulging, sightless eyes of her victim. She knew she would relive his last thrashing, choking moments over and over again, most probably for the rest of her life.

Emma dressed then sat in the armchair opposite the bed. Every minute trapped in this room felt like an age, each passing sound, every creak upon the old wooden floorboards outside, convinced her the SS were about to burst into the room.

There were still three minutes to go before the half hour minimum Walsh had ordered but Emma could take no more. She rearranged the body on the bed, turning the professor's head away to make it look as if he was asleep then arranging the bed clothes so they obscured his body and the ligature marks around his neck then she made for the door, opening it just a fraction before making a play of closing it very quietly behind her.

'He's sleeping,' she explained to the guard in a hushed tone, as if sharing a confidence with him, their earlier clash forgotten, 'they usually do.'

'I see,' he said, regarding her closely once more, as if he understood why Gaerte might be in need of a nap.

'Goodnight then, Captain,' she said.

'I'm just a sergeant… miss,' he didn't seem to know what to call her.

'Well now,' she said coquettishly, 'I'm told they really run the army.'

'Oh, they do, miss,' and he gave her a mock salute, 'they do.'

Emma slowly walked away. When she reached the end of the landing, she turned back and smiled.

Emma began her slow descent of the hotel's staircase. The German officers were still drinking in the lobby. For a second time their conversation ceased and all eyes went to her as she walked down the stairs. Were these the looks men would usually give an attractive, young woman of her profession, as she emerged from an assignation, or was there more to it? Were they somehow suspicious of her now? Was the kill written indelibly on her face? Emma tried to walk slowly and calmly, keeping her face forwards as she reached the bottom of the stairs and her body upright as she walked through an agonising silence across the hotel's lounge and passed the young officers who eyed her jealously.

She was still yards from the front door. What would she do if one of them spoke to her? It had never crossed her mind until now. Her heart was pounding and still she had not yet reached the door. What if they commanded her to stay and have a drink with them? What if one of them then tried to take her to bed with him? He would hardly expect her to refuse if he offered a sufficient fee. She felt a sharp pang of fear for it had never even occurred to her that this could happen. What excuse could she give when there was none?

She was perhaps five paces from the hotel door now, could see the shoulder of the guard who had admitted her and kept her gaze fixed rigidly upon his frame as she drew closer to him… four paces… three… nearly there and she knew if they spoke to her now her voice would crack and she would be incapable of reply… two paces… one… and then, gloriously, she reached the door and pushed it open and the burly guard moved to one side to allow her to leave.

Pure instinct made her halt in the doorway next to the guard and she reached into her coat pocket. She took out a packet of cigarettes and a lighter like she had all the time in the world. Without looking behind her, she removed a cigarette from the packet and raised it to her mouth. Emma had to make a conscious effort to stop her hand from shaking as she raised the lighter and lit it. She took a deep drag on the cigarette, inhaled the smoke then let it out. Only when she had taken two long drags did she allow herself to walk away from the building, knowing that her unhurried exit was the best cover she could have given herself yet all the while experiencing a state of abject terror.

As instructed, she walked for three blocks, taking care to avoid ruining everything with a wrong turning in her panic. After what seemed like an eternity but must have been less than five minutes, she reached a small square that housed a market during the daytime but was dark and empty now. There, tucked away in the farthest corner was the little, green delivery van, a sight which made Emma's heart soar.

She knew Simone was hiding in the back and Emma did not hesitate. She crossed the road, gave a knock on the side of the truck and Simone emerged. They both climbed into the cab and the French girl drove the truck away, leaving the quiet streets of Rouen behind them, both girls praying the professor's body would not be discovered until they were far away from the city.

Picnic weather, thought Emma and it would have been in a different life, had she been back in England before the war changed everything. The early-morning sun shone brightly down on them, birds were chirruping in the trees and brightly coloured wild flowers swayed in the breeze. It could have been a picture in a magazine.

Emma felt numb.

'I know what this is,' grimaced Cooper as he slid painfully into the passenger seat vacated by Emma, 'revenge for Yugoslavia.'

'No,' replied Walsh, 'I still owe you for that.' He pushed the truck door shut for the American then spoke through the opened window, 'I'm sorry you can't come with us but…'

'I'd be picked up in minutes,' Cooper told him.

'Yes,' agreed Walsh.

'So, what's it going to be? A Lysander in the middle of the night? That's risky with the Germans crawling all around here right now?' Walsh knew Cooper was fishing but he wasn't going to answer. 'Or over the Pyrenees into Spain? I suppose you could head to Switzerland… but it's a very long walk, my friend, either way.'

'You don't need to know that.'

'No,' he agreed, 'I guess I don't.' He knew Walsh meant that was one thing they could keep from him in case he and Simone were caught.

'Take care of him, Simone, don't stand any nonsense.'

'I won't,' the French girl beamed at him from the driver's seat.

'Well, you did it, Harry,' said Cooper, 'you achieved the impossible.'

'Not me,' said Walsh and they all looked over at Emma who was standing back from the van, arms folded, a distant look on her face. When she realised they were regarding her, she raised a hand and gave them a grim smile.

'One in a million that one,' said Cooper.

And Walsh did not contradict him.

42

'Better a living beggar than a buried Emperor.'

Jean de La Fontaine

Kornatzki had seen his master in a rage before. He had witnessed him tear into subordinates till they literally quaked beneath the force of his demented fury. He'd watched as Tauber confined incompetent or merely unfortunate underlings to God-awful posts in the east without a second's thought. Kornatzki had been at Tauber's side the day he had taken his grim amusement from the execution of the maquisard by his own hand. He had stood by and watched as the Colonel calmly tortured young Olivier beyond the limit of all human endurance, but he had never seen the man like this before; for Tauber was scared. He was terrified in fact.

As Kornatzki listened to Tauber's seemingly endless tirade, following news of the discovery of the Professor's body that same morning, he began to realise it was the first time he had ever seen the Colonel close to breaking point. This was going to be bad, thought Kornatzki, very bad indeed.

'I want that guard on Gaerte's door… that… that soldier,' stammered Tauber, 'I want him stripped of his rank and shot. Court martial him today, immediately, then shoot him, for dereliction of duty. No, don't shoot him. That's too quick. I want him to suffer. Demote him to the lowest rank then ship him off to the Eastern Front! Find me the coldest spot there is. I want him in a punishment battalion by the end of the week, with all the murderers, rapists and sodomites dredged from the worst corners of the Wehrmacht. I want him to suffer and then die. I want him to have time to *know* he is going to die, is that clear?'

'Yes, Colonel,' Kornatzki stood rigidly to attention, ignoring the spittle that flew from Tauber's mouth and rained on his face.

'And the captain of the guard, I want an example made of him too; stripped of his rank, Eastern Front, punishment battalion. Do it today!'

'Yes, Colonel.' Kornatzki had no time to worry about unfortunate wretches who would soon join the suicide missions that always fell to punishment battalions. They were already full to bursting with men who had committed capital crimes, defied orders, deserted or simply messed up important tasks, such as guarding prominent scientists. Two more souls would disappear into their swollen ranks soon enough and be killed without meriting a further thought from anyone.

For the most part, Kornatzki was relieved he was still in a position to carry out the Colonel's retribution and was not yet a part of it. He knew Tauber was ultimately responsible for the safety of the professor, which meant Kornatzki could easily have filled the role of scapegoat.

Tauber ceased shouting to take a breath. He stopped pacing the room and stood by the side of his desk then he seemed to pitch forward and, for a moment, Kornatzki felt a guilty elation, for he actually thought the Colonel might be having a heart attack, which would surely prove to be the best solution for everybody. Instead Tauber merely spread his arms and put his weight against the desk, gripping the edge of it in his palms, squeezing the wood hard in his rage.

'I don't believe this, I can't believe it! A girl! They let a girl walk into his room and kill the man! All those guards, all those precautions, and the Englishman simply sent a girl to kill the professor and she walked calmly away afterwards! They say she even lit a cigarette in the doorway! What kind of a woman is she? It's beyond my comprehension!'

It had been Kornatzki's unfortunate duty to report the events of that morning and he had dreaded the task. He was forced to tell Tauber that the whore was not a whore but an assassin, sent by his nemesis the English agent to kill Gaerte. To make matters worse the crime had only been discovered when the professor failed to appear for breakfast the next morning, so the killer had the whole night to get away. Shortly after the body was discovered, a hand-written note reached the hotel notifying them of the whereabouts of the terrified Madame Dechabert and she was able to fill in all of the gaps.

'I want every man in that guard duty punished, every man, whether he was on duty at the time or not,' and Tauber banged his fist onto the desk, 'why should I take all the blame?'

Oh God, the blame, thought Tauber. My responsibility, this is my responsibility, and he desperately searched for a way out of his quandary. He needed time to think but Berlin would surely hear of this fiasco soon enough. They had eyes everywhere. Tauber had to come up with a plausible story that would shift the fault elsewhere. The captain of the guard would not be enough to pacify Berlin and he had already decided to offer them Kornatzki's head as well. Retribution was needed of course and he must pledge to hunt down the terrorists and show them no mercy. In the meantime, a hundred civilians executed by firing squad in the city centre would be the kind of gesture expected of him. That would be a start. But could he convince his superiors it was enough? Whatever would they do to him if he could not? Tauber needed time to think. He had to get away and think, damn it.

Just then there was a soft knock at the door and a terrified subaltern entered the room. The young officer actually swallowed before he spoke. He looked as if he were about to break some truly terrible news but surely no family bereavement could possibly trouble Tauber more than the death of the professor.

'What is it, man?' Tauber demanded.

'It's Berlin...' the youth struggled to complete his message, '... Reichsmarschall Goering asking to speak to you.'

Tauber visibly slumped. He brought his hand up to his eyes then pressed his thumb and forefinger together to pinch the loose skin at the top of his nose between them. His head throbbed and his face flushed, making him feel simultaneously both faint and nauseous. He tried to compose himself in front of his subordinates but realised it probably didn't matter anymore.

'Get out,' he said quietly, 'both of you.'

'But, Colonel... the call...' protested the boy.

'Tell him... tell him...' Tauber sighed and there was a very long pause then, until, in a dead voice, he said, '... put it through.'

They left Tauber alone in his misery. He knew he should be using the last remaining seconds before the call came through to compose an explanation that might in some way miraculously save his life and military career. Somehow though, all he could think of was the message Madame Dechabert had given him. The words went round and round in his head all morning, mocking him.

'Harry Walsh says hello.'

And Tauber wondered if the Englishman was laughing at him right now.

43

*'When you go in search of honey you must
expect to be stung by bees.'*

Joseph Joubert

The guard on Gaerte's door that night had compounded his sin by leaving the professor undisturbed until breakfast, giving them nine hours to make good an escape before the body was discovered.

The Germans threw up roadblocks all over Normandy and beyond. They searched every vehicle, took countless civilians in for questioning and wasted hours delaying every young couple they found. At the same time, they halted all passenger trains travelling through the region and scrutinised the documents of everyone on board. They searched each load of freight to ensure there was no one stowing away in a consignment of coal but of Harry Walsh and Emma Stirling they found not a sign.

As soon as they had said their goodbyes to Simone and Sam Cooper, Emma and Walsh made their way to Elbeuf where they holed up for the day in a warehouse by the river. That night, under cover of darkness they boarded a fishing boat. The captain of the vessel was one Pascal Montueil, cousin of the Maquis leader. He had been mooring overnight at Elbeuf for weeks, in between forays out into the Atlantic and trips back along the Seine to sell his catch in Rouen. If the crew were puzzled by their new routine, they knew better than to question Pascal Montueil. If the Captain wanted to sell his fish in Rouen instead of Le Havre that was his business.

On the subject of the new hand who joined them late one night at Elbeuf, the crew were similarly mute. No one had actually seen him board but he was there in the morning, large as life, helping to repair the nets. The new man kept himself to himself, aside from one or two monosyllabic grunts directed at the men in his immediate vicinity but he seemed to know what he was doing so that was sufficient.

Pascal Montueil had greeted Harry Walsh and Emma Stirling alone when they boarded the boat that night. The crew were all bedded down in Elbeuf by then for an early start the next morning, as *Le Chapardeur* would be away at first light. Pascal had commanded the change of routine weeks before to prevent any suspicion falling upon a new boat some eighty kilometres from its usual port. By now the presence of *Le Chapardeur* was known and accepted. Walsh and Philippe Montueil had met with the captain and agreed the Englishman's passage out of France, along with Cooper, Valvert and Emma, should they all survive the mission.

Walsh had returned to the captain to break the sad news of his cousin's disappearance, Valvert's death and Cooper's incapacity, then he'd booked the illegal passage for Emma and himself for the night Gaerte was scheduled to die.

Now Walsh worked hard on repairing the nets, a job he had been taught by Montueil years earlier on a very different trip when he was spirited away weeks after the collapse of Dunkirk. Emma hid herself away in the Captain's locked cabin. Pascal had prepared a hiding place for her beneath his bunk with a false side that could be removed and replaced in a hurry should they be boarded by the Germans, though this would only withstand the most cursory of searches. One of

Pascal's usual hands had been persuaded to remain behind at Elbeuf, so Harry could pretend to be that man if questioned but they all prayed it would never come to that.

Emma watched nervously from the tiny porthole in the captain's cabin as *Le Chapardeur* pulled out from the riverbank and made its unhurried progress along the meandering Seine, keeping back so she would not be spotted from the shore or any passing vessel. To begin with, German patrol boats on the river allowed the fishing boat to go about its usual business and Emma had actually begun to half believe the unthinkable, that they might get away. It was then that she spied the dark, low shape of the E-boat. It was coming straight towards them and coming at speed.

Walsh spotted the E-boat too and his mouth turned dry, because the deviation in its course sent the torpedo boat straight towards them. Why would it make such a detour unless the Germans were suspicious of *Le Chapardeur* and intent on boarding her? There was no hope of avoiding or outrunning the military craft, so their boat kept to its course at a slow and steady pace.

The S-100 Schnellboot was aptly named, for it had a top speed of over forty knots and could overtake a fishing boat without even taxing its three Daimler Benz engines. Primarily intended to harass Allied shipping in the Channel, the Schnellboot operated mostly at sea but today it was making short work of the deep River Seine. As well as four torpedo tubes, it was armed with a single 20mm machine gun and a 40mm Bofors gun. The only weapon on board *Le Chapardeur* was the Luger. Walsh had time to get off the deck and out of sight but elected to stay where he was. He knew binoculars would be trained on the deck of the fishing boat and did not want to increase suspicion with a sudden departure below deck.

The Schnellboot was almost upon them now. Walsh could

easily make out its four torpedo tubes and the twin machine guns, one of which had been manned by a uniformed sailor in case it was suddenly needed against the crew of *Le Chapardeur*. The captain of the vessel was standing on the deck surveying the fishing boat keenly. Walsh was just waiting for the barked command through a loudhailer to stand by for boarding and his mind raced as he tried to work out what he would say when he was questioned. Would Emma even have time to hide beneath the bunk? Her presence on the boat could not be explained. The Schnellboot drew within a few yards of their boat.

Just then Pascal Montueil appeared at Walsh's side and did something strange. He raised a hand towards the German manning the machine gun, smiled and gave a manly wave of greeting. The gesture seemed so innocuous and unassuming that Walsh thought it was probably the calmest thing he had ever witnessed. The German behind the gun did not respond but the Captain noticed the wave and turned to one of his men, speaking quietly. The Schnellboot first drew level with *Le Chapardeur*, passing within feet of its hull then it swept majestically past the fishing boat, sending a wash of water out from its side which gently nudged the *Le Chapardeur* as the two craft went their separate ways. Suddenly Walsh could breathe again.

The Schnellboot was looking for something out of the ordinary that day, not a craft they had witnessed ploughing the same lonely furrow for weeks. The calm wave from a familiar figure had been enough to convince the E-boat captain that his time would be better served elsewhere.

It was only when they finally emerged into open water at the mouth of the river, however, that Emma could dare to hope once more. She knew it wasn't over. All the local fishing boats were routinely followed and scrutinised by German patrol boats while they were out at sea but Montueil's cousin knew the way they operated and he was confident he could slip through the cordon to get enough miles out at sea until they could meet a British ship then signal it to take Walsh and Emma on board before slipping back home unnoticed. They had even kept a portion of the previous day's catch back on the boat, packed in ice, so it would look as if they had been busy fishing all day.

When she realised they were finally at sea, Emma immediately lay back on the Captain's bunk. She needed to talk to Harry, had something important to tell him in fact, but that would have to wait for now. Was it all finally over? Maybe. Emma instantly fell into an exhausted sleep.

44

'I'm intact and I don't give a damn.'

Arthur Rimbaud

'I'm to congratulate you, Walsh,' said Price blandly, before adding, 'apparently.' The Major was seated at his shabby little desk in Baker Street, just as he had been on the day, a hundred or so years ago, when Gubbins had first summoned Walsh. Price was attempting a brave face that morning but Walsh was under no illusion. His survival was an inconvenience to the Major and he could easily imagine how galling Walsh's recent elevation from F-Section-pariah to hero-of-the-hour must have been to his commanding officer.

Price adopted a falsely cheerful tone, 'You're quite the blue-eyed boy all of a sudden. It seems we have discovered a whole new talent of yours. So, how did it go? Nice clean kill, was it?'

The tiredness he'd held at bay for so long began to overcome Walsh just then. All of a sudden, he lacked the energy for the verbal sparring that characterised his debriefings with Price. 'There's rarely anything clean about killing,' he offered flatly.

'Quite,' taking his lead from Walsh's tone, Price decided against pressing him further, 'doubtless I shall read the details in your report, as it seems I am now finally permitted to know what has been going on in my own section.'

Gubbins had only revealed the true nature of Walsh's

mission to Price once it was over, and this clearly rankled with his commanding officer. Walsh would normally have taken pleasure from Price's exasperation but he was far too weary to care.

'You will spend this morning writing that report and you will have it on my desk this afternoon. Is that clear?'

'No, sir,' answered Walsh, his eyes burning with tiredness.

'No, sir?' Price could not quite believe the impertinence. 'What on earth do you mean by "no sir"?'

When Walsh spoke, his words were slow, measured and deliberate for he feared that, if they weren't, he might finally explode, possibly beating the man in front of him to a pulp in the process. His eyes locked on to Price's and never wavered for an instance. 'I have not eaten hot food in days, I haven't slept in forty hours and you may have noticed I am badly in need of a bath. So now I'm going to leave here, I'm going to take that bath, eat a large meal, drink a beer and then I'm going to sleep for a day.' Price just gaped at him. 'You can have my written report then and only then and if you don't like it, you can take it up with Gubbins,' then he finally added, '... sir.'

Price's face actually twitched then. He looked as if he was struggling to comprehend the words he had just heard. The Major opened his mouth, trying to find the right response to such open defiance and Walsh readied himself for the onslaught, the tirade about dumb insolence, insubordination, shoddy soldiering and general poor character that would surely follow. He was about to experience the full wrath of his superior and he didn't give a damn.

But the moment passed. Though red in the face and clearly seething, Price must have calculated that reporting Walsh's rudeness to Gubbins would do him no favours. He knew how the CD would view that one. Gubbins would be astonished Price could not command a hero for one day on the peaceful side of the Channel without prompting an almighty row. Walsh was flavour of the month for now, and Price's reputation would be harmed by an unseemly spat, not his. He might also have calculated that it was better to bide his time, wait until Walsh's achievements had been forgotten, then strike.

In the midst of his humiliation, Price eventually settled on an exasperated, 'Do you have any ambitions beyond the rank of captain?' and when no answer was immediately forthcoming, 'well, do you, Walsh?'

'No, sir.'

'And why not?'

'Because it would be a waste of time.'

'Well, at least you understand something about this man's army!' Price attempted to compose himself. 'Now get out of my office before I completely lose my temper.'

Walsh rose wearily to his feat. He neglected to salute his CO and instead turned his back on Price before walking out of the office and along the drab grey corridor. He had won and could actually get away with such behaviour for once. As for the future, no doubt it would prove to be a Pyrrhic victory but, for the moment, he wouldn't dwell on that.

Professor Gaerte was dead and the Komet project had been severely derailed. Improbably, he'd managed to get both Emma and himself out of France alive, running his commanding officer ragged in the process, but Walsh wasn't thinking about that right now. As he walked, it was Emma's words that came back to him. As soon as they were safely on English soil she had taken him to one side. 'I don't want them to know I did it,' she said. Emma looked exhausted, all in. 'I don't want them to know I killed the professor.'

'Why?' he asked.

'Because they will want me to do it again,' she said flatly, 'and I don't think I can.'

She was right. They had already turned Walsh into an

assassin and, if she allowed it, they would do the same thing to her. 'I'll tell them I killed him,' he offered.

'How will you explain that?'

'I'll think of something,' and she had nodded her acceptance.

There was a silence between them for a while and, after a time, she asked him, 'You're not going to end it with me, are you, Harry? Not this time?'

'No, I'm not,' he replied without hesitation, 'not this time.'

Emma nodded slowly, 'I thought not.' Then she looked past him, avoiding his eye, and said, 'Then I must. I'm sorry, Harry, but I can't be your mistress. I could do it in France, when each day could have been our last but not back here, not in London. You understand that, don't you?'

And it was absolutely no consolation to Harry Walsh that he did.

Walsh knew that it was no use brooding about Emma. That wouldn't get him anywhere. He'd just have to take it and accept her decision to end things, which was entirely her prerogative. All he could do was try to put her out of his mind. There was work to be done after all; they'd give him another mission before too long, there was still a war to be fought and a traitor to find. Then he could finally avenge the deaths of so many good men.

Every new day the world would continue to wake up around him, the people in it as hell-bent on destroying each other as ever. Next to that, Harry Walsh was forced to admit, his own problems didn't count for very much at all.

As Walsh reached the end of the corridor he heard a muted crashing noise from an office some way behind him. It was the sound of someone kicking out at a hard, metallic item, a waste paper bin perhaps, and sending it across the room in impotent fury.

THE END

'The life that I have is all that I have
And the life that I have is yours.
The love that I have of the life that I have
Is yours and yours and yours

A sleep I shall have
A rest I shall have
Yet death will be but a pause,
For the peace of my years in the long green grass
Will be yours and yours and yours.'

Code poem written by Leo Marks for SOE agent Violette Szabo, murdered by the Gestapo in Ravensbrück concentration camp, 1945.

HISTORICAL NOTE

The Me 163 Komet finally became fully operational in 1944 but it was never produced in sufficient numbers to influence the outcome of the war. Like many of Hitler's much vaunted miracle weapons its impact was too little, too late. Fuel shortages prevented many of the planes from seeing combat and the Germans never did overcome the problems of excess weight and combustible fuel mixtures that so frustrated the fictional Professor Gaerte. Just sixteen confirmed kills were attributed to Komet attacks, all of them Allied bomber planes. It is thought a larger number of Komets were destroyed in crash landings.

Jedburgh teams played an important role in the aftermath of the D-Day landings, with more than ninety teams parachuted into occupied territory, to form a link between the Allies and the Resistance, then cause havoc for the retreating Germans.

Kim Philby was a lecturer at SOE's training schools before rising through the ranks of MI6 following the war then gaining lasting notoriety in the 1960s as an unmasked KGB mole planted deep into the heart of British Intelligence years earlier.

Ian Fleming worked for Naval Intelligence during World War Two. It is said that Elder Wills, the creator of SOE's 'props', was the model for Fleming's character Q in the James Bond stories. Vera Atkins is cited as an inspiration for Miss Moneypenny. Elder's 'little inventions' did indeed end up in a glass case somewhere – during an exhibition in the Imperial War Museum.

Emma Stirling's codename 'Madeleine' was actually used by SOE agent Noor Inayat Khan, the first woman wireless operator to be sent into France. She was eventually discovered by the Germans, enduring eleven months of captivity, before being taken to Dachau Concentration Camp. On 12 September 1944, along with three other female agents, she was executed. Their tragic deaths are a reminder of the incredible courage of the men and women of the SOE and the very real danger they faced behind enemy lines.

Sam Cooper's employers the OSS were the forerunners to today's CIA. It would be another sixty-one years before Sam's beloved Boston Red Sox won the World Series again in 2004. I like to think he might have lived just long enough to witness it.

ACKNOWLEDGEMENTS

This is my fifth novel with the lovely people at No Exit Press and I would like to thank everyone there for publishing *Ungentlemanly Warfare*. In particular, a special thank you to Ion Mills for his faith in my writing and for getting me started as an author, a journey that I am still constantly surprised to be on.

I would also like to thank the rest of the guys at No Exit; Claire Watts, Steven Mair, Clare Quinlivan, Clare Holloway, Jayne Lewis, Lisa Gooding and Katherine Sunderland. You are all an absolute pleasure to work with, every single time.

A huge thank you, as always, to 'Special Agent' Phil Patterson, who, as well as being my brilliant literary agent, also shares my minor obsession with all things WWII related and, like me, can recite virtually every line from *Where Eagles Dare*. May he always be there to remind me which side of the square the cathedral is on.

The following people have given me help, support and inspiration during my writing career and continue to do so, every day. Thank you, Adam Pope, Andy Davis, Nikki Selden, Gareth Chennells, Andrew Local, Stuart Britton, David Shapiro, Peter Day, Tony Frobisher, Eva Dolan, Katie Charlton, Gemma Sealey, Peter Hammans, Emad Akhtar, Joel Richardson and Keshini Naidoo.

My lovely wife Alison gets a special thank you for putting up with me and all of this writing. I may be a bit strange but all I can say in my defence is, at least I only kill people on the page.

My amazing daughter Erin continues to inspire me every day. She makes me laugh and puts everything neatly in perspective. I'm in awe of her intelligence and constantly cheered by her kind heart. Love you always Erin.

TWO MEN… ONE MISSION… TO KILL THE MAN WITH THE IRON HEART

Based on true events, this gripping historical thriller is the culmination of Howard Linskey's fifteen-year fascination with the attempted assassination of Reinhard Heydrich, the architect of the Holocaust. With a plot that echoes *The Day of the Jackal* and *The Eagle Has Landed*, *Hunting the Hangman* is a thrilling tale of courage, resilience and betrayal.

In 1942 two men, trained by the British SOE, parachuted back into their native Czechoslovakia with one sole objective: to kill the man ruling their homeland. Jan Kubis and Josef Gabcik risked everything for their country. Their attempt on Reinhard Heydrich's life was one of the single most dramatic events of the Second World War, and had horrific consequences for thousands of innocent people.

2017 marks the 75th anniversary of the attack on Heydrich, a man so evil even fellow SS officers referred to him as the 'Blond Beast'. In Prague, he was known as the Hangman. Hitler, who dubbed him 'The Man with the Iron Heart', considered Heydrich his heir, and entrusted him with the implementation of the 'Final Solution' to the Jewish 'problem': the systematic murder of eleven million people.

9781843449508   £7.99

NO EXIT PRESS
UNCOVERING THE BEST CRIME

'A very smart, independent publisher delivering
the finest literary crime fiction' – *Big Issue*

MEET NO EXIT PRESS, the independent publisher bringing you the best in crime and noir fiction. From classic detective novels, to page-turning spy thrillers and singular writing that just grabs the attention. Our books are carefully crafted by some of the world's finest writers and delivered to you by a small, but mighty, team.

In our 30 years of business, we have published award-winning fiction and non-fiction including the work of a Pulitzer Prize winner, the British Crime Book of the Year, numerous CWA Dagger Awards, a British million copy bestselling author, the winner of the Canadian Governor General's Award for Fiction and the Scotiabank Giller Prize, to name but a few. We are the home of many crime and noir legends from the USA whose work includes iconic film adaptations and TV sensations. We pride ourselves in uncovering the most exciting new or undiscovered talents. New and not so new – you know who you are!!

We are a proactive team committed to delivering the very best, both for our authors and our readers.

Want to join the conversation and find out more about what we do?

Catch us on social media or sign up to our newsletter for all the latest news from No Exit Press HQ.

f fb.me/noexitpress **𝕏** @noexitpress
noexit.co.uk/newsletter